PIT AND
A PEACH

Titles by Anna Pollock

When the Summer's Over
Scout's Honor: Part One

PIT AND A PEACH

ANNA POLLOCK

BRASEBERRY
 PRESS

Cover art by Jess Cruz
cruzdigitalstudio.etsy.com
Instagram: @jesscruz_design

ISBN 979-8-9891195-4-7
eBook ISBN 979-8-9891195-5-4

This story is based in Minneapolis, MN, or Bde Óta Othúŋwe.
Its geographical location is near B'dote, a sacred land of the Dakota
people where the Minnesota and Mississippi rivers meet. It is the site of
some of the most violent treatment of indigenous people in Minnesota's
history and is on stolen land.

It's important to note that even fictional places are based in real
history filled with genocide and forced removal of
Dakota and Anishinaabe peoples.

To my future peach.

Chapter 1

I HAVE NO IDEA WHAT'S GOING ON. Right now, at least. Not like, generally.

I'm sitting on some rooftop bar in the North Loop with my girlfriend of six years and eight other people I genuinely wouldn't be able to name if my life depended on it. We were all invited here because each of us has some sort of following on social media or is associated with someone who does. There's a rookie Twins player on an off-night with a blonde sitting in his lap, two middle-aged TV personalities from the local news station, Kare 11, and the rest are overdressed, glammed up twenty-something social media influencers. Including my girlfriend, Lacie of @LacieEats.

She's wearing my favorite mini skirt and it's giving me enough hope that I'll get laid tonight. Her blown-out blonde hair is cascading down her bare back in a way that confirms it.

She looks hot, and she knows it.

"Oooh, ooh! Get a photo of that!" she nearly shouts across the table as the server drops a brightly plated appetizer of caprese salad. They aren't even going to eat it. I'll bet on it.

No less than three people get up from the table, adjusting the other plates, glassware, and bright lights of their phones shining on the newly placed props. That's what they are at this point. Props.

Lacie started her "journey" on social media (her word, not mine), about five years ago. We had been interns together at my now job during our senior year at the University of Minnesota. She was in the marketing department, and I was in the graphic design internship at *North Star Magazine*, a lifestyle publication that is one of the last pieces of printed media that represents the entire state of Minnesota, rather than only the Twin Cities. I worked my way up to be their director of production and now deal with a thing called pagination. Just a fancy word for the layout of each section and how it gets put together. Every ad, column, and feature runs through my desk, and I get to find a way to make it all fit.

Lacie, on the other hand, finished her internship at North Star, then proceeded to focus on her Instagram account with her newfound online interest in all the food trends Minneapolis and St. Paul had to offer.

A night like this isn't uncommon. Lacie knows everyone by name and rarely introduces me. She has a rule about never sharing about her personal life on her account and that rule bleeds into real life, meaning I never truly feel a part of these outings, only on the sidelines cheering on. It's probably for the best seeing as I don't have more than an inactive Facebook page that I haven't checked in at least a year. But this is Lacie's livelihood, and like a good boyfriend, I hold her purse, watch her snap at least three hundred photos of the food on the table, and wrap my arm around her when she sits back down.

The table goes silent, faces illuminated by phone screens and thumbs tapping to edit and post photos. The whole point of these dinners is to cross-promote or die.

"Come here, cutie, let's get a pic." Lacie leans out of my arms and into the girl next to her. I'm almost positive her name is Sonja and she has twice as many followers as Lacie. I know she's mentioned her a few times. They snap around thirty pictures, *I'm not joking*, before landing on a few they like.

The whole thing is still bizarre to me, but somehow familiar. Lacie has been doing this for years and recently started making some decent money from it. I'm proud of her in a way. We've both come so far from the two nervous interns at *North Star Magazine*.

I almost manage to slip away completely before the rounds of goodbyes, but I catch the tail-end and Lacie meets me at my car.

"So great to meet you, Connor!" someone yells. It's Conrad. My name is Conrad. And I have never meant it more when I say I don't care enough to correct them.

I look at Lacie to give her an eye roll, but she's too preoccupied getting into the passenger seat of my SUV, so I shut the door a little more aggressively than I should and meet her in the front. As usual, the car ride consists of Lacie on her phone and my thumbs thumping the steering wheel along to the song in my head. Frank Ocean's "Pink + White" this evening. It makes me nostalgic for something I can't pinpoint.

I pull up to the house she rents with three other girls, and I know what you're thinking. *Six years together and she hasn't moved in?* Well, we're working on it. 102k followers on Instagram doesn't pay the bills like you'd think.

I give her a smile. I lean over to give her a kiss goodbye and ask if she wants anything more, but she takes a deep breath, as if to psych herself up for something.

"We need to talk." She stares out the windshield. Before I can ask what she means, she says, "I want to break up."

And I kid you not, I think she's joking. "Hah, okay."

"Con." She's serious, and in fact, I realize she looks more nervous than the time I accidentally let slip that I voted for

Bernie in the 2016 presidential election at her dad's house. "I've been thinking about it for a while. I have so many decisions ahead of me, and I feel like I'm on the cusp of something really big with my personal brand."

The laugh that is bubbling up feels highly inappropriate. I'm actually thinking she's pulling a prank on me for some video she's going to post.

"Babe, what does that have to do with me?"

"Well," she starts, fidgeting with her nails. Pale blue, but she calls them *blueberry milk*. "You've been at the same job since we met. You never want to go on brand trips with me," — she's been invited to *one* and it was during deadline week — "you don't have social media, and I just know that things are going to be picking up soon, and I can't have a partner that doesn't actually believe in what I do."

Alright. This isn't funny anymore.

"Lace, I've been supporting you for *years*. What are you talking about? You can't actually be doing this."

She opens the door and with a look that has less than an ounce of actual remorse, she steps out of the vehicle with nothing more than, "I'm sorry. I think I need a clean break. It'll be easier for both of us this way. I love you, Con, but it's time to start living my life."

What the fuck just happened?

Chapter 2

IT'S MONDAY. I DIDN'T SLEEP AT ALL LAST NIGHT. And for the first time in six years, I wake up single.

Single.

I don't even remember what it feels like to be single.

I didn't cry on the drive home, or while I lay in bed, tossing and turning the night before. It still doesn't feel real, even as I pour a cup of the muddy water they call coffee at the office. My phone still has zero notifications. That hasn't changed since the last time I checked it ten seconds ago. And five seconds before that.

I'm so dumbfounded that I considered calling my mom, which, if you know me, is completely out of the question. I haven't spoken to my mom since last Christmas and I know her words wouldn't be comforting right now. If anything, she'd probably blame me for the breakup. Lacie never really got along with her, and on top of it, my sister, Georgia, couldn't stand being in the same room as Lacie. They have nothing in common except for their love of pink but in different ways. Lacie has a millennial pink purse she totes with her everywhere she goes, while Georgia sports bubblegum pink hair most days. To each their own. We spent way more time at Lacie's parent's house in Edina, and the thought makes me mourn the loss of the free dinners, yearly vacations, and good whiskey at every family function.

Honestly? I'm trying not to think about it. She'll come back. We've had bouts of separation here and there. Lacie's probably just having a bad week. Lost a promo op, or looked at her engagement percentages and needs to take it out on someone. I'm always an easy target. I've never put up much of a fight with her, and that's probably why she knew she could dump me out of the blue and it would still be the path of least resistance. Whatever. She'll come around.

As I carry these thoughts back to my desk, I see Zakariya blocking my path. He's the managing editor and is in charge of all content both digital and print. I don't envy his workload. He has tight curls that bounce around his face and reminds me of a dark-skinned Justin Guarini circa the first season of American Idol, which ages me in a way I feel like it shouldn't.

He's standing with a girl. Tall, light brown hair, wearing khaki overalls and a white t-shirt underneath. She exudes the energy of someone who goes on morning hikes, vibrant and calm all in one. She's sunburnt on her cheeks and it confirms her outdoor nature. Nothing like Lacie.

"Conrad, hey!" Zakariya greets me with a smile. He's such a happy dude, I don't know how he does it. "This is Maeve, our new associate editor. I'm taking her around the office to introduce her to everyone."

She produces a smile that tells me she is also probably a happy person or something. "Hi! Nice to meet you."

"Morning, hi. I'm Conrad." I squeeze around them to hide back in my desk, but Zakariya keeps talking while his elbow leans over my cubicle wall.

"Conrad does everything. He's the person who puts the entire magazine together every month, so all things run through him. You work a lot with sales, right?" he asks, as if I have time for this. Sales is in fact on my shit list this morning. And most mornings.

"Sometimes it feels like I work *around* sales, but yes," I answer. "I have to get all the ads in but I usually don't get confirmations on what's been sold until deadline week."

Zakariya's smile fades. "Best not to piss Conrad off during deadline week, or any time for that matter. Deadline week's when we print out the upcoming issue, spread it out on the production table, and everyone tries to catch typos and misspellings. Can't wait for you to be here for one!" he cheers. Again, they're both smiling and entirely too excited to be talking about something that makes me sweat profusely.

"Speaking of sales, I need to hound Amy about the half page that she told the client was a three-quarter. Let me know if you ever need anything, here to help," I try, putting my best smirk in the direction of the new editor while I nod Zakariya off.

They're whispering as their footsteps align, disappearing into the back corner we call the Editor's Den. They've always been cliquey. It's a constant battle between who's more important, the writers supplying the content, the graphic designers making it look good, or the sales team that keeps the lights on. No one ever thinks of the person who actually puts the damn thing together.

Lacie sure didn't. I bet if I was a writer she'd still be with me. They're always getting into things for free in exchange for an article or a review. Pathetic.

Before lunch, I send out a round of passive-aggressive emails to the account executives with clients who still have outstanding ads for the next issue. It's the second week in September, so they have one more week to fart around for the October issue. Next week is deadline week and I am taking no shit this month.

A headache creeps in and makes a home behind my eyes until the day closes. I'm so excited to get back to the apartment to wallow in more self-pity that I forget to check in with my boss all day. He's been quiet since I leaned into his office this morning to tell him about the breakup. Jesse is a sensitive guy, and I think that's what makes him well-liked around the office. For the most part.

He's on the phone when I pop in. "*Hey, heading out,*" I mime.

His eyebrows turn up. "One sec, hon. Yep, one sec. Just one sec," he repeats, pulling his phone away from his ear. "You good? Anything you need from me?"

"Nope. Another day in paradise. Finally replaced Lisa in editorial, huh?" I quip, sarcastically.

Jesse chuckles. "Yes, Maeve has big shoes to fill. Exciting stuff." He points to the phone. "I should get back. Drive safe," he whispers before turning his back to me. "Alright, when does he need to be at tennis, then? I don't know if I could get there in time with downtown traffic."

I chuckle on the way out, dreading my own commute. Working downtown has its perks. For one, if you want to go to an impromptu happy hour or dinner, you're already there. And two, the lunch options are fantastic when you want to pay $18 for a salad. But, if you need to get anywhere from 4 pm to

7 pm on a weeknight, good luck. My watch currently reads 6:21 pm.

On my way out the door, the mid-September heat reaches my lungs and warms my overly air-conditioned nostrils. Smog and baked cement linger in the air. I'm assuming it was a scorcher. I didn't get a chance to leave for lunch today.

I pass a few bus stops on my walk to the cheapest parking garage eight blocks away. I sometimes pass a co-worker or two, but seeing as I was one of three people still at the office, I don't see anyone, until I recognize the tan overalls a block ahead. She's sitting at a bus stop bench with her notepad resting on her thigh while she scrolls on her phone, pausing every few seconds to write something down. She's left-handed.

As she looks up, she catches me watching her. Well, not like *watching*. I was just noticing that she was there. *Ugh.* Now I have to say hi or it'll be weird.

"Hey, you're the new editor, right?"

She smiles up at me, removing one of her earbuds I didn't notice until now. "Oh! Yes! And you're... oh gosh. I'm so sorry, I met so many people today."

"Conrad."

She snaps and points at me, still smiling. She has one dimple on her left cheek. *Not weird, just noticing.* "Conrad, that's right. Pagination, deadline week, don't piss you off."

"You're already getting the hang of it." I actually feel myself smile slightly, but immediately I'm exhausted. "Well, I'll let you go. Hope you had a good first day."

"It was great! Thanks, Conrad." She waves me off and instantly places her earbud back in, returning to her notepad.

At last, I am finally free from any and all social obligations. My couch is the sexiest thing keeping me company when I get home and I try not to think about how depressing that is the rest of the evening. And I *definitely* don't think of getting an Instagram account so I can see what Lacie is up to.

Deadline week this time around is the worst I've had since I got promoted to this role two years ago. I'm not exaggerating.

Out of the forty-three ads in the issue, twenty-nine of them are late. Editorial can't decide which feature to run since the one that was supposed to go live this month has been pulled due to some newsworthy scandal at the organization being highlighted, and the marketing and events team wants to wait on some in-house ads until the last minute because "some exciting news" might be confirmed soon. *What does that even mean?*

I stomp into Jesse's office, ready to sound off.

He beats me to it. "Before you start, I know," he sighs at his computer. "October's issue is always a mess. Coming out of the summer is a bitch for sales. This happens every year."

"Bullshit. Twenty-nine ads, Jesse. This is ridiculous. You realize how much work this is putting on me?"

Jesse turns around, giving me his *I hear you* upside-down smile. "I know, I know. Let me know how I can help."

"Get a new sales team," I spit under my breath, walking out pissed off as ever. And even as I huff and puff at my desk, four ads have already hit my inbox and it lowers my blood pressure slightly. By Thursday, we're only missing five plus the feature, and I have to swallow my pride. By Friday at 5 pm, we're still missing three and I'm about ready to burn the place down.

The one thing that this mess has done is take my mind off Lacie. She always knew deadline week was a week to back off. And now I'm sitting at my desk, calling and emailing the account executive who just happens to be off-site at a meeting and is the culprit for all three missing ads. I feel myself being awful. But if people got their shit done, maybe I wouldn't be so wound up every time. If this issue doesn't go to the printer by 10 pm tonight, we're screwed. I feel the pressure forming behind my eyes. Sweat is dampening my undershirt and my mood. It's a quarter to seven.

Jesse calls me on my cell. "Hey Conrad, had to pick up the boys from a birthday party. Any updates?"

I roll my eyes. "I can't get ahold of Hank. All three of the ads from Master Pool and Spa are missing." I bite my tongue from saying, *"I have a life, too, you know,"* but it's not true. I have no plans. And without Lacie, it feels like I actually have negative plans.

"I think he's been at the Mercedes-Benz end of the summer event. I'll give him a call, okay? Have you heard anything about the feature?"

The feature? The feature was submitted already, why would I have heard anything about the feature? "Uh, I...what about it? It's already in."

"That was last month's as a placeholder. See if Zakariya is still there. It should be done. Don't panic."

I panic.

I'm going to *kill* Zakariya.

More stomping.

I make it to the dumbass cozy corner that the writers have made for themselves and find everyone's cubicle light is off but one.

"Zakariya, what the hell?"

A small voice startles me. "Zakariya left. Just me back here. I'm working as fast as I can!"

It's Tan Overalls. Well, not today. Today she's wearing olive green pants and an off-white top. Her nose is about six inches from her computer screen, and immediately, I feel like an ass.

"Uh." I'm trying not to be awful. "I'm... sorry, but I really needed that like, well, to be honest, last week."

"I swear I'm almost done. Eighteen minutes."

Eighteen minutes will hopefully give me enough time to get the stupid ads from Hank. "Okay. Uh, yeah," I sigh. There is so much more I want to say but she's been here, what, less than two weeks?

I have a missed call on my office phone back at my desk. Three seconds later, my cell rings, and what do you know, it's Hank.

"Hank."

"Conrad, hey! So sorry, buddy, just got done with a work event." *I know what you just got done with, Hank, I can practically smell the Coors Light over the phone.* "I've got the ads in my inbox, I'll send them over now!"

Oh, so he's had them this entire time. Awesome. "Yep, that would be appreciated, Hank. I'm held up here at the office until I have them."

"Ah, shoot. Sorry about that, Conrad. You'll get them within the hour!"

No!

He hangs up before my mouth can catch up. "Within the next five *minutes*, Hank," I mumble to myself, whining futility.

I use the time to check the edits on the marked-up pages from the production table. Everything, for the nineteenth time, looks fine. I pull up my email and finally, *finally* the ads are in my inbox. *Was that so fucking hard, Hank?* I double-check that they align with their contract, and a voice bursts over the cubicles and through my concentration.

"Done!"

Exactly eighteen minutes since I spoke to Tan Overalls, the feature is in my inbox, formatted correctly, and ready to print. I hear footsteps as I import everything into Magazine Manager.

"Does it look alright? Zakariya's going up North with girlfriend's family this weekend. I didn't want to call him."

So everyone has a life but me, cool. "It looks just fine—"

"Oh! Is that the whole issue? Can I see? This is the first one with my name in the masthead!"

This is the last thing I need. The clock on my computer reads 7:16 pm. She steps into my cubicle. No one steps into my cubicle. "Can you not? I should have had this sent three hours ago and I don't need someone breathing down my neck while I wait for the export."

She swallows and nods, muttering, "Sorry," before stepping away and disappearing from my view. A minute or two later I see her head to the elevator that takes her twelve floors below to the slowly dwindling traffic outside, the only silver lining in my commute home tonight.

After another sweep over the issue, everything looks perfect. This is my favorite part. I preview the book, flipping through the digital pages and it all flows great. With a final export, I email Sandy, my contact at the printer, with the usual apology and a link to the export. It's right around 7:54 pm, and at long *fucking* last, I shut my computer down and head out for the weekend. My armpits are soaked, I have a headache, my shoulders are tense. I feel like I just ran a marathon.

The air outside is muggy and warm, a stark difference from the air conditioning that didn't do much to prevent my sweaty pits from the last three hours. This one was *hell*. The streets of downtown Minneapolis are in that weird lull between the evening commute and the bustle of a Friday night. Marquette Avenue specifically has an identity crisis, unable to determine itself as a hip, sparkly catwalk or the landing strip of a business class Delta flight.

Right as I turn onto the street, I see her. This time she doesn't have a notepad on her lap, just a bouncing knee and a blank stare ahead. A twitch of guilt in my stomach reaches my mouth and I purse my lips. Once again, she sees me and we make brief eye contact, contractually obligating me to acknowledge her. I guess it also gives me the opportunity to say sorry for how I acted earlier as if the universe is giving me a second chance at the day.

"Hey," I say as I approach her. She waves weakly. "Sorry about earlier, I didn't mean to be rude," I say as I approach her.

She offers me a flat smile and takes one of her earbuds out. "It's okay. Are you just now taking off?"

"Yeah, had to double-check everything and exporting takes a bit of time. The good news is that we have an October issue." I try to let out a laugh, but it sounds more like an aggravated grunt. "Have you been waiting for the bus this whole time?"

I look around. She's the only one here.

She lifts her phone. "Mhmm. I missed the 6:27, so I was going to catch the 7:27, but the app says it broke down, so I'm waiting for it to update."

"Oh, uh. When's the next bus scheduled?"

"Not until 8:27, but they sometimes add a bus if the one that broke down is beyond repair. I don't know," she said, shrugging.

If the universe isn't slapping me upside the head, I don't know what is. "Do you, um, need a ride home?"

Please say no, please say no.

"No."

Thank god, but also, ouch? It was a little harsher than it needed to be, and *oh my god, listen to me.* "You sure?"

"Yeah, I'm sure. I live all the way in Golden Valley."

I live in Golden Valley. I'm no longer receiving a smack upside the head, the universe is pushing me off a cliff. She could have lived anywhere in the Twin Cities metro. There are probably over a dozen neighboring towns and suburbs, and she lives in the exact one I do. The hell?

"I live on the Westside, too. Honestly, it's not a huge deal. Least I can do after tonight. We both had a late night," I say sheepishly. I'm, like, nervous all of a sudden.

She hesitates, and I wish I had kept walking. All I want is to be inside my car, blasting the AC and listening to sad Frank Ocean songs for the rest of eternity. I plan on doing just that until she stands up with upturned eyebrows.

"Actually? If you're sure, I would really appreciate a ride home. Only if it's okay."

"It's okay." I nod and reluctantly motion her to follow me.

We walk silently, and my fried brain can't muster up even one topic of conversation other than complaining about today. I've talked to this girl three times. I have no idea who she is or what she's about. All I know is that we both were at the office until after 7 pm, I kind of yelled at her, and it's her second week on the job.

We finally get to the parking ramp and the silence is making my skin itch. "Sorry you got handed the task of editing the feature on such late notice. I'm sure that was a bitch."

She exhales with relief as if she's been holding her breath, too. "It wouldn't have been if it was fact-checked. Zakariya thought it already was. He gave it to me this afternoon, otherwise I would have had it to you way earlier. Still the new kid, I guess." Her tone matched her expression, full of guilt with a sprinkle of fear. "I'm sorry I pissed you off during deadline week. My first one, too."

I unlock my car ten feet ahead of us, feeling like shit. "This one was a particularly rough one. All good. Promise I won't hold it against you." She gives me a weak smile and her left dimple appears. "Alright, what's your address?" I ask, and the universe offers its final blow.

She recites my own apartment address back to me.

Chapter 3

I'M ALREADY THINKING OF WAYS I can avoid this being a *thing*. I could drop her off, drive around the block, enter the underground parking garage, and probably be fine. I could go to the grocery store. Pick up dinner somewhere. Or I guess I could be a normal fucking human for once.

"You live in Weston Village Apartments?"

She eyes me from the passenger seat. Weston Village Apartments aren't well known or anything. It's a dinky four-story apartment complex surrounded by high-rise condominiums near the General Mills campus. It's also across the street from a movie theater and a killer Chinese restaurant.

"Yes?" Her eyebrows lift and excitement takes over exhaustion on her face. "Do you?!"

"For like, four years."

"I've lived there for almost a year!" she cries, shifting in her seat to face me completely. "What are the odds? That's crazy!" Our chuckles dissipate as I merge onto the highway from the Ramp A parking structure. She continues the conversation. "So have you always lived in Minnesota?"

If you're from Minnesota, it's a weird question to ask. "Yep. Born and raised. Grew up outside of Duluth. You?"

"No, I came out here for school, then just kind of stuck around. It's hard to leave Minnesota for some reason."

"That's what I hear." I ask the next question in the queue. "Where'd you go to school, then?"

"Macalester. I majored in Journalism with a minor in Anthropology. You?"

"U of M. Strategic Communications," I answer, glancing at her across the center console.

I was always proud to go to the U of M. When I moved to Minneapolis, it felt like I had finally "gotten out." It was hard enough growing up with a mom who was working during every parent-teacher conference and a dad who was never around. We weren't poor thanks to our dad's child support, but it was obvious Georgia and I were on our own most of the time. I swear kids can pick up on it. They get a whiff of something that marks you as a sob story and boom, I'm sitting alone at lunch all four years of high school. Mix that with an emotional attachment to any woman that gave me the time of day, and oof. Yeah. The U of M was a chance to reintroduce myself to the world.

The car is quiet for a few minutes as if she knows I'm reflecting on something. Maybe we both are.

"I really, *really* appreciate this by the way," she says. I half-ass a smile. "I'm hoping to get a car in about six months. By then everything will change." I catch her smiling out the window as I glance over. "Things have already changed with this job. The bus line is so much more convenient. I used to work in North and there wasn't a good line that ran near my office. I had a twenty-minute walk to the bus stop. Whenever I had to work late it was..." She trails off and looks ahead. "I got my backpack stolen off me one night."

I'm somewhat frozen. The last thing I need is her life story, but damn. That had to be terrifying. "That's fucked up."

"It sure was," she says and nods. I'm hoping that's the end of the conversation, but she's got more in her. "So, tell me. Now that deadline week is over, what's your pit and peach of the day?"

"My pit and peach?"

She nods, smiling. "Like, have you ever heard of a rose, a thorn, and a bud? Something positive about your day, something negative, and what you're looking forward to tomorrow?"

"I have not."

"Well, this is like that without the bud. A pit and a peach. It's kind of fun to say. Pit and a peach!"

I give her what I hope at best could be a neutral look, but I feel myself scowling. "Uhh."

"Just go for it. Pit and a peach isn't sacred. It'll only exist in this car, and then we can roll down the windows to let it out."

I have no idea why she's doing this, but the vision of chucking my day out the window feels delightful. I am so tired. I feel the rumble in my belly and concede. I'm so sick of fighting with anyone and everyone today and I just want to go home.

"I don't know. Um, my pit is everything."

"No, you can't say *everything*," she argues. "It has to be a specific thing."

"I don't need to get specific."

"No, you do! Something small."

I grunt. *Nothing* feels small today. "I don't have anything—"

"Come on!"

"How specific do you want me to get, then? Huh?" I snap with the weight of it all. "Fine! Here's specific, I got dumped two weeks ago after giving the better part of my twenties to someone who won't even answer my texts. My job is a constant battle of getting people to respect me, oh and I get to go home to an apartment with no Netflix account because my ex changed all the passwords to everything. And I don't *care* if I can afford my own accounts, I don't *care* that it'll take me two seconds to create them. I deal with enough account fucking management, I could be an account executive! Then I wouldn't have to do *anything*. I definitely wouldn't have to do my job! I'd get to be at the Mercedes-Benz dealer with a stick up my ass playing beer pong with my fellow washed-up fraternity brothers! There, how's all that? Specific enough for you?"

Tan Overalls looks at me as if I just spontaneously combusted. And then she has the audacity to *laugh*.

"Is there steam coming out of there?" She peers into my ear, bobbing her head side-to-side as if to get a better look. "I think a vein popped out on your neck."

"Alright. You know what? Nevermind. Thanks for the assurance, really needed that."

"Oh, no. I'm sorry." She faces ahead. "I didn't mean to downplay any of that. Breakups are tricky. That's actually a lot for one person. And on a deadline week."

I exhale as I veer onto the 169 exit.

She's still smiling as I check over my shoulder at my blind spot. "So, what's your peach then? You always have to end on a peach. That way you're left with good vibes." She wiggles her fingers. Is she *choosing* to ignore everything I just said?

"I don't have one." My tone has shifted from shrill and combative to cutting and bitter. I'm done with this conversation.

"Okay," she responds so softly I barely catch it and proceeds to look out the window for the rest of the car ride. All five minutes of it. We're quiet until we're both waiting for the elevator in the lobby, huffing from silently climbing the metal stairs from the parking garage. It dings and we almost run into each other getting inside. She hits Level 3, I hit Level 4.

Defeated, I finally reciprocate her question. "What are yours?"

She takes a deep breath and still somehow manages to smile as the doors open to her floor. "Weirdly enough, I'd say that car ride was both my pit and my peach. Thank you for driving me home. Hope you feel better, Conrad. See you Monday."

As the doors shut, I realize I can't even recall her name, and it reminds me how much of an absolute asshole I can be when I try hard enough.

Monday morning, I'm back in the Editor's Den, building myself up to have a "chat" with Zakariya. He gives me a guilty smile when I peer over the partition of his cubicle.

"Got a second?"

Zakariya lets out the breath he was holding. "Yeah, I knew this was coming." Of course he does, he knows better than this. He's been working here for two years.

"Don't do that again. Don't send me shit that isn't supposed to be in the issue. If I would have received Hank's ads before I found out about your little placeholder thing, that shit would have gone to print. And it would've been on my ass. I don't have time to read every word that you guys write to make sure it's not a duplicate from last month."

"Sorry, man. Honestly, I know this issue was a mess."

I give him a vacant glare because he doesn't know the *half* of it. "Yeah. Don't do it again. Got it?"

"Yep. Got it," he affirms, and I spin myself around and almost run face-first into Tan Overalls. I really need to get her name.

"Conrad, hi," she whispers. Why is she whispering? "Can I ask you something?"

You just did. "Uh, yeah. Can you walk with me? I'm grabbing coffee and have to stop at my desk first."

I stride off towards my cubicle to grab my thermos. Even though she's tall, her stride has nothing on me, and she has to jog to keep up.

"So I was running some numbers last night. It's $3.25 one way to ride the bus to work, so over $6 a day, $130 on average a month. Just to get to work."

I nod as we land at my cubicle, seeing a few new emails from our marketing team roll in on my computer. I avoid them like the plague and head to the kitchen. She's still following me and I'm following her train of thought. I'm already preparing my rejection. How is this my problem?

"So, I was wondering if you'd be willing to carpool." Here we go. "I'll pay you $100 a month for gas and parking so it's even."

I sigh, pouring the office sludge into my travel mug. The commute sucks, yes. Forty-five minutes each way for a trip that should take fifteen is dumb, but those forty-five minutes are mine. I get to listen to music, plan out my day, and cling to the last few moments of solitude before being bombarded by incompetence at work. Not to mention, the ride home is usually saved for decompressing, not meaningless conversations about the highs and lows of the day.

She cuts off my inner thoughts. "Plus, we'd be able to use the HOV lane. Which you have to admit, will save us both time in the morning."

I consider her, and she catches on all too quickly.

"You're thinking about it!" She snaps and points again, standing on her tiptoes, and I fight the urge to take a step back. "I can pay upfront. Just let me know." She walks away, still smiling and I'm left with a shitty cup of coffee and a crossroads.

On one hand, this makes total sense and would help her out. I've never taken the bus before, but from what I can imagine it's probably hell. On the other hand, I don't owe her anything. And that's the problem. Either I'm going to look like a complete ass, or my mornings are no longer mine. Guilt wraps around my esophagus with that thought. The memory of nearly screaming at her in my car on Friday sends a ping of regret up my throat. She must be desperate if she wants to be in the same car with me again. I guess I'd be desperate, too, if I had been jumped at a bus stop.

Once I'm back at my desk, I go into weirdo mode. I need to find her name. After pulling up the company directory, I find the editorial team and recognize all but one name; *Maeve Thomas*. I head to LinkedIn and find her from remembering she graduated from Macalester. There she is. She used to work at a nonprofit before this centered around food security. Hmm.

I'm about to open my fourth tab on the subject before I cut myself off. I had already made the decision. And for the second time this week, I feel the invisible hand of the universe pushing me towards the edge of something. Maybe it's because I miss Lacie, maybe it's because I secretly want to have someone around to tamper my thoughts. Or maybe this isn't my problem and she can continue taking the bus like countless other people in Minneapolis. I'd be an actual ass to say no to this, though. The girl got mugged.

I think I've grown soft in my old age. (29.)

My pride tries to stop me on the way to her desk, but I keep walking, smelling cinnamon once I enter the Editor's Den. There's a candle lit somewhere and I'm pretty sure that's absolutely not allowed. I find it on Maeve's desk as I peer over the cubicle wall, only it's not a candle, it's one of those wax warmer things. I resist the urge to scoff as an opening to the conversation.

"Okay, I'm in— *but* I have a few conditions." I plow through her wide-eyed reaction and suck in a breath. "I don't know how late I'll be today, but I leave at 7:30 am every morning, not a second later. And I stay at the office late sometimes, so you'll have to work around that. My job isn't very predictable, as you saw on Friday."

"Got it, absolutely."

"And I can't be driving you anywhere else," I say, not really understanding why I'm bringing this up. "To and from work, that's the deal."

Her eyebrows knit together and it looks like she's trying not to laugh. And then it's me who has to fight a grin. She salutes and nods stoically. "Ten-four."

"Alright, listen—"

"I'm kidding! Understood. Let me know when you're ready to head out today."

With an unamused huff, I walk back to my desk to grab my thermos. It's my third cup today.

♥

I know it's my own fault, but I'm already regretting this decision. It's half past five and most folks are packing up for the day. I could, too, but I'm stalling. Stalling because I'm trying to come up with an excuse to get out of this. A family emergency, I forgot I have plans tonight, my dog needs to go to the vet, but none of it's true. My mom lives in Duluth and last texted me a picture of Lake Superior six months ago with the caption, "Blessed today and every day, praying for you to seek the TRUTH." I don't have plans for the foreseeable future, and I've never owned a dog. More of a cat person.

Jesse rips out of his office like a pistol. "Gotta jet, I'm late to pick up the boys. Totally forgot it was my turn today. You good?" He raises his eyebrows in my direction, already halfway to the elevators.

"Yep!" I reply, going back to the LinkedIn page open on my computer. It's embarrassing that I haven't closed it. I don't even know what I'm looking for anymore.

Tan Overa— *Maeve* appears from behind the wall of my cube. Her eyes peek over my computer screen. I frantically close tabs and stare intently at the default background image of a starry night on my desktop.

"Yes?" I mumble, trying to seem unfazed and totally normal.

"Hey, just checking to see where you're at. I'm finished for the day, so grab me whenever." And then she was gone, caught in Jesse's jetstream.

I wait ten minutes on principle, and soon we're back on the hot pavement of Marquette, making our way to Ramp A. She has her headphones in, and I consider it a peace offering. As we follow the same choreography of getting into my parked car, it's not until we're on the highway again when she speaks for the first time, taking her headphones out and putting them neatly in their case and into her small grey backpack.

"You know what's coming," she teases, smiling devilishly. I actually don't. "Pit and a peach?"

I scrunch my nose. "You can't possibly think I'm willing to entertain this again."

"Excuse me." She fakes offense by placing her hand on her chest. "Fine, I'll go first."

I groan.

"My pit is that today I had to write an advertorial on this new furniture store opening in Wayzata. Wanna know who their target audience is?" She pauses, raising her eyebrows at me before answering her own question. "*Recent divorced*

PIT AND A PEACH

housewives. Their cheapest couch is, like, six thousand dollars. Can you imagine?"

I can imagine.

"Luckily it's only half a page, so like, twenty-five-hundred words. Not awful. But my *peach*," she effuses, her voice going high-pitched and squeaky as I speed past hundreds of cars to enter the HOV lane, "is that I submitted my review of the new tapas place in Loring Park. Zakariya and I scoped it out last week and it *slapped*. It was so good. And I got to meet the owners and I told them a little about what I do, and they tried to comp my meal. It was so sweet. Anyway, so I wrote up the piece and got it to Zakariya, and he loved it. He said it might even be printed instead of digital. I'm so pumped. I can't wait for the first issue with my name on a byline."

Her energy is radiating in the car. I wouldn't describe her as bubbly, she's too aggressive for that, punching the air and clenching her fists. But she can't stop moving. Both her knees bounce and her heels jump up and down on my floor mat. She watches the cars whiz by before turning her attention to me. It's like having a spotlight pointed at my face on a dark stage.

"Okay, you've gotta give me something now."

"Please, no."

"Dude! I'm not asking for an in-depth analysis of the day. A little high, little low. Easy come, easy go, ya know?" She stares at me as if I'm supposed to respond. "Freddy Mercury?"

"Yeah, I understood the reference," I sigh and push myself back against the headrest. "I don't know. I guess my peach is—"

"Nope, pit first."

I don't have the fight in me anymore, and the eye roll just happens. My pit is Lacie. My pit is being single in the real world after college when I'd go to a party and get three girls' numbers in two hours. My pit is that I have no idea where to go from here, but all I can think of is how disappointing my lunch was today. "Fine, my *pit* is that they were out of my favorite soup at Allie's Deli."

"Oh, that sucks. What kind of soup?" I turn to give her a glare, but I don't find the sarcasm that I'm expecting.

"Creamy tomato."

"Yum." She nods sincerely. "And your peach?"

I think hard. I guess today wasn't the worst day ever. "Uh, well since it was the Monday after deadline week, it was a bit slow today. Caught up on emails." *Read your LinkedIn eight times.* "Managed to get a head start on November's issue."

More sincere nodding. "Nice. That sounds like a good break from last week." She smiles and settles into the passenger seat, seemingly satisfied with my answers.

I'm content with the quiet, and before I know it, I'm taking the Betty Crocker Drive exit (I'm serious, that's the exit name), and turning into the underground parking garage. We split on the elevator, but not before Maeve shuffles through her backpack and pulls out her wallet.

"For your troubles."

Before I can thank her for the five crisp twenties, she's off on the third floor without a backward glance, and for some reason, I can't stop smiling on my way to the fourth floor with "Bohemian Rhapsody" stuck in my head like an earworm.

Chapter 4

LACIE AND I STILL HAVEN'T TALKED. And that's weird, right? I feel like I'm going crazy, but there's been nothing. She hasn't spoken to me since her surprise dumping over a month ago. And for someone I've spent almost every weekend and major holiday with for the past six years, it feels like a certain kind of fuck-you-ery to not even send a text saying something like, *"Hey! Hope I didn't ruin your life too much! Sorry about the lack of orgasms. xoxo, Lacie."*

Which makes me want to hate her, but I kind of miss her. And for that, I feel a weird sense of guilt and rage. If she would have talked to me when she was first having second thoughts, we could have probably pushed through it. I would've listened.

I would've changed. But she didn't give me the chance, and it's unfair that I'm the one left on read.

It's my pit and has been since the first drive home. I have a hard time not bringing Lacie up in every conversation that I have with Maeve, *see I remember her name,* seeing as she's constantly asking me what the best and worst parts of my days are.

In all honesty, the drives have been going fine. It only took three mornings for her to ask why I drive in silence, and I had been this close to telling her how Lacie didn't *like* my music before she reaches for the dials herself.

"It's *awkward*," she tells me, like I'm the crazy one, but I'm pleased with the result nonetheless. The music gives us both an excuse; Maeve sometimes catches a few more moments of sleep, and I get to prepare for my day. She's quiet in the mornings, allowing me to listen to my music without interruption. The silence is almost comfortable. Almost.

Evening commutes are not as peaceful. While *my* days tend to beat me to a pulp, hers usually get her going like a wind-up toy. She's loud and animated, telling me about something as dull as an interview with a business owner or how a croissant tasted in Stillwater and how she's excited to write about it. And each day, it's the same game she refuses to let me forfeit.

"Pit and a peach?" Her eyes widen curiously. We haven't even left the parking garage, yet.

Today was particularly frustrating. Jesse "took action on my feedback" by bringing me into the sales meeting to talk about the importance of telling their clients about the ad deadlines upfront, and that the account executives are *fully capable* of uploading ads themselves into Magazine Manager. As if I haven't had this exact conversation one-on-one with every person in the room. Hank was conveniently offsite, while the rest of the team looked either half-dead or were on their computers. It was exhausting.

"Just give me, like, three minutes," I plead.

"For what?"

"I don't know, to get my seatbelt on?"

She laughs, with a singular, "Hah!" and puts her phone in her grey backpack, leaning forward to focus on the conversation. "I can start today."

"Okay, you start today."

"My pit is that I ran out of coffee today at home, so I had to drink the stuff at the office." She makes a face like she just smelled something awful. "That shit is gross. Gave me heartburn."

I furrow my brows. "Excuse me, I drink that *shit*. It's not that bad, and it's free. So..." I pause, feeling myself smile. "Be grateful."

"Grateful?! For battery acid? No. I'm pretty sure you're the only one who drinks it." She looks out the window, smiling to herself. "And my peach is...hmmm." She looks back at me, confused. "Gosh, I don't really know. It wasn't a bad day, just can't think of something. Oh! You know what, I tried out Allie's Deli for lunch today and the person working was really nice. You know how you have those interactions with people and you walk away thinking, 'Wow, that's what it feels like to be human.' It was like that."

I have no idea what she's talking about. I don't think I've ever thought twice about what it means to be human after something as impartial as paying for lunch. "Um, what?"

"I know. It was an older woman and she called me honey. I wanted to hug her," she says, and my stomach is doing weird things. "Okay, your turn. It's been at least three minutes."

We're already in the HOV lane, passing the crawling traffic on the 394 exit to 100. I'm so glad I'm not sitting in that, which I suppose is half the answer to her question. "Alright, pit is that I had to go to the sales meeting today. Brutal. I can't imagine being an account executive."

"They have the *worst* jobs," she agrees.

"And peach is that I'm not sitting in traffic. Because that also looks particularly brutal today."

"Nice," she exhales and nestles back into the seat.

The mood settles alongside her and the opening notes of "Kill Bill" by SZA play softly underneath the rattle of the highway. The volume is almost so low you can't hear it, but that doesn't stop Maeve from sitting up once again.

"Oh! I love this song," she mumbles, fiddling with volume as she tries and fails to hit every word that SZA has perfected into a song that's gotten me through most nights lately. "I don't know the verses," she laughs to herself, then proceeds to sing the chorus as if she's been dumped by David Carradine himself.

The masterpiece ends the second I get into the parking garage. It's one of those moments that feels planned, perfectly synced up as the engine comes to a halt. She smiles at me with her mouth agape in surprise. "I love when that happens! New peach."

I chuckle, grabbing my overstuffed backpack from the back seat and we climb the stairs in silence, breathing a little more labored as always. We both head to our mailboxes, a routine that has been set up now for the past two weeks, and I see a box by my feet with my apartment number written in thick black marker on the top. I haven't ordered anything and vocalize that to Maeve before I realize what it is. The return address is for a house in Northeast where four girls live, including my ex-girlfriend. I sigh and try not to let Maeve catch my reaction.

"I think I have a new pit."

The box was light enough to carry on my own, but large enough to make riding the elevator with Maeve awkward and uncomfortable.

"I was going to ask about how that was going when we were in the car, but it felt a little on the nose during that song." She glances at me as if I'm about to explode again.

"It's going about how you would think it's going." I readjust the box and rest it on my hip. I don't remember leaving that much shit at her place. I was never there. "It sucks."

The elevator dings and she turns around with a forced smile. "Sorry. See you tomorrow morning."

The box almost drops again, and I have to hoist it back up. "Yep," I say, because I'm somewhat at a loss for words.

I exhale once she's out of the elevator, but I wish she didn't leave. I don't want to do this alone. I don't necessarily want to do this with her, either. I just miss having someone next to me who knows me like Lacie does... or *did*.

I set the box down on my couch and debate staring at it for the rest of the night. I might as well rip the bandaid off. I grab a beer from the fridge, because that's for sure going to help, and sit down on my coffee table, swigging half of it down before taking the scissors from the kitchen to get on with it. Her handwriting is squiggly and loopy as ever. I don't know why I thought it would have changed.

There's a mess inside. Whether she tried to organize it neatly, or chucked everything in like an afterthought, I'll never know, because the United States Postal Service doesn't care if a package is full of sentimental pieces of a relationship. It gets jostled about anyway.

The first thing I notice is a sweatshirt. I don't recognize it right away, but once I see the U of M logo, I'm immediately taken back to senior year. We're on the front lawn of one of her friend's houses, dressed in maroon and gold waiting to go to a Gopher football game. We'd been seeing each other for a few weeks and realized that we lived on the same side of campus. She had more friends than me, so I was absorbed into her friend group by association. I was attached to her side and she seemed to like that. By the end of the night, I had given her my sweatshirt to wear over her bright yellow tank top. We cuddled next to a fire, too drunk to do much else than sit and laugh and watch the flames flicker alongside our new relationship. I catch myself smelling it before I chuck it across the couch where it lands haphazardly, half on the armrest, half on the floor. I haven't seen that sweatshirt in years. She doesn't wear things like that anymore.

There are two other pieces of clothing, and I pull both out at once, rolling my eyes and groaning to the ceiling. This was petty as fuck. She knows I don't need these back. Lacie had a thing for wearing my boxer briefs as pajamas. It only lasted two years out of college, but she liked keeping them for when I stayed over, even though they were too small for me now.

They're not the only thing she could have thrown away. A box of condoms peeks out from the wreckage along with an old toothbrush I kept there for emergencies. And call me whatever you want, but I throw the toothbrush wrapped in the boxers at the sweatshirt, and the condoms get placed to the side. Who knows.

Then things get real. I used to read a lot. In college, it felt like a party trick. I'd show up to a group hang with a book and girls immediately want to talk to me. Sit outside the library with anything by Toni Morrison and it took less than a half an hour to get a girl's phone number. I continued the hobby well into my mid-twenties (because I actually like Toni Morrison), but haven't found the time or passion to start anything and commit. My copy of *The Alchemist* by Paulo Coelho is bent out of shape and folded at weird pages while my hardcover of *The Tipping Point* by Malcolm Gladwell held up well on the journey.

I keep out *The Alchemist*, trying to straighten it back in place, but chuck the hardcover at the pile accumulating on the end of the couch. I wouldn't mind disappearing into the mind of Coelho right about now.

The next gut punch is a stack of photos, held together with a pink binder clip. Upon first glance, I realize they're the pictures that once hung above her bed, strung together with twine and mini clothespins. I helped put it up when she moved in. We weren't the fighting type, but we bickered a lot that month, arguing about whether or not we should live together. I practically begged her to move in, but she wasn't ready. She wanted more time with her friends, which I had a hard time contending. Looking back, it was the beginning of the end. In the pictures, we look happy. Smiley, relaxed, and young. I don't remember where most of them were taken. A house party here, a tailgate there. A few of them were in her old apartment from senior year. One is of us in her bedroom cuddled up together under her purple duvet. The moment I spot it I'm flush with visions that make my stomach drop and my legs feel heavy. Lots of memories on that purple duvet. Memories that only her and I share.

The words are on repeat in my head.

I love you, Con, but it's time to start living my life.

She was living her life. We both were. How could someone look at these photos and think she— *we* weren't already living?

As if the photos weren't enough, there's a small box and a handwritten card left, and I know immediately what's inside. With shaky hands, I open the flat white velvet jewelry case and chew the inside of my lip. It's the butterfly necklace I gave her when she graduated. She always said she was waiting to spread her wings one day. I always knew she'd fly. I just didn't know I would be the thing she left behind. I always figured I'd fly with her.

I finish the rest of my beer before opening the card, transitioning to the couch, surrounded by reminders that I'm not someone's someone anymore. Her curvy handwriting surprises me once again, but this time it's because I'm taken aback by the amount of it. The card wasn't enough, she included a separate piece of notebook paper, folded and tucked into the crease. I bite my lip a little harder and blink away what I've been avoiding for the last month so that I can read clearly:

Hey Con,

I'm moving out soon and wanted to return some of the things that you might want back. But I also wanted to write you a note.

I know I cut things off really quickly, but everything I read online told me that would be the easiest thing for both of us. And to be honest, things had been stale for so long that I figured maybe it was an out for you, too. Maybe I was wrong about that, but I'm standing by my decision for a clean break.

I will always love you, Con. You were there for so many of my favorite memories in the last six years. Graduation, moving off campus, vacations with my family, new jobs, weddings, and even just getting dinner together on a Thursday night. But when I look back on those times, I also get this sad kind of feeling because as much as I love to think about the past, I could never see my future with you. I'm just being 100% honest.

I don't want you to think that it was any one thing you did or said that made me walk away. I haven't been feeling it for months, and I'm sorry that I didn't talk to you about it first. At some point I didn't think talking about it would change anything.

I hope one day we can be friends, but in order to do that, I need some time to live my life without you. Thank you for respecting that.

xoxo,
Lacie

Friends. With someone I spent the last six years with. How would that even be possible? I don't know whether to be blinded by my anger or my heartbreak. Six years wasted on someone who *couldn't see her future with me* for god knows how long. What a blow to the gut. Meanwhile, I envisioned my entire life by her side. Not one anticipated milestone existed without her; getting married, buying our first home, growing grey and wrinkly and still being in love. I don't want to live life without her. Without *someone.*

The inside of my lower lip is raw from how hard I'm fighting it, holding it all in so it doesn't feel real. Up until now, I thought if I didn't cry about it, maybe it was just a story, like it wasn't actually happening to me and was some bit I'd made up in my head. But the letter was right in front of me, trembling in my hands.

It all came out. I let it. It was over.

And all I had left was a pile of trash that smelled like her.

Chapter 5

MY EYES ARE SWOLLEN THE NEXT DAY. I've never woken up with a swollen face from crying in my entire life. It's stupid and embarrassing. I'm waiting for Maeve in the lobby of our apartment complex, and I'm hoping with enough weird face exercises, the puffiness will go away. Especially after last night, I don't need her asking more questions about how things are going with the breakup.

I check my watch. 7:32 am. If she bursts through the elevator, I would consider it still "on time," but she's cutting it close. And sure, I don't really have anywhere to be. My first meeting of the day isn't until 9 am, but still. Getting to the office early with Maeve has been kind of fun. When it's just us, sometimes she'll shout a random news headline or work-related update over the cubicles.

A few more face stretches and I'm getting antsy. I wish I could say I'm too tired to get angry about this, but my chest is starting to get that sinking feeling. How hard is it to be on time? How difficult is it to give someone a heads-up text if you're running behind? Well. She'd have to get my number in order to do that. The thought gives my chest another pulse.

It's 7:50 am and I'm over it.

I lean my entire body into the heavy metal door with force, pushing out my frustration and stomping down the steps as they echo in the stairwell. I'm fighting with my emotions from last night, battling two conflicting feelings of wanting Maeve to be stomping down the stairs with me, yet annoyed by the fact that she's not. I want to be alone, I want to have someone next to me. I want to shut up and never speak again, I want to talk about it until I'm hoarse. I want Lacie back, I want my future back. The past, present, future. It doesn't feel like mine anymore without her.

I slam my driver's side door and feel the crunchy pearls of flesh beneath my teeth. My lip is so raw that I've moved to my cheek. My entire face is sore. I'm angry and I place it all on the fact that I am usually at the office by now. That's the problem in front of me. That's the thing I can fix. With a shortened breath, my car roars and as I look in the rearview mirror, there she is. Her backpack is dangling from her forearm and her hair is wild, flying around her as she's running toward my car.

"Conrad! Wait!" Her muffled yell makes it inside the car. I want to peel out of the garage to leave her behind; I want to stop, sit in silence with her, and cry the rest of the morning. I do neither. I do the right thing. She hoists her backpack up and opens the door, smiling and huffing.

"I thought you were gonna leave me."

I had every right to. "You're twenty minutes late."

"I know, I know." She clicks her seatbelt and takes out a small bag from her backpack. "I was up late last night. And remember how I told you I ran out of coffee?" she says as if that explains the entire morning.

I'm still struggling not to lose composure, so I don't answer her. For the most part, we're silent on the way in, save for the sedative sounds of Augustine's airy album *Weeks Above The Earth* centering me back into the commute.

Now that I've calmed down a bit, it's comforting to have Maeve in the front seat, putting on makeup haphazardly. From what I notice, Maeve spends the first five minutes of our commute aggressively rubbing some kind of lotion on her face, applying blush, and flicking on mascara. I know you're getting sick of hearing it, but it reminds me of Lacie and just how different the two are. Lacie used to take hours before events to get everything just right. A wave of anger hits me all over again and I have no idea why.

We're exiting from the highway when Maeve speaks for the first time since the garage.

"You're quiet today."

"Hm."

I can sense her watching me for a second before turning to look out the window. I'm blinking hard and trying to think about something that won't make the clench in my throat worse. Emails, taxes, rent. Pointless distractions that feel sterile compared to the thoughts swirling in my mind.

We're spiraling up to the sixth level of the parking ramp, and her tone changes beside me. "I'm sorry I was late."

"It's fine," I mumble.

"Is it? Because you seem very determined to be upset about it."

"I promise it's not about you," I push out with more verve than I feel. Anger is so much easier than whatever is going on right now.

She nods and fidgets with the button on her linen shirt. It's oversized and light grey. "Is this because of last night? The box?" she asks.

I nod and taste blood. My poor cheek.

"Have you talked with her at all?"

I shake my head. Having someone else talk about Lacie is bringing it all up to the surface. Maeve doesn't know her name, but she knows she was mine. Knows that we probably loved each other.

The sixth level is fuller than normal because of the delay, which gives us more time to awkwardly sit in silence as I weave through the rows of cars and musky cement pillars. I finally find one I'm satisfied with and I shut the car off. Neither of us move.

"Are you okay? Do you want to talk about it?"

I can't answer that. *Don't do this, Conrad. Keep it contained.*

"Okay," she whispers. At least three full minutes go by. Her hand makes contact with the bare skin on my forearm.

"I'm sorry."

I'm not biting my cheek anymore because it's not working. Nothing's working. The tears are already to my chin and I have to find interest in the car next to me in order to turn away from her gaze.

"Is there...do you want me to...hmm." There's a rustling in the seat next to me, but I'm trying way too hard to look the other direction at the red sedan on my side.

I want her to stay.

I want her to leave.

"I'll be outside. There's no rush."

That's somehow both. How is she so good with managing my emotions? I sure can't. I nod to the red sedan and hear the door shut with a thud that shakes the car, and my face falls.

"Fucking ridiculous," I cry to myself, letting my head hang until it rests on the steering wheel.

I'm trying to piece together how I got here. The last month took nothing out of me. The day after the breakup, I was fine. Angry about work, but fine. These last few weeks were somewhat normal, which only confirms that something was wrong with Lacie and me. How strong is a relationship if your day-to-day barely changes when it's over? I don't know why all of a sudden it's hitting me like a bus. I'm single, but I'm more than that. I'm alone. I don't have someone to call, someone to spend my time with. Do I even have any friends? I don't have any fucking friends. I don't have a life.

It's too hot in the car now. My clothes are too close to my skin and my eyes hurt. My head feels too small. My sinuses are hammering at my skull to expand. Tears are sticking to my steering wheel and I need to blow my nose more than I need air. It's all just a bit too much. I can either spark the engine and sit in air-conditioning to wallow indefinitely, or I can get my shit together and walk with Maeve to the office.

With a quick glance around the parking garage, I can't find her. Makes sense. I've been sitting here for over ten minutes. I shouldn't expect her to wait for me to finish with my toddler-like meltdown.

The nip of the fall air hits my flushed cheeks and I instantly feel better. My car has been a chamber of weirdness lately. From Lacie dropping the breakup bomb to Maeve planting peach trees, it just feels good to get out.

I don't find her until I reach the skyway, right as she turns a corner with two to-go coffee cups and a clump of napkins in her hand. I must imagine the way her eyes light up when she sees me. It's not real. Because if I was her I'd be weirded out by me right now.

"Hey." Her eyebrows drop and she gives me a smile that sort of makes my skin itch. I feel the shame in the back of my throat. "I got you a coffee."

"You didn't need to do that."

"I know. I did it anyway," she counters, handing me a cup with focused eyes. I take a few napkins instead.

"One sec," I say, scurrying away like some gremlin to avoid her hearing the sounds of me clearing my nose. I'm an absolute mess and it's not even 9 am. I turn around and realize she's following me. "I'm good, I'm fine." She hands me a coffee, and this time I take it with a small, "thanks."

There's no denying how nice she's being. It feels like pity, but her eyes are forward. There's no upturn of her eyebrows, no carefulness to her gait. She catches me looking over at her and it sparks a conversation I regret instantly.

"You can talk about it if you want. If you don't, that's okay, too."

"I don't." Now my eyes are straight ahead. I can't stand being consoled. My parents got divorced when I was four. I don't remember anything about it, but even in college, my mom made doughy eyes at me and my younger sister whenever my dad got brought up, as if we'll burst into tears with the mention of him. He's in DC now, has another family, another life. I don't even think about him. Still, Maeve knows this matters to me. How could she not by my spontaneous display of human emotion?

She shrugs. "Okay. Door's open."

My phone vibrates in my hand. It's a calendar notification for a department head meeting that starts in fifteen minutes.

"Ah, fuck," I inadvertently whisper out loud. Maeve catches on but says nothing. I tear off with my coffee, and she's on my heels.

I think I've fully decided that I wish I was alone right now. If I didn't have to wait for Maeve, I would have been here almost an hour ago. There wouldn't have been a twenty-minute delay to get on the highway. The HOV lane wouldn't have been so busy. The parking ramp would have been emptier. And I could have avoided falling apart in the car because no one would have bothered me to ask *"Are you okay?"* or *"Do you want to talk about it?"*

Why would I want to talk about it? Look what happened when I just *thought* about it. The only thing I should be focused on is gathering my thoughts for the Thursday department head meeting. A meeting that I should have been preparing for all morning.

Zakariya, Jesse, and our marketing director, Kathryn, are all waiting for me as I rush into Jesse's office. I'm only three minutes late, but for someone like me, that feels like a lifetime.

"Ah, Conrad, there you are. I was just about to text you," Jesse says, gesturing to my usual seat next to him. We post up at the small table across from his desk. Jesse's office is three times as large as anyone else's. Publisher's privilege. Kathryn has her own section of the office with Kiara, and Zakariya's cube is the largest in the Editor's Den, but for me? Well, my cube is directly outside of Jesse's office with how often we have to check in about the issue thus far. I can see my desk through the small window in Jesse's door, untouched from the wild morning I had.

We begin the rounds of updates, each of us editorializing the best parts of the week and making excuses for why things aren't submitted yet. I'm always the bad guy in these things. The problem is that we don't have an account manager. Jesse has acted as that for years since the last publisher left.

"Alright, so. Sales are looking good. We're out of the summer slump and into the fall. We're already halfway to our advertorial goal about 'Fall Favorites for the Home,' so those should be trickling in," Jesse reports, making sure to look everyone in the room in the eye. He's been to too many leadership trainings.

He lands on me. It's my cue. I pull what I can from the top of my head. "Yep, we have a forty-page book. Last I checked, there are thirty slots in this issue, and sixteen of them are in. Four of them are half pages, two full pages, six-thirds, and two eighth pages ads. That was yesterday, I haven't taken a look at my email this morning, though."

Jesse writes all that down. "Excellent. Better than last month at least. Alright, Kathryn, anything new?"

Kathryn doesn't interact with me much outside of timid hello's and apologetic emails. "Um, yes, so, it's not announced to the public yet, but we're at a point that I can share with the folks in this room that we've started a contract with a pretty high-profile talent agency for online influencers."

I can't fucking catch a break today.

She beams around the table with a nervous smile. "Mainly we're hoping for a few ghostwritten columns, some exclusive reviews, and some bigger brand partnerships. More to come!"

"Who are the influencers?" I ask, trying to contain the heat that's rising in my neck. I know it came out harsher than I meant it.

Kathryn glances at Jesse. "Uh, well. I can't share individual names yet, but we're focused on the local mid-tier level market with a following between fifty thousand to two-hundred-fifty thousand followers. And um, food and lifestyle are our targets." Cool, so, exactly Lacie. I'll ask Jesse about it later. "The talent agency we're working with specializes in—"

"What's the talent agency?"

Jesse clears his throat and it's my signal to calm down.

Kathryn's eyes widen. "Um, it's called Agenzia. They're out of Edina and have offices here in downtown."

"Of *course* they do." I didn't mean to say that out loud.

"Alright, Conrad." Jesse gives me a stern look before softening at Zakariya. "Zak?"

He smiles and I swear his hair animates and bounces alongside it. He reads from his notebook. "Yeah! So, we're finally back up to a full editorial staff this issue, so that feels good. I have Jordan covering Hennepin Theater Trust since they announced their winter season. I think she'll be stopping in St. Paul at the Ordway, too. Their upcoming season was announced and there's some controversy with one of the shows they chose. I don't know the name of it though." He threw his hands up, his smile bright as ever. "Sua's been cranking out the newsletter like a champ, and advertorial is being covered by our intern, Grace, with the help of sales and Kiara for social media.

"I've been digging into some legislative stuff on the elections coming up in Greater Minnesota, and Maeve is on all things food." My ears perk up like a dog before I'm even conscious of what I'm doing. Suddenly I'm fully invested in what Zakariya has to say.

"There's a new spot in Uptown called Bordeaux. French cuisine, insane wine collection, the works. But, I don't know." He loses steam and scratches his temple. "I can't really justify reimbursing her for a three hundred dollar meal when I know that the Strib and every other magazine in the area is going to send a writer to type up the same thing, just reworded."

Jesse nods, grimacing. "I hear you and completely agree. I've been wrestling with the same thing."

"Me too," Kathryn chimes in, following Jesse's lead. "Kiara has noticed that every time a new high-end restaurant opens, we're competing with the same posts on our competitors' pages. Sometimes it feels like we're all saying the same thing!" She lets out an anxious laugh.

"Then what if we just...don't?" I say, adding nothing to the conversation. Zakariya gives me a placating glare, but I keep going. "No, like, what's telling us we have to write about every new restaurant that opens?" I point at Jesse. "You've said before that we're not a news organization. We curate content for our audience. People aren't looking to us to be their first source on things, they're looking to us for quality shit." I'm on my high horse, but I believe in our strategy. It's why people still read our magazine. We talk about the good stuff. The *peaches*, if Maeve were here.

"I don't disagree," Zakariya says, a bit puffed. "But we may seem a little irrelevant if we're not at least talking about the things everyone else is."

"Then put it into a listicle of new restaurants in town! Not an entire feature." I'm out of breath for some reason.

Jesse puts his hand out to de-escalate the situation. "Okay, I think there are two excellent points being brought up," he says. Kathryn is avoiding eye contact with anything in the room.

"I'm just saying. What about the restaurants that have been open for ten-plus years, owned by families and competing with all these new flashy places with seventeen-dollar cocktails?" I pulled that number from the rooftop bar the night Lacie broke up with me. It's not like *she* was looking at the prices.

"I don't want to write hit pieces," Zakariya pushes. "We're not food critics."

"We don't have to be!"

I need to calm down, but I can't.

I continue, "If we don't like something, we don't publish it. There's gotta be some hidden gems that no one's writing about anymore."

Zakariya shrugs. "Yeah, you have a point, I guess. My adeer owns a place in Cedar-Riverside. Customers are loyal but there aren't many new ones. I could see if Maeve wants to write up a piece about it." Her name is the most comforting thing about this conversation.

"That's awesome, excellent work!" Jesse cheers, smiling at Kathryn who's since reanimated. "Once it's up, we can share on our socials, maybe get some good photos of the owners and the food."

This is the rooftop all over again, and I want nothing to do with it. I share out the deadlines for the issue before we break and Jesse pulls me back.

"I gotta ask, Conrad. What's going on today?"

Oh, as if the puffy eyes and runny nose weren't a dead giveaway. "Just a rough morning. Still dealing with the breakup."

He nods solemnly. "Look, your ideas are great, but the way you present them isn't. We all have bad days. You need an afternoon off, you just tell me, okay?"

"I don't need an afternoon off. I have to pull reports for last month's distribution. I'm fine."

With a sigh, he says, "Alright," and gives me a pat on the arm. "Let me know if you need anything from me."

There is one thing. "Do you have a list of names that agency works with? My ex does that kind of stuff."

Jesse hesitates but gives in with a nod to follow him around to his computer. He furrows his brow and pulls up their contract, listing names of potential influencers that we would have "access" to per the language of the agreement. I skim them and find a few names I've heard before, Sonja one of them, but notably not Lacie. I don't know if I'm relieved or disappointed.

"Thanks," I mumble, making note of the pictures of Jesse's family on his desk. A husband, two kids. They even have a golden retriever. I can't help but compare his perfect life with the one I thought I was building with Lacie.

There's so much I was subconsciously planning for whenever I envisioned our future. Marriage? Yes. Kids? Probably. A good 401k? Well, not on my side, but I bet her family would've had a nest egg set aside for her. How can someone just walk away like this? Since I was a kid, I've never understood it, and always blamed myself. And in this instance, it's hard not to fall into that trap all over again.

I'm already writing the script for the car ride later. This is my pit.

"What if we got ice cream tonight?" Maeve asks on the walk to Ramp A. "I know it's against the contract, but I'll pay."

"Contract?" I question. "There isn't a contract with this."

"Oh, really? You had a lot of stipulations for there not to be some sort of contract written up in your head," she says matter of factly. She mocks me, "'To and from work, that's it.' But this is kind of that. It's just a pit stop. Plus this is me owing you for being late this morning."

This is the closest I'm going to get to having plans this week. "Fine. Ice cream and then home. That's it."

"Roger. Okay, so the place is only ten minutes from the apartment, it's called Honey & Milk. It's—"

"This is premeditated!" I catch on quickly. We stop at a crosswalk and wait for the traffic of Hennepin to pass. "You had this planned all along."

She laughs. "Sue me! I want ice cream. Have you looked at the weather? It's supposed to be in the fifties next week. Summer is almost over."

It's deadline week next week. That's the only thing on my radar.

"Plus, they have the best vanilla ice cream in the world."

I grimace as we cross the street. "You're taking me to a place because of their *vanilla* ice cream?"

"You don't get it. For an ice cream shop to be known for its vanilla is such a flex. They don't need all that gimmicky stuff. It's *that* good."

The passion behind every syllable makes me want to believe her. I will still be getting the cookie dough flavor because I'm not an idiot. And that would be great and all, but once we get there, I learn they have nothing of the sort.

"They don't have normal flavors." I bend down to whisper to Maeve in line. It's nearly out the door and suspiciously aesthetic for an ice cream shop. The walls are beige and there's a lot of wood.

"What are you talking about?" She points up. The flavors read vanilla, chocolate, strawberry, pistachio, coffee, black cap raspberry, and *sweet corn*. Huh? "It's all made with local ingredients. Well, I'm sure the chocolate and pistachio aren't. But it's delicious."

"Sweet corn ice cream?"

Her eyes challenge me. "I dare you to get it."

I can't resist a chance to prove someone wrong. "I will, just so you can have a bite and see how gross it is."

"It's *not* going to be gross. They wouldn't sell it here if it was."

We'll see. Ten minutes later, we're handed our ice cream in tan paper cups. Maeve got olive oil drizzled on her vanilla. (Disgusting.) And since she was paying, I asked for honey on my sweet corn flavor for a whole extra *dollar*. (Also disgusting.) Jesus Christ. I'm prepared for this to be revolting.

She makes me take a bite before we get into the car. "You can try mine first since I know you'll like yours more."

"Doubtful," I counter. My chest is doing a weird thing that makes me feel light and airy. Ever since this morning, there has been something different about being around her. It doesn't feel like an obligation. For either of us. I thought maybe she would treat me differently because of this morning, but nope, it's been sunshiney Maeve as usual. That's all I'm feeling, I just like the familiarity now. I like being around her. She's becoming a part of my routine.

We each take a spoonful of each other's scoops. I try to hide a smile while I move around the oil to get a spoonful without it. And fine. It was smooth and creamy and somehow rich and bright. I got a drop of olive oil on the edge of my spoon and the nuttiness of the extra virgin olive oil I'm finding out is quite amazing. The whole thing is good in an unexpected way.

"That's *incredible*!" she announces, pointing her soon at my ice cream. "Do you like the vanilla?"

"It's okay," I lie.

She eyes me. "Mhmm. Whatever. Oh! Do you have a pit and a peach for the day?"

"I was beginning to think you'd forgotten."

"Never."

We settle into the driver's seat of my SUV and turn the car on just to roll down the windows. The sun is out, but the breeze feels good. I'm dreading the winter like every other Minnesotan.

"I think it's obvious what my pit was. The hours of seven and eight this morning."

"Right. Checks out," she says. I'm too busy shoveling spoonfuls into my mouth to respond. "Are you feeling better?" I nod. "That's good. And your peach?"

"Peach is..." *This ice cream, damn.* "Alright, this peach is more like a silver lining than a full-blown peach, but during our department head meeting this morning, Kathryn in Marketing said we were working with this agency for influencers. My ex is an influencer, and I was like, here we go, it's just my luck, but I saw the list from Jesse and she doesn't work with them." I'm suddenly aware that I'm talking too much and take another spoonful to shut myself up. It's too easy to tell her everything. "Dodged a bullet."

"Your ex is an influencer?"

"Yep," I sigh. "LacieEats is her handle. She posts about food and like, lifestyle stuff I guess? Minneapolis content."

Maeve blinks at me, her spoon hanging in her mouth. The breeze grazes the wispy strands of hair around her tanned face.

It's in a loose braid today. Summer looks good on her. Summer looks good on everyone.

"I think I follow someone called LacieEats." *Oh god.* She picks up her phone and with a few thumb thumps pulls up an Instagram page. "Is this her?"

It's her. Her bio says, " ☀ BIG ANNOUNCEMENT COMING SOON ☀ " and I can only imagine it's some collab she's not getting paid for with someone who has 100k more followers than her. The most recent post is a classic posed smile, shoulder popping out just right, plates of untouched food on every photo of her carousel. I recognize the arrangement from the rooftop bar. I'm sure she's been juicing that night dry for the past few weeks. My hand is visible on the booth next to her and my chest sinks. I blink away from the screen. I'm absolutely not doing this again.

"Yep, there she is." I want to be talking about anything else. "Your turn."

"My turn for what?"

"Pit and peach, Sherlock. Keep up."

"Oh! Hmm." She puts her phone down on her lap and takes a bite of ice cream. "Pit is...um, let me think." She glances at her phone and then out the window. "Honestly, it's the same as yesterday. I miss my coffee. I'm so tired," she says with a full mouth. "And then my peach is that I was assigned to write

December's food feature, which I'm nervous as heck about, but I am so excited."

"You'll do great." And I mean it. Although, I haven't read anything of hers. There's a certain amount of pride in my chest knowing that I had a small part in her peach today.

We sit in the car and finish our last few bites. I'm not about to drive with the best-tasting ice cream I've ever had and be distracted by the traffic on Highway 55. I can't really hide my satisfaction; my entire cup is gone before she's eaten half of hers.

"So you really didn't like the sweet corn ice cream, huh."

I scoff with my last mouthful of dreamy, creamy goodness. "I was hungry."

"Sure," she chuckles. "Oh! That reminds me. Next Wednesday, I won't need a ride home."

I am overcome by a mixture of disappointment and curiosity. But I don't ask. I just nod and consolidate my trash before starting the car again. My stomach is doing weird things now that it's satisfied and what comes out of my mouth has perhaps a bit to do with it.

"I should probably have your number, that way you can text me and actually give me a heads up in case you're late again."

"Oh my *god*, how many times do I have to say I'm sorry," she remarks with an eye roll but smiles and opens her phone for me to type into her contacts regardless.

When I get home that night, I can't help myself. Sure, I pretend to read something from my bookshelf, but my mind is too busy to register the words on the page. In a moment of weakness, I download Instagram and create a throw-away account with some letters and numbers. I've never had anything other than a Facebook, so it's clunky and hard to navigate once I find Lacie's profile. I instantly go to her followers and type "Meave" into the search.

Nothing.

Chapter 6

THE FOLLOWING WEDNESDAY MORNING, I find out why
Maeve doesn't need a ride home. Tonight she's headed to the
restaurant that Zakariya mentioned in our department head
meeting last week. And I learn on the way into work that not
only is she going to the restaurant to write the December
feature, all of the editors are going and are being hosted by
Zakariya and his family's friend. Even our social media
manager, Kiara, was invited. I've never spoken to her outside of
work.

"I can ask Zakariya if you want to come," Maeve asks in the
front seat as we merge off the HOV lane and into crawling
traffic. She must still be waking up because she's not making
sense.

My eyes widen involuntarily. "Nooo, no thanks. Even if I wanted to go, I highly doubt Zakariya would say yes to that. He hates me."

"What, why?" She genuinely looks puzzled.

"Do you not remember me yelling at him about October's feature your second week on the job? Also, I kind of snapped at him last week in our department head meeting."

She gives me an upside-down smile. "He's never mentioned anything about hating you. I mean, I think half of editorial is afraid of you, and don't get me started on Kathryn in marketing, but I think he'd be okay with you coming."

"Afraid?"

"I don't know if afraid is the right word, but intimidated at the very least."

Our conversation is just getting going and I'm already pulling into Ramp A. Lately it's been feeling like the fifteen-minute car rides aren't long enough. Sometimes I wish we had hours.

"I don't know how anyone would be intimidated by me. Do they know I've been sulking over an ex who dumped me in less than five minutes over two months ago?"

"Um, well."

"Wait, do they actually know that?"

"I may have mentioned you're going through a breakup," she admits, sucking in air through her teeth.

"Oh, great. How long have they known?"

She buries her head in her hands. "I told them the day after I found out."

"Maeve!" I haven't said her name in a while and it feels good to feel my front teeth against my lower lip.

"Well, I didn't know you! I wasn't about to get into the car with a complete stranger every day without knowing a bit about you. I asked Zakariya and Kiara, and they both said you seemed a little more stressed out than usual."

I'm parked and she's grabbing her backpack as I swing mine over my shoulder. The air outside has shifted this week. It's sweet and crisp and reminds me of apple pie and the pumpkin spice lattes that Lacie got every year. I hate that the good memories are now tainted with her. It's like nothing is mine anymore.

"And so you told them I got dumped?" I ask.

"No, I asked them what you were like. They said you keep to yourself and that you're no-nonsense. But that specific deadline week you had been particularly...rude."

"Rude."

"But then I explained your situation!"

"Oh my god," I groan, pushing open the skyway doors. "That's why Zakariya was so nice to me after I yelled at him."

"I had just told him that morning." There are little crinkles in her eyes as she smiles, and her left dimple is facing me as we walk.

Maeve is the only thing shiny enough to distract me from the Lacie situation. This past week has been full of weird revelations. When we parted on Thursday, I genuinely wondered what she was up to so late the previous night. Then it happened again over the weekend. She had my number, I didn't have hers. The temptation of texting her was futile, but there nonetheless. Every night when she exited on the third floor, a full-body curiosity took over me. I wanted to ask her what she was doing, and who she was doing it with. Did she live with anyone? Oh god, was she dating anyone? There's no way. I've never seen her with someone. I've also never asked.

Having these thoughts feels foreign. For the last six years, I didn't have to worry about other women. Some would try to hit on me when Lacie was doing her thing at bars, taking photos of every drink and dish. But our relationship spoke for itself. Lacie was gorgeous. Always done up whenever we left the house. The second anyone saw her, they got it. I got it. I knew I was lucky. I don't know why I was the one she chose. She said it was my green eyes. You know how many people on this planet have green eyes? She had to be lying. There's nothing that physically special about me. I'm 6'1" on a good day, can't gain muscle worth shit, and my mousy brown hair could be described as wavy or curly depending on what mood you're in. People tell me I look like a young Steve Hartman, the guy from CBS. As if everyone is supposed to know who that is. Have you ever heard someone say their celebrity crush is Steve Hartman? Exactly. I could never pinpoint a reason why Lacie was attracted to me other than proximity.

We never really fought, but we had plenty of bad days. And during those bad days, she always wanted space. So that's exactly what I gave her. I came to predict it, stepping back the moment I could feel the earth shift, preparing for a tsunami that usually knocked us out for a day or two, even if there wasn't an earthquake of a fight beforehand.

I ask Maeve the question that's been top of mind since last week. "How are you getting home tonight, then?"

"Well, the light rail runs right by Cedar-Riverside."

"But that area is a little rough at night."

"And so I was going to ask Zakariya to drive me to the train stop. From there, I just have to time it right to catch the 9:27 in downtown back home."

There's no way that's happening. After knowing she had gotten mugged once already, I'm surprised by her ignorant courage in taking public transportation that late. I have two options; I can either offer to drive back to the Eastside to pick her up, or I can suck it up and go to the dinner.

"Ask Zakariya if I can come."

Her brown eyes sparkle. What? It was the lighting. "You want to come?"

"I want to make sure you get home safe."

"Of course you can come to dinner tonight!" Zakariya's dark curls bounce up over my monitor. Maeve must have talked to him already. "It was your idea, anyway."

"Was it? It's your friend's restaurant." I'm trying to smile at him to match a fraction of his energy. The guy must've gotten laid last night. His luminous smile is bursting out of him.

"My uncle's. It'll be great. We're leaving here around five, but there's no rush. We'll be there for a while. I know it's deadline week."

I nod, giving him an unconvinced expression.

"Did you get the feature? Looking alright?" he asks.

The pagination is actually coming together quite easily for November's issue. The feature fits fine and only six ads are missing this time. "Yep, it's looking great. Thanks for sending it early."

"You got it!" He points at me and bounces away as quickly as he appeared. "See ya tonight!"

I don't leave the office until a quarter after 5 pm. I watch the editor clique leave together laughing and shouting about who would be driving with whom. Haha, so funny. I don't know how they all have so much to laugh about.

My stubbornness in leaving after them makes me about twenty minutes late to the restaurant. It's a hole in the wall. There's no traditional signage. Nothing more than a lit-up neon sign that says OPEN on a metal screen door with the correct building number. I don't know what language the name of the restaurant is written in and overall I feel like I'm intruding on something I'm not supposed to be at. I pass the threshold and it's clear this is a whole occasion. There is no one else in the restaurant besides a large table with the editors and a few other folks from different departments I don't interact with.

A short, filled-out woman wearing a hijab greets me with a wide smile and a thick accent. "I'm sorry, tonight we are closed for a private party."

Zakariya makes eye contact with me and senses the situation. He's already halfway to where we're stopped by the entrance. "Eedo, he's with us!"

She retracts as if she has insulted me and tries to get everything out in one breath. "I'm so sorry! Oh, yes. You are welcome, yes, of course. We are so excited to host you, yes!"

"Might want to wash up first. This is going to be a hands-on meal," Zakariya says, wiggling his fingers in front of his face.

I do so in a dingy, poorly lit bathroom, and after I smell like tangerine hand soap, I approach the table hoping to find a spot next to Maeve, but the only seat available is the head seat of the table in between Zakariya and someone I don't recognize. Zakariya is waving me over and as I sit down. The stranger on my left is next to Jordan from editorial. She's in an animated conversation with the girl next to Zakariya and some intern. Greta, maybe?

Zakariya takes the lead on introductions. "Conrad, this is Chris. Chris, Conrad."

Chris reaches his large handout and gives a firm shake. Even while he's sitting down, I can tell he's tall. Really tall. His brown skin is darker than Zakariya's and contrasts with his white Nike shirt.

"Hi," his low voice booms out over the conversations happening across the table. "I'm Jordan's husband."

"I've known Chris since grade school. It's how Jordan found out about the job," Zakariya adds.

Jordan whips around with the sound of her name. "You're talking about me?" The girl next to Zakariya laughs.

Chris pulls an arm around her and says, "Yeah, about how I got your job for you."

"Uh, hardly. You didn't even know the name of the magazine," Jordan sneers, garnering more laughter from Zakariya and the girl.

Chris shrugs. "Yeah, I don't keep track of that stuff."

I look around the table and Maeve is at the opposite end, sitting next to Kiara in Marketing. They're giggling about something. Maeve is showing Kiara her phone screen, and a few seconds later Kiara is leaning over the table, feigning a dramatic eye roll and jutting out her bottom lip. Maeve's expression settles and if I knew her better, I might say Kiara's reaction was less sincere than Maeve wanted it to be. But a millisecond later, she's resting her head on Kiara's shoulder playfully. I didn't even realize they knew each other.

I wish I knew what they were laughing at and why Kiara was giving her a look of sympathy. I wish I was sitting next to her. Maeve is beautiful, smiling and laughing with a friend, and I could be seeing it up close. Something kind of clicks. Shit. Do I like Maeve? What would that even look like?

"Conrad." Zakariya's voice brings me back to my side of the table. "This is my girlfriend, Lena." His arm is wrapped around the woman next to him and she beams at me. Her hair matches his, only her spiral curls are more blonde and blend in with her sepia skin tone. She's glowing when he introduces her. This must be the source of Zakariya's brightness.

"You're the director of production, right?"

Oh god, has he talked about me? "Yeah, yeah. Nice to meet you." I don't know what to say next, but I realize why we're here. To eat food. "Should I be looking at a menu?"

"We already ordered. I got us a round of shaah and the food should be out in a bit," Zakariya said.

"Shaah?"

"Oh, it's great. You like chai?"

I nod.

He turns to Lena. "I tried to tell them not to serve us anything off the menu, but I highly doubt they'll listen."

Lena laughs and her teeth are white and straight. I didn't catch what's so funny. "I swear they think we have a hidden stomach somewhere," she says.

Once the food arrives, I understand what she means. At least six different dishes are overflowing with on-the-bone meat that's skewered, stewed, and barbecued. It's paired with enough rice to feed the entire U of M football team. There's something that looks like spaghetti, but it all smells like cumin and pepper and oregano. Everyone is oohing and ahhing, but my focus is now on the plate that's directly in front of me, where nine bananas are arranged in a spiral formation.

"Bananas?" I ask Zakariya.

"Ooh, yeah, who here hasn't eaten Somali food before?" he asks the group. Chris and Lena keep their hands down, but the rest of the table either shoots their hand up (Maeve) or feebly raises a few fingers (me). "Okay, awesome. So, first things first. We eat with our hands, our right hands. You can take some injera, the rolled-up pancakes, and use that to grab stuff if you want. Otherwise, the rice is a good vehicle. Oh, and we always eat a banana with a meal like this. Take one and pass it around."

He's in his element. We take his lead while Chris and Lena help. It's not until the first few bites that I realize I stumbled into something really, really special tonight.

First, the food is phenomenal. There's no getting around it. They went easy on us with the spice level, but there's this green hot sauce that I'm putting on everything because it's bright and full of cilantro. My hands are filthy, my napkin is in shreds, and my nose is running, but I'm determined to handle it. And second, Zakariya's uncle comes out every ten minutes to check on us, and eventually the woman who greeted me before makes an appearance, too. They're so proud. It's written all over their faces.

I can't help but watch Maeve interact with the owners, too. Her demeanor changes when she's talking to strangers. Her chest is lifted and her hands are clasped in front of her. The woman gestures to follow her and they disappear behind the counter. Everyone's talking and laughing and I'm just sitting there watching it all happen, wishing I knew where Maeve was.

A total wave of realization sweeps over me as if I just became sentient. I'm enamored by Maeve. I can't wait to have her alone in the car. I want to know everything about her. I want to hear her talk and laugh and watch her eyes as they light up. I want to know what she spends her time thinking about;

what she's afraid of; what she's inspired by. And most immediately, I want to know what her pit and peach are for the day.

Chapter 7

EVERYONE IS SENT HOME WITH SAMBUSAS, and if I wasn't so full walking to the car with Maeve, I'd be eating them right now with how good they smell. She's a few steps ahead of me, words spilling out of her as I listen happily.

"And they have this whole community of restaurant owners — entrepreneurs, really — that all help each other out when supplies are low or they can't get the right spices. Some of them have their own gardens to grow certain peppers. Isn't that cool?" She looks at me for affirmation and I nod while raising my eyebrows. "But damn! It was so good! That was the most amazing meal I've had in years. Zakariya said his cheeks hurt from smiling so much. This is going to be incredible to write about."

She's in a good mood. I test my luck. "The night is young. Wanna get a drink before heading home?"

She turns around and her hair blows a bit in the wind. She looks ethereal. It's just wind. "I would, but my mind is racing with ideas of how I want to write this feature."

The feature isn't due for three weeks. "But you have time, don't you? Can't you pick it up in the morning?"

"That's not really how it works," she says with a smile. "I want to capture the feeling I have right now. All the details are swirling in my head, and I know exactly how I want the structure to be, and I don't want to lose it. It's hard to turn back on. Writing isn't like a faucet for me."

"Hmm," is all I give her. I guess I never thought about the fact that writers can't turn it off and on. My job doesn't require anything more than deadlines and telling people about those deadlines. I bump my shoulder against her because, well, touch barrier. "We got a workaholic on our hands."

"Hardly." She rolls her eyes and we silently get into the car and onto the road. She's a bit quiet now. Her eyes drift from the windshield to the passenger window. I don't have any music on, and I could, but nothing started playing from my phone. My mind was too busy to notice, but now it makes the silence even louder.

"So," I start. She turns to face me. "Aren't you gonna ask?"

"Ask what?"

I furrow my brow. "You feelin' alright? Pit and a peach."

"Oh! Right, okay, you first."

"No way, I asked you first."

"Conrad," she says, and I really like when she says my name. It throws me off my game and I comply.

"Fine, okay. Hmm. My pit today is finding out the editorial team knows that I got dumped by my ex-girlfriend." I pause to give her time to laugh, but she doesn't. She just rolls her eyes and shakes her head. Okayyy? "And my peach is the food tonight. Probably that green hot sauce."

She nods her head slowly and takes a deep breath. Her contented smile falls. "My pit is stupid, I know it, so you don't have to tell me, but it's been tugging at me all night." Her gaze is on her short fingernails, fiddling with the hem of her shirt. They're painted a chipped orangish-red. Like, terracotta or something. It's weird that I noticed this stuff now that my brain is excited to be around her.

"You said a pit and a peach isn't sacred. Who cares if it's stupid?"

"Right." She cracks a few knuckles. "So, my boyfriend is in the Peace Corps—"

What.

My brain instantly fries. It's not excited anymore.

Boyfriend?!

"—and usually we can only talk once every other week because of all of the volunteering he's doing. Tonight was supposed to be a night we talk, but he can't do it because he's traveling with his host family. And I'm just sad." She sighs. "Long-distance has its ups and downs. We've kind of been in a down this month."

What the flying fuck-er-ino is happening right now?

"You have a boyfriend?" I blurt. I have no control over what's happening to my body.

"I do. His name is Sean." She smiles. Goddamn smiles. Like she's in love. God fuck.

It's like I've been floating tonight, and with this new information, gravity is punching me back down to Earth. You'd think she would have talked about him even in passing. Did I even give her the chance? Do I talk too much? This is just like when I called her Tan Overalls the first week I knew her.

"You've never mentioned him," I mumble.

"Well, I guess it's never been brought up. And seeing as he's in Albania—"

"He's in *Albania*?" I realize I sound like an angsty teenager once the words leave my mouth. As if I'm disgusted by Albania. I probably can't even locate it on a map.

"Yes, jeez," she laughs. "He's there to do work with their health education. He teaches people about sex." She laughs again. Goddamnit. "Not really, but he does do a bit of training to teachers on how best to teach reproductive health to youth. He loves it. He's always working, plus he doesn't get cell service very often."

"How long has he been there?"

"A year and a half."

"When does he come back?"

"Four months, two weeks, and six days." *Oh, shut the fuck up.*

"How long have you been together?"

"We were together for six months before he left. So almost two years. We were friends before that. Since, like, Freshman year of college until I finally came around. Most of our relationship has been long-distance, though. It sucks."

I'm all out of questions. Not because I don't have any more rattling around in my head, but because I know I'm starting to sound insane.

"I guess it's weird to just be finding out about this now."

She knits her brows together but doesn't make eye contact. "I mean, he's not really a part of my day-to-day life right now." *I know how that goes.* "But when he moves back, we're planning on living together and getting a car. It feels like that's when my life will start. There's so much we're waiting on until he comes back. I can't wait, god."

Her life has already started. Why do people keep saying shit like that? Life is happening. And now I'm thinking of Lacie.

This is bullshit.

"Anyway, I'm just having a day. We were kind of supposed to have an important conversation tonight. He hasn't missed a call in months, and I'm trying not to think about it." She purses her lips.

I try her at her own game. "Wanna throw it out the window?"

The spark in her eyes from the sidewalk is back, and she instantly presses the motorized button to stretch her neck out until her hair is whipping around her face. I crack mine down so my ears don't hurt and swallow a laugh as she screams into the highway and the darkness of the night.

"LONG DISTANCE RELATIONSHIPS SUCK!"

Couldn't agree more.

Her eyes are wild when they look at me. "Okay, your turn."

"I'm driving." We're almost to the exit.

"Just do it! Come on!"

I comply, rolling my window down all the way while trying to keep an eye on the road. "Long distance relationships suck!" She laughs and I have her right where I want her.

"No! You have to throw your own pit out the window."

"Oh, oh right." I turn again. "MAEVE LIKES TO AIR MY DIRTY LAUNDRY TO THE ENTIRE OFFICE!"

"I do not!" She throws her head back, and my belly is warm even though my car is now chilled inside. This feels so good.

It's so nice to be in my car with Maeve. This is her life. We're already here.

Come on, Maeve. Feel the heat of the seat warmer, the dry hot air blowing on the car vents, the damp October night. Listen to the highway and the sounds of the city. Squint your eyes at the splotches of light from downtown reigning overhead. We're alive.

We're both laughing and the cold sting of the wind has my eyes watering. At any moment, I could start crying. My throat pinches with the familiar feeling, and then I realize we've missed the exit.

"Oh, shit! The exit!"

She's already noticed and is laughing harder, wiping her eyes with her sleeve. The sight of her opens up the valve in me and I let it out as we slow down to catch the next exit. It's only adding maybe six minutes to the drive, but it continues to tack onto the chaos until we're finally at a standstill at the light. Why does Maeve have a fucking boyfriend? What is the universe trying to do to me?

Tears are streaming down my face and I'm doing nothing to stop them. She glances over, and when our eyes meet, her eyebrows turn up. As I pull into a left turn, she buries her head in her crossed arms resting on her knees, and we don't really speak until we're in the elevator. Both of our faces are red, I'm still sniffling, and her mascara is smudged. My chest hurts from the emptiness it's experiencing without someone to love.

When she leaves, she reaches out for a hug, and I'm somewhat caught off guard. It's over before the elevator door shuts, and without a word, I'm ascending to the fourth floor alone, left with a barely there scent of something like vetiver. That was the first time she's hugged me.

I end up taking the hottest shower I can stand, and I gotta tell you, there is something fucked up about jacking off to your ex when you just found out the one person who might help you get over her all of a sudden has a boyfriend.

Fuck Sean.

Chapter 8

NO, BUT ACTUALLY, FUCK SEAN.

Two weeks later, like clockwork, she's late. It's past 7:30 am on Thursday and I know exactly why Maeve hasn't met me in the lobby yet. And before I can ruminate on her and Sean's late-night conversation, whispering sweet nothings to each other, my phone vibrates in my hand.

7:36 AM 360-555-4773: Running late sorry snarfing down breakfast in 311 if you want to wait up here

I try swallowing, but my throat isn't working. This feels like a breach into new territory for our friendship. Ever since Cry Night (that's what I'm calling it) in my car, there's been this silent understanding that we're friends. Best friends. Hah.

Okay well, I don't think she'd say that about me, but she's mine. She's my best friend, because who else would it be? Silence is comfortable, conversation is easy, and damnit, the best part of my day is always our car rides together. But going to her apartment? This feels intimate.

And now I have her phone number. I type out three responses with differing versions of, "I can wait downstairs," or "I'm good in the lobby," before my curiosity gets the best of me. And spite. Even if she was up late talking to Sean, *he* isn't the one knocking on her door before 8 am.

She greets me with a bowl in her hand and a mouth full of cereal. "Sorry, gimme five minutes."

As I enter, I am transported to another dimension. First, it hits my nostrils. Cinnamon and clove mixed with orange and pine waft me into her living area. Her apartment's layout is the same as mine, but that's where the similarities end. She has artwork on the walls, plants on shelves, piles of books everywhere. There are pumpkins scattered about on couch pillows and in picture frames. My apartment looks like a vacant dorm room while hers looks as if someone actually spends time here.

"Huh," I involuntarily let out. She eyes me from the kitchen, where she's packing a lunch on a countertop littered with glass leftover containers.

"What?" she says, about to accuse me of exactly the thing I am guilty of. "Don't judge me, I like seasonal decorations."

"I'm not judging. It's just, a lot of... pumpkins." It's the week before Thanksgiving. To me, it's a week before deadline week, and that's been the only thing on my mind lately.

She rolls her eyes as she puts away the containers and closes the fridge, but stalls next to the small island in the kitchen. Her brows knit together and she's smiling. "You look very uncomfortable."

"We're ten minutes late!"

"*Okay*!" She finally animates, running to her bedroom, and she returns with her grey backpack in hand. Her coat is draped over an armchair next to the couch, and when she laces up her boots, I feel each knot looping into my stomach. This feels so domestic. It reminds me of Lacie. (Sorry.)

The anger I've been feeling about the whole *Lacie Situation* has turned from the sting of a burning nettle to the annoying velcro-like burr that's on every Sherpa jacket sleeve I own. I carry it around like some rash beneath my clothes, itching constantly yet invisible to everyone else. I don't miss *her* anymore, I just miss the whole thing. I miss the relationship.

We're out the door, and she sighs up to the ceiling. "My coffee." I give her an unamused glare, but her tired eyes plead up at me. "Can I run back and grab it?"

"Fine." I exhale all the air in my body and wait for her to return. And with that, we're finally on the road.

The weather lately has been on our side. Every so often we get a couple inches of snow that accumulated in the ditches and curbs, but for the most part, the roads have been clear. Everything people hear about winter in Minnesota is usually a bit exaggerated, but one thing is true; the cold rips through your skin and settles deep into your bones. Maeve and I are lucky enough that the only time we are exposed to the outside elements is for a few blocks from the office to the skyway system. It's technically connected, but we'd have to go through three other buildings to get there.

In the warmth of the upper-level walkways, she turns to me, finally awake. "What are you doing for Thanksgiving?"

"Uh, nothing."

She takes a sip from her thermos. "What do you mean nothing?"

I mean *nothing*. I've spent the last six Thanksgivings with Lacie's family, and this year, I won't. I don't even like the holiday. It's a day centered around eating a meal and...colonization? Dramatic, sure, but pair that with nearly every Thanksgiving lining up with a deadline week, I'll take any excuse not to drive up to Duluth alone to visit my mom. My sister, Georgia, hasn't spoken to her in years.

"Next week's deadline week," I say, scratching my jaw. My face is itchy now. "I always have to get the issue to print on Black Friday if we want to get it out by the first week of December. And seeing as sales weighs our entire advertorial budget on gift guides, the earlier the better."

"God, don't remind me." She puts her hand on her forehead. "I have to submit my feature by Monday and have about six product blurbs left to write by tomorrow to send to clients. Is December's issue always like this?"

"Yes." I let out a huff and I'm so close to smiling, I have to bite my cheek for a new reason. "Fun, huh?"

She rolls her eyes and takes another sip of her coffee, but her left dimple is visible and I know she's smiling, too.

This month's deadline week finally feels like a fucking break. This is what happens every November. Jesse usually incentivizes sales by giving them Wednesday off if all of their ads are in. All means all. Not one ad can be missing by Tuesday at 5 pm, so the only thing that I'm holding my breath for is the feature. Maeve's feature.

I don't tend to read the content that comes through my inbox, hence the shit that Zakariya pulled a few months back with the October feature, but this time my knee is bouncing at my desk waiting for the email. It normally comes from Zakariya, but there's a chance it'll come from Maeve directly, too. I'm thinking entirely too much about it. I can't stop, though. I can't wait to read it.

Just before I get up for lunch, it hits my inbox. Her email makes me smile and this time I don't even bite my cheek. This is the first time I've ever been this connected to the feature and now I'm basking in the excitement.

From: Maeve Thomas <mthomas@northstarmag.com>
To: Conrad Sutherland <csutherland@northstarmag.com>
Date: Monday, November 22nd, 12:13 PM
Subject: My First Feature!!!

Hi weirdo,

Attached is the feature. Check out the byline!!!! Aren't the photos amazing? Zakariya had our photographer stop by to get shots of the food. Let me know if everything looks alright! Zakariya looked it over and said it was fine but wanted to check. Ok thanks!

Getting this done is my peach!!!!

M

Maeve Thomas (she/her)
Associate Editor, *North Star Magazine*
mthomas@northstarmag.com
612-555-0281

For some reason, I stare at the "M" for a few seconds. I wonder if she signs all of her emails like that or just this one. I wonder if people call her "M" in real life. Does Sean? I hate thinking about Sean. And yet, I seem to do it a lot.

The amount of exclamation marks makes me want to roll my eyes, but like, sincerely. I remember the first time I got a physical copy of the magazine with my name on the masthead. I saved my first year's worth of issues. Now they just sit in my closet collecting dust.

I respond back as enthusiastically as I can to match her energy.

From: Conrad Sutherland
<csutherland@northstarmag.com>
To: Maeve Thomas <mthomas@northstarmag.com>
Date: Monday, November 22nd, 12:15 PM
Subject: RE: My First Feature!!!

Let's get ice cream to celebrate.

C

Conrad Sutherland
Director of Production, *North Star Magazine*
csutherland@northstarmag.com
612-555-0271

I press send and open the attachment. Design had a field day with the layout. There are illustrations of spices and vegetables that trail around the page and provide the perfect line for the eye to follow. Maeve is right, the photos are great. Zakariya's uncle has a wide smile and who I presume is his aunt is holding a plate of the stewed lamb in front of her. It looks just as delicious as I remember.

The first few sentences pull me in instantly. She opens up with a story about Zakariya and how everyone knows him as our Managing Editor, but this time Maeve talks about his role as nephew, and then ties it to the way she felt a part of the family the moment she walked inside. When she gets to the food, I'm taken right back to my seat next to Zakariya and Chris, smelling the coriander and cumin as if it were here in the office.

I'm reading about the sambusas that Maeve and I took home (there's no mention of me), when a voice makes me flinch so wildly, you would have thought I was watching porn at my desk.

"Everything looking alright?" Jesse mumbles. He's holding a few pieces of paper and watching me curiously. "You've been staring at that feature for a while."

Reading features is not my job. "How long have you been standing there?"

"Longer than I needed to." He seems stressed and at the very least, unimpressed. "We've got a situation. Amy just sold a last-minute package to a dentist group in Wayzata." He hands the paper to me, outlining their contract for two half-page, two quarter-page, and four eighth-page ads. He continues, "Our book is at forty pages, and the package is going to add two full pages—"

"So we'll have to cut two or add four."

We can't add four pages this late in the game. Where are we going to pull two pages worth of content? Out of our ass? Editorial would kill me. Creative would be the getaway driver.

Jesse nods. "Work with creative. The ads are already submitted, so at least we won't have to wait on anything."

Right. The only thing we're waiting on now is me. This happens every once in a while, but it's never happened for the December issue. The week of Thanksgiving is supposed to be a breeze. We're only missing two ads from one client and the issue was finished, and now Halson Dental Group has gone and messed everything up.

On normal weeks, it's a puzzle. I have the task of moving things around to cause as little disruption to the content as possible, but when the equivalent of two pages in ads gets added four days before going to print, it's an all-hands-on-deck emergency that sounds off alarms in almost every department.

I pull up the pagination as it currently stands. A few internal event ads can be brought from a half-page down to a quarter-page. Easy. Kathryn in Marketing can handle that. The next one to go is creative design. Content is king around here, so I do anything I can to save what the editors have written for this issue, sometimes to the detriment of an illustration or a photo. Editorial and creative love working together on these things, but we don't have time. I need shortcuts. And unfortunately, there's only one department left who can provide that.

I smell her desk before I see it. She's got a candle warmer going that smells like a calm winter morning in the woods, er, pine or whatever. I peer over her cubicle wall.

"Well, look who it is," she says, already smiling.

"Gotta favor to ask."

She places her hand on her chest, covered by a turtleneck sweater. "Yes, I can pay for your ice cream."

I know I could lighten up and play the game with her, but I'm already sweaty. This has to be figured out by tonight so sales can sign off on the book tomorrow. (Because it's looking like they'll all get Wednesday off.)

"I meant about the issue." She finally sits up straight. "Is there any way you can cut your feature by half a page? I'm headed to Tara to see if any illustrations can be changed to make room for more text, but we just got a sales package that's bumping two pages out of the issue."

Her elbows land on her desk as she cradles her forehead. "Are you kidding? I already had to chop it down from five pages to four."

Zakariya pops up from his cubicle. "What's going on?"

"Last minute sales package. It added two pages, but we're already at forty pages this issue."

He's been here before. "Dang it. I can help!"

"Okay, call me stupid, but why can't we just have forty-two pages in this issue?" Maeve asks.

Zakariya lets out a sigh, but he's still more patient with her than I would have been. "Because the pages are folded. Each piece of paper has a right outer and inner and a left outer and inner. The number has to be divisible by four."

Her eyes trail around, and I can see her mind's eye trying to visualize it. "Ohhh."

I shrug. "Yeah. Anyway, sorry, but it's not like we can say no."

"We'll figure it out." Zakariya nods.

Phew. I move out of the Editor's Den and into the set of cubes across from them that make up our creative team. We have three interns, two graphic designers, and one art director, Tara. She used to be my boss when I interned here, but now she's part-time and freelances on the side. She's got a dozen pictures of her poodle, Dash, on her desk, and her thick-rimmed glasses always match her outfit. Today they're red and her ensemble is white and black. She reminds me of Carla Hall back when I had access to a Netflix account to watch Top Chef.

"Tara, hey," I start, trying not to be too confrontational. "Got some changes for this issue. We need to consolidate two pages."

"Of course we do. Which sections are you looking at?"

"Any of them. Mainly the feature. I just told Maeve I needed at least half a page, but I'll let you work with her on it. There are a few internal ads that I'm going to work with Kathryn on. We'll need it done by tonight so I can have sales sign off on it tomorrow. I think most of them will be gone on Wednesday."

She removes her glasses and rubs the bridge of her nose, something she did often when I was an intern. "Don't get me started. Must be nice to be rewarded for doing your damn job." Tara is half the reason I loved my internship. Well, that and Lacie. "I'll get with Maeve. She's a peach, isn't she?"

The word choice throws me off enough to stick around and engage in a conversation. "Yeah, she's... The feature she wrote was good." *Good*. That's all I can say? It was brilliant, warm, and inviting. Everything writing should be.

"Oh, it was phenomenal." Tara brightens and puts her glasses back on with a flourish. "We're lucky to have her. Okay! Better get going on this."

She rubs her hands together and has Adobe Illustrator pulled up before I leave her cubicle. She's insanely good at what she does.

On my way to Kathryn, I grab a refill of coffee from the kitchen and run into Kiara. She's heating up some sort of noodle soup that smells delicious and reminds me I haven't had lunch yet.

"Hey Conrad!" She greets me like we see each other every day. It catches me off guard. I didn't realize she knew my name.

"Oh, uh—"

"I hear there are some last-minute changes to the issue. Let me know how I can help!" she says and slowly walks away, eyeing her steaming bowl carefully.

I wish I would have had half a brain to respond, but I'm stuck staring at my thermos. Why is everyone being so nice to me today? Am I being nicer than normal? Usually if something like this happened in the past, everyone would be avoiding me, trying to pass the problem off to another department. It would take an entire afternoon just to get people on board, but if everything goes to plan, we should have a finalized book in a few hours.

I still have to talk to Kathryn.

Marketing's cubicles are on the other side of the kitchen, which means it's a low-traffic area. Tablecloths with the North Star logo are thrown about along with drink koozies and chip clips. They work our events and I do not envy their jobs one bit. Faint music from the local top 40s radio station is playing while Kathryn is folding invites at her desk. It's a mess, as usual.

She jumps more than I did when Jesse caught me reading the feature. Kathryn is a little ball of energy. Short, plump, with fiery red hair that pops with her bright red lipstick. I don't know if I've ever seen her without it. Around me, she's a bit wide-eyed, and now I know it's because she's afraid of me.

"Conrad! Hi. Did you need something?"

"Yeah. The ads for the New Year's Bash need to be cut down." I continue to tell her the same story I told everyone else; two pages, big sales package, etc. "Think you could send those to me within the hour? Sorry about the turnaround."

She relaxes and finally exhales. "That's no problem at all. We've started making ads for events in every size. Just in case."

"Oh, okay great," I say. "Thanks, Kathryn."

She holds up a New Year's Bash invite. "I haven't seen your RSVP come through, yet. Are you going?"

I've been avoiding this event like the plague. Every year *North Star Magazine* invites our ad clients to showcase their products at our Annual North Star New Year's Bash. It's like a glitzy trade show cashing in on vendor sales and getting people so drunk they'll spend all their money on cocktail mixers and artisan marshmallows. It's kind of the "Event of the Year" for the magazine. *No one does New Year's like North Star!*, per the tagline of all the ads and social media posts about it. Which of course means that Lacie was in attendance all six years we were together. This is the first year I'll be going alone.

"Haven't decided yet. When's the deadline?"

"Next Monday!" She gives me a jerky nod with a tense smile and I'm finally back at my desk to work on the cluster that this issue has turned into.

If we can get all the internal ads cut down, we'll be golden, but there's a pit forming in my stomach the size of Lake Superior as I read the rest of Maeve's feature. I have no idea how she's going to cut any of it out. Each sentence feeds right into the next, each new idea not only makes me crave the food we ate, but it leaves me thinking that food is so much more than food. It's a community. It's home.

Growing up, food always meant Georgia. The amount of dinners I made for two could have been sold in a couple's cookbook. We always had the same tastes. Not a huge fan of eggs, but cereal was a favorite. Once I was in high school, pancakes were out, french toast was in. So many memories of us in the kitchen laughing and smiling. Nothing else mattered. I was feeding my sister and doing a good job. Food was a love language. Lacie never made me think of food that way. To her it was income.

The shift in perspective pushes me to think a little harder. If I move around some of the ads later in the book, I can revamp our listicles to fit into a vertical one-third ad, and that would give room to add something near the table of contents. It'll be tight, but it could work.

I notice a margin is off by an inch on one of the pages from Editorial, which also frees up some room towards the bottom. It ties in perfectly since the article is "Can't Miss Theatrical Performances!" and the ad is from the St. Paul Conservatory. It's coming together. Maybe Maeve has nothing to change. I ping Tara and include editorial.

From: Conrad Sutherland <csutherland@northstar.mag>
To: Tara Hope <thope@northstar.mag>
Cc: Zakariya Abdullahi Ahmed <zahmed@northstar.mag>,
Maeve Thomas <mthomas@northstar.mag>
Date: Monday, November 22nd, 1:49 PM
Subject: Pagination Update

Team,

Looks like we'll be able to keep the feature at its current length if we can skim off some of the art and fit two eighth-page ads in there. I adjusted the listicle to fit into a third, too. PDF attached.

Let me know.

Conrad Sutherland
Director of Production, *North Star Magazine*
csutherland@northstar.mag
612-555-0271

Would I have done this for anyone else? Maybe. A response comes in from Maeve, but it's just to me.

From: Maeve Thomas <mthomas@northstar.mag>
To: Conrad Sutherland <csutherland@northstar.mag>
Date: Monday, November 22nd, 1:52 PM
Subject: RE: Pagination Update

YOU'RE MY FAVORITE HUMAN RIGHT NOW! Ice cream is
definitely happening today.

M

Maeve Thomas (she/her)
Associate Editor, *North Star Magazine*
mthomas@northstar.mag
612-555-0281

I'm not reading into it. Yes I am. I know she's exaggerating
to be dramatic, but every time she says stuff like this, I want it
to be true.

🍑

"Wait, they don't have the sweet corn flavor anymore?"

Maeve caught on immediately. "Aha! I knew you liked it."

The seasonal flavor today is pumpkin. Notably *not*
pumpkin spice, just...pumpkin.

I scoff, which makes Maeve's eyes roll.

"Maybe you'll like it," she says with a smirk that does
something so alarming to my stomach, you would think she
punched me in the gut. "You should get it."

I, of course, oblige.

"I have a feeling this whole thing is just so you can try new flavors of their ice cream."

"You wouldn't be wrong."

"Yet, here you are, ordering vanilla again," I say with a huff and pay for both of our scoops.

"Exactly. One that we know is good, and one wild card. It's enjoyment insurance." I should have teased her about coming up with the term, "*enjoyment insurance*," but I didn't. I was trying too hard not to smile.

The line was shorter this time around. The temperature outside has been hovering around freezing, but inside it's warm with cozy tables perfect for couples to gaze into each other's eyes. There was even a small fireplace. It's fake. But still. The whole thing screams date night. We sit at a table by the window and I feel myself relax. December's issue was finalized and already printed out on the production table for the sales team to approve tomorrow. Wednesday will be an easy day in the office, Thursday is a holiday, and Friday is my favorite day of the year. A quiet office with one, two other people at most. It's going to be heaven. Actually, heaven is already here, because the pumpkin ice cream is somehow better than the sweet corn, but I can't tell Maeve that. I don't have to.

"Your face," she says. "Your eyes just rolled back."

I clear my throat. "I don't know what you're talking about."

"You love it! Let me try." Her spoon hits my cup before I can protest. As if I wanted to anyway.

It feels like a lifetime since Lacie left me. Weeks since I last touched someone or held a hand that wasn't mine. Months since I've been laid. But sitting in this weird ice cream coffee shop combo and watching Maeve's used spoon scrape against my cup is intimate enough to send me into overdrive. My body admits it for me. I am insanely attracted to Maeve, and I can't do a damn thing about it.

Chapter 9

THURSDAY OFFICIALLY MARKS the Bermuda Triangle of Thanksgiving, Christmas, and New Year's Eve. It'll be my first holiday season single, and by that, I mean alone. Unless you count the five blades on my ceiling fan staring back at me.

If I was still with Lacie, I would have woken up on silk bed sheets in her parent's house in Edina. There would be fresh coffee and expensive pastries. Her mom would've made eggs and bacon and they would have been undersalted, but at least I wouldn't have had to cook. Lacie's family was easy to be around. Her brother, Sam, and I got along, even if he remained a perpetual frat boy in year seven of his finance degree. Her mom loved to buy me things I didn't need. Her dad and I didn't always agree, but at least he was there. I never had a dad around during holidays growing up. It wasn't something that I thought about until the first Easter I spent with the Daltons and he refused to let me address him as "Mr. Dalton" anymore. I never called him "Dad" or anything, but calling him by his first name was close enough. I've never called my real dad by anything else.

Her seven cousins were a blast, too. She was the only girl on her mom's side, so Thanksgiving was filled with afternoon backyard football and evening cigars. Yeah, it was *that* kind of family. The liquor was top shelf, the food was plentiful. Coming from a family that rarely had more than three people at the table, it was nice. It was like all of the movies I grew up watching. For six years. And now? Nothing.

Before noon I get a headache from the lack of caffeine, but I can't get out of bed. I should be dreading conversations with Lacie's dad about whatever atrocity he believes the Democrats have pulled this legislative season. I should be drowning myself in gravy and cranberry sauce and sweet sparkling wine because that's the only stuff her mom drinks. At the very least I shouldn't be alone. Anger starts to flood my eyes, and then I get a text from Maeve that has me smiling in record time.

11:23 AM Maeve Thomas: Have you eaten? Wanna see if anything is open for takeout?

I remember when she asked me if I was doing anything today. I never asked her what her plans were. Guilt sparks on my fingertips as I type back a response.

11:25 AM Conrad Sutherland: I'm down. Haven't even had coffee yet. When are you thinking?

11:26 AM Maeve Thomas: I just made a fresh pot! Come over whenever

I'm showered and dressed in record time. I have my favorite jeans on with an Adidas crew neck that Lacie used to love me in. But as soon as I step off the elevator on the third floor, I panic. I check my phone and it's been twelve minutes since she texted me last. *Come over whenever,* probably doesn't mean come over in twelve minutes, right? That's desperate. That's I'm-obsessed-with-you. Not to mention, I'm still damp from the shower and my clothes are clinging to me as if I got caught in the rain. I turn back. No, I stay there. I'm losing brain cells over this, I can feel it.

God, just be normal for once, Conrad.

Fuck it.

With a deep breath and a bit more composure than I had originally, I finally make it to the door of 311.

"Conrad!" She opens the door in pajamas and an apron.

Cool.

It smells like a bakery and it might be coming from a candle because it also smells like something's burning.

"Come in, come in. Coffee's still hot I think." She's somewhat frantic. There's an energy about her that doesn't quite feel like the excitable and warm Maeve that waved goodbye the day before.

"Everything good? Are you baking something?" I ask, trying to be nonchalant and super laid-back.

She wipes at her forehead and immediately searches her hand before searching me. "Did I just get flour on my forehead?"

"No," I answer, feeling a smile rise in my cheeks because there is already flour all over her chin. "What's going on? Is something in the oven?"

Her shoulders fall. "I tried to bake a pumpkin pie."

"Tried?"

She motions me to the oven and cracks it open. Inside a glossy orange pudding is surrounded by a browning ring of crust, burning by the second. "I have no idea what I did wrong."

I shrug and grimace. "I'm not much help. I've never made a pie in my life."

She doesn't react the way I expect her to. I normally would anticipate an eye roll or a smile with a shake of her head, but she ignores my comment and takes a mug from the cupboard. The kitchen is somewhat of a mess. A dusting of flour remains on the island countertop, and the sink is full of slimy orange bowls and dirty measuring cups.

"Coffee?"

"Sure, yeah." I'm stuck watching her pour me a cup from her fancy-looking coffee machine.

"Do you take cream or sugar?"

"No, I'm good."

She gives me a smile more half-baked than the goopy pie in the oven, but the first sip hits hard. I've never been a smoker, but this feels like the equivalent of the first cigarette of the day. I inhale the familiar aroma, sighing out on the exhale. Now I understand why she doesn't drink the stuff at the office. I wouldn't either if I could drink this every day.

I finally see her genuine smile when I open my eyes. "It is so obvious when you like something." I furrow my brow to egg her on. "It's just like the sweet corn ice cream. And the pumpkin one. Your shoulders relax and your eyes squeeze shut, and then they roll back when you open them."

I gotta say it feels good to be observed by her. By someone. "Okay, it's good coffee, sue me. Where is it from?" I ask.

"Home." Her smile falters as she wipes down the countertop. "My mom and dad sent me a box for Thanksgiving. Normally I get a local dark roast, but these beans are from Seattle." Seattle. I had no idea she was from Seattle.

The entire mood in the apartment shifts. Her mouth is twitching downward and I have no idea what to do with my hands. "Do you normally spend today in Seattle?"

She nods. "Yeah," is all she can get out before her mouth tightens and she tries to swallow. She opens the oven to take another look at the somehow overdone and underdone pie before giving me a teary smile and crumbling.

"Hey, hey, hey. What's up?" The words tumble out of me and I'm reaching for her shoulders to dock into my chest. And then we're hugging. This isn't like the hug after Cry Night. It's not a punctuation, it's the entire sentence. It's an exposition, a rising action, as if both of our bodies exhaled into one another, comforted by a touch we weren't expecting. I've never had a hug like this with a co-worker. Not even most of my friends. Instinctively my hand reaches up to cradle her head, and something deep in my bones wants me to kiss the top of her scalp like I used to with Lacie.

"I'm just missing a lot of people right now," she mumbles.

Of course she is. I shouldn't do this. She has a fucking boyfriend. Once again, fuck Sean.

I deflect the second we pull apart. "You said something about takeout. Should I see if King's is open?" King's Palace is the Chinese restaurant across the street. I get takeout from there at least twice a week.

"Is that okay?"

"Hell yeah. It's my favorite. I'll order. You allergic to anything?"

She gives me another fumbling smile. "No."

I step back to keep myself from giving her another hug. It felt so good to have her that close. "I'll be back."

In the elevator, I notice two small dots of tears on my shirt along with the faint residue of the flour from her chin. And even as I frantically shove a beanie over my ears and slip each arm through my coat, I'm smiling. The sky is cloudy and the wind whips on my red cheeks as snow crunches under my boots, but it might as well be a Saturday in June with how warm I am inside.

I might have overdone it on the Chinese food, but I couldn't decide what to get. And in my defense, I wanted to get everything on my rotation so that Maeve could try it all. Which means I am awkwardly balancing three bags between two hands as I try to knock on her door forty-five minutes later.

"It's open!" she yells from inside.

I manage to hang all three bags on my numbing right hand and make it into the apartment once again. This time, she's in jeans and a tight maroon turtleneck standing in a clean kitchen. She has a bottle of wine in each hand.

"Oh, Conrad, hello. This is the first time I've seen you all day, welcome," she says with a sarcastic and airy tone. "What can I get you to drink?"

I set the food on her coffee table with a smirk. "I'm easy. Whatever you got."

"I have a Riesling and another bottle of a different Riesling." Her smile turns shy. "I'm sorry about earlier. I just cried to my mom on the phone for fifteen minutes, cleaned the kitchen, and changed. I'm a whole new person. I don't know who that was before." She's back from the kitchen with a twist-off and finally notices the amount of food. "What did you all get?"

I shrug sheepishly as I announce the kung pao chicken, fried pork dumplings, Szechuan green beans, spicy cucumber salad, scallion pancake, xiao long bao, and egg tarts. "I went ham."

"*Oh* my god. This looks amazing."

We dig in, not bothering to get plates or use anything other than the cheap wooden chopsticks that came in the bag. Four pairs are left discarded while we sample each dish, and it's at this point when I realize how much I enjoy watching Maeve enjoy something, too.

My shoulders might relax and my eyes may squeeze shut, but when she loves something, her whole body squirms. She balls up her fists and furrows her brow as she chews, like she can't believe it. By those markers alone, I can tell the kung pao chicken is a favorite followed very closely by the xiao long bao.

It's not lost on me that this scenario mirrors ones I had with Lacie. Only whenever we had plates of food surrounding us, we rarely touched them. Her fellow "influencers" rarely ate in front of each other; it was all for the photos. I was never a participant, only a front-row observer in the stands. Today, I'm on the field.

She takes a sip and pauses. "So is this what you normally do on Thanksgiving?"

Ah, so it's my turn. The almost three glasses of wine have made me a bit more loose-lipped than I want to be. "Not quite. First time in a while I'm not with Lacie's family." She nods and it looks sincere, so I unload. "For the last six years, I've spent every major holiday with her family in Edina. It was incredible. They always spent so much money on the food and drinks. And I mean, I've had to work Black Friday since I've been in production, so it's not like tomorrow will be much different. But waking up alone in an empty bed versus waking up to coffee that's already made and Lacie's mom making me breakfast, well, it's just stirring up everything."

I'm rambling. *I can't fucking stop.*

"And I haven't spent a holiday with my own mom for years. I mean, she went a little nuts during the 2016 election, if you know what I mean, and I don't know. I feel like I kind of lost her around that time. Which sucks because that's when Lacie and I were getting serious. But, whatever. My sister is no-contact with her, so it's not like I have much of an obligation. She's in— er, *they*, she goes by they/them, fuck! *They* go by they/them now, but they said they'll always be my sister, so that's why I call them my sister. Sorry, I feel like I have to explain that."

Maeve is nodding and I won't shut up. What is happening to me?

"Anyway, they're up in North Metro and manage a Swedish clog outlet. Isn't that random? Hah."

I finally take a breath and will myself to look up from my empty wine glass. Maeve is just sitting there, a relaxed smile on her face, leaning back against the couch cushion unfazed.

"I love Swedish clogs. Like with wooden soles?"

Thank god *that's* what she asked about. "Yeah, like the ones with leather on top and wood on the bottom. Georgia swears by them, says they're the only shoe they can wear all day on the sales floor."

"That's so cool. I've always wanted a pair." Maeve rests her head back on the couch. "Families are hard. I'm really lucky. All of my sisters get along for the most part. And our parents were the quintessential Seattle parents growing up. We went on weekend hiking trips, drank coffee at fifteen, did beach clean-ups as a family, all of it. My older sisters are both still in

Seattle, but my younger sister is in Colorado. I miss her the most." Her eyes are misty.

"How many sisters do you have?"

"Just the three. It goes Stephanie, Anna, me, and Valerie." She holds up her fingers and I can tell the wine is getting to her, too.

Outside, the sky is darkening. The food surrounding us on the coffee table is nearly cold, there's barely a dent in each of the boxes, and the second bottle of wine is half empty. I'm so full, my pants are tight around my belly. I'm about to announce this, but Maeve cuts me off. "The pumpkin pie kind of turned out. Should we try it?"

I widen my eyes. "You're not serious."

"Come on, just a bite." She hurls herself up and extends a hand. I take it, not knowing what exactly for, but she shifts her weight back and heaves me up off the couch. I follow her into the kitchen where said pumpkin pie is covered with aluminum foil. "My mom told me to cover the crust with foil if it was burning." She peels it back and underneath is a pumpkin pie with a crust so brown, it's approaching charred territory. "I think I was a little late."

The giggles just happen. It has to be the wine. We're both laughing and leaning into one another and suddenly her open palm is resting on my chest. I can't help but feel guilty for how good it feels to be in her kitchen, sharing laughter over a botched pumpkin pie, while her boyfriend is somewhere over in Argentina. Or Alabama. No, Albania.

She takes two spoons from the drawer and hands me one with a "Cheers!" and a metal *tink* before scooping up the filling directly from the center.

"Maeve!"

"Wuhh?" she says with a full mouth, "Iss *my* puh-ie."

She smiles but her cheeks are puffed out like some adorable chipmunk. I follow suit and take my own spoonful. It's creamy, heavy in my mouth, perfectly sweet. We eat in silence for a moment until I'm about ready to combust both physically and mentally. I'm almost positive Maeve and Sean had their biweekly chat this week.

"Did you talk to Sean yesterday?"

She swallows her bite and chucks her spoon back into the pie like a dart. "Well, that's the other reason why this morning sucked. I fell asleep last night before he called. I woke up *fifteen* minutes late and tried calling him, but he, um. He didn't pick up. I stayed up for an hour waiting and nothing." She sighs and buries her head in her hands. "Then I woke up early to see if he texted me overnight and he did, so we talked for like five minutes this morning. We um, got into a little bit of a fight."

Relief isn't what I'm supposed to experience right now. I know that. But it overwhelms my body. The tightness in my chest loosens. My shoulders relax. I scoop more pumpkin filling onto my spoon so that my smile doesn't show. "Sorry to hear that."

"I just don't think he understands the amount of sacrifices I have to make sometimes. First of all, waiting two weeks to speak to your boyfriend over the phone? What am I, a regency-era English housewife? And second, if I fall asleep for *fifteen minutes* and that's enough for you to cancel the whole phone call, then what does that tell you?" She takes another bite. "Wednesdays are his only mornings off. I know he has to focus on his service work and integrate into the community or whatever, but hello?!"

I don't say anything back. I know myself enough that I would want to say something like, *He's an ass, you should dump him*, or *That's fucked up, you know who wouldn't make you wait two weeks to talk to them? Me.* But I hold my tongue because she keeps going. Maybe I'm not the only one who rambles after three glasses of wine and six Chinese food entrees.

"We put everything on hold because of this. It's hard to like, see what life will look like with him when the majority of our relationship has been phone calls and spotty facetime chats. And I mean, this was the deal when he got selected, but I constantly feel like I'm waiting to start living my life."

The exact phrasing does something to my throat and the words are out before I stop myself. "That's not— *No.* This is your life. This, this, this." I pat the countertop, my chest, biceps, and gently land on her shoulders. "You're living your life right now. Look around. You're alive. What about your life right now doesn't feel like living?" I've been reading too much Coelho. "It's already happening. Always. So start fucking living, babe. Okay?" I shake her shoulders to distract from calling her babe. I have no idea where that came from. "Okay?!"

"Okay, okay! I'm alive!" Her laugh is melodious. She takes another bite and I can already hear the *Oh!* she wants to say, but can't with her full mouth. Her eyes are saying it for her. "What's your pit and peach today?"

I don't want to say mine yet. "You first."

Her eyes narrow. "Hmm. Guess. I think you know."

This feels like another line of intimacy we're crossing because, for the first time since I met her, I do know. And I love that I know.

"Pit was your fight with Sean, I'm sure." She nods for reassurance. "And your peach? Your peach was the kung pao chicken. Xiao long bao are a close second."

She hides her smile behind her hands. "I was literally going back and forth between the two. How'd you do that?"

I shrug and we lock eyes. We're both tired, satiated from the meal and each other's company. I can't stop idly smiling, and she seems to be in the same boat.

She points a weak finger at me. "Your pit is not having coffee until noon and your peach is the scallion pancake."

I shake my head.

"You're lying," she says, reaching to pinch my chest, but I back away just in time. If she touches me right now, I might black out.

"Nope."

She scrunches her nose and steps closer to me. Her body language is telling me everything. She's leading with her hips, her shoulders are open, showcasing her collarbone beneath the tight fabric of her turtleneck. I know we're flirting. Neither of us says it.

It's time for me to go home.

I break our bubble and set my spoon in her sink. I feel her eyes on me as I walk to the couch where my beanie and parka are. If I had even one more glass of wine, I don't know who I'd be right now. I'm being vindictive, but damn, I would love to fuck something up the way that Lacie fucked me up. I can't do that to Maeve, though. She matters too much to me.

She sits on the edge of the armrest while I loosely tie my boots and I steal one more forbidden smile before I open the door.

"My pit was seeing you cry this morning." Her face falls and she swallows hard. I can't tell if she's surprised in a good way or a bad one. "And my peach was not spending the day alone." I can't look at her anymore. "Thanks. For everything. See you in the morning."

The door latches before she can respond because, with this much food and alcohol in my system, I don't trust myself not to do something really, really stupid.

Chapter 10

SO I MAY HAVE A HUGE THING FOR MAEVE. I can't stop thinking about her and wishing I was still in her apartment as I toss and turn in my bed. When I wake up, I'm excited to drive to work with her. And then when I realize it will probably just be the two of us in the office, I'm excited all over again.

Excitement wilts into nerves waiting in the lobby at 7:23 am. What if she picked up on the shift in tone last night? What if she brings it up? I'll get a rejection before even asking the question. *You know, Conrad, I have a boyfriend, and maybe we shouldn't hang out anymore outside of our commute.* I can hear the regret in her voice. I can see the upturn in her eyebrows. I can feel the consolation touch on my forearm. *You even said only to and from work. I think we should stick with that.*

I'm barely over the hump of the breakup with Lacie, and I'm already developing feelings for someone who A) has a long-term boyfriend; and B) doesn't want me in that way, obviously. We haven't even established that we're friends outside of work. I'm just the transportation. A utility.

I adjust my beanie and use the knitting to scratch my forehead. Everything feels hot and sweaty in the warm lobby with my parka. The elevators ding and my mind is immediately cleansed of my internal temperature. With wide eyes, I watch the doors open.

"Conrad!" Maeve's face illuminates. She's somehow carrying two thermoses and an overstuffed tote bag. I remove the coffee cup that's pinned up against her chest by her elbow and take the tote bag.

"What's all this?"

"I brought you coffee! And I thought we could bring the leftovers to the office. Kiara will be there and I think she said Zak is working today, too."

My stomach swoops. *Goddamnit.* Why couldn't she follow the script? Now all I can focus on is the way her face brightened as she left the elevator and the fact that she made me the best cup of coffee I've had in years. A tingle warms my belly when I envision her morning. Guess we both woke up thinking about each other.

Having Kiara and Zakariya in the office isn't as disappointing as I thought it would be. This month's issue is done, already sent off to the printer, which allows me to catch up on cataloging our database. Maeve still yells things over the cubicles to me like she does in the mornings when we're alone. The office is quiet, and when lunch rolls around, Kiara of all people is the one who grabs me from my desk.

"Hey," she starts, hooking her hand over the top of my cubicle half-wall. Her nails are long except for her middle and pointer fingers, and it looks like they have charms on them or something. "We're going to heat up the food Maeve brought. Wanna join us for lunch?"

I nod. Anywhere Maeve is, I want to be.

I walk into the kitchen and our takeout containers are littered about, rotating in and out of the microwave. Sitting in the middle of the table, however, is a plate of sambusas. The same ones I binge ate for breakfast the morning after dinner at Zakariya's uncle's. Next to his plate is a glass takeout container full with what looks like homemade sushi. I silently take a seat and don't really know if I should help or stay put. There's one microwave and four of us.

"What did you do for Thanksgiving?" Kiara asks as she rounds the table. Her hand just touched my shoulder, so I'm assuming she's asking me.

"Oh, uh." I look at Maeve whose eyes flicker over to me but land on Kiara. Am I not supposed to say that we hung out? "I don't really celebrate, so I just laid low."

Maeve takes over. "You can thank him for all of this food. We ordered takeout since we live in the same apartment complex." She's notably not making eye contact with Kiara or me.

"Oh shit, Conrad came through," Kiara says. "I brought some kimbap that my mom made if anyone wants some." She points at the glass container. "I would've brought some cornbread from my dad's side of the family, but my brother took the rest of it."

"How is Derek liking the married life?" Zakariya asks, taking out a piping hot container of what looks like eggplant in some sort of red sauce.

"Oh he's loving it. I think my mom asked his wife no less than three times when they were going to start having children."

"But he wants them, doesn't he?" Maeve asks.

Is Derek Kiara's brother? I'm so lost. How do they all know each other like this?

Kiara pulls out a chair and reaches for a piece of kimbap. "He wants, like, six. I don't know why."

"We'll see if his wife wants that," Maeve adds.

Kiara pops the whole piece into her mouth. "Exactly."

The last of the food comes out of the microwave and we all sit at the table, Zakariya on my left and Kiara across from me. It's pathetic how disappointed I am that Maeve isn't sitting next to me again.

"How do you all know each other?" I ask and immediately feel like an idiot. All three of them give me a look.

"We work together, buddy," Zakariya answers.

Kiara raises an eyebrow. "For two years."

"But Kiara and I went to school together at Macalester," Maeve adds and momentarily rests her head on Kiara's shoulder. "She's the one who told me about this job."

So I have Kiara to thank.

"Huh," I let out involuntarily. They're plating up food and all I can do is watch. I don't know anyone at the office well enough to ask how their brother is liking his marriage. I don't know my co-workers' relationship status, let alone their siblings. And since Maeve is in the vicinity, I have to open my big mouth.

"I've been working with Jesse for six years and I don't even know his husband's name." The only reason I know he's married is from the pictures I stare at in his office every week during our one-on-one.

All three of them answer as if they've rehearsed it, "It's Tom!"

"How do you know that?" I match their energy.

"Because he talks about him all the time!" Kiara says with an amused laugh. "You're clueless."

Maeve hits her arm and they giggle towards each other the same way they did at dinner last month. And damn, the thought that I've been stowing away like a forgotten suitcase in baggage claim finally surfaces again; I don't have friends at work. I don't have friends at all.

I look over at Zakariya, but he just shrugs and asks, "Are those dumplings filled with pork?"

Maeve nods.

"Dang it!"

Two weeks before Christmas, I get a text from Georgia that fills me with a sort of dread only family drama can bring. I'm already in a weird mood because Maeve had a happy hour with the other editors, so I didn't get to tell her that my peach was reading her listicle, "Twelve Best Cookies Found in the 'Burbs."

8:23 PM Georgia Sutherland: Are you going to Lacie's for Christmas?

8:24 PM Conrad Sutherland: I'm not. Bit of an update there. We broke up in September.

I should have expected them to call immediately after, but the buzz in my hand still makes me flinch.

"Hey George."

"In September?!" they say, foregoing any real acknowledgment that we haven't talked in a month or so and haven't seen each other since early July. "What happened?" I can already hear the smile in their voice.

"I just, well, *we...*" I sigh, losing steam. Might as well just say it. "She broke up with me out of the blue. I didn't see it coming for the life of me." I tell them about the *personal brand* comment and wanting to *start living her life* and like a good sibling, Georgia laughs at how pathetic it sounds.

"That's so like her. *God,* this is good though, right? You must be so relieved to never see her family again."

A part of me wants to say yes, but the truth is, I miss a lot about being with Lacie. Being a bystander in someone else's family is so much better than not having one of your own.

"For the most part, yeah."

"Are you seeing anyone new?" they ask.

Maeve's image drifts into my mind like a fog machine. I answer, "No," batting it away until it dissipates. It's artificial anyway.

They let out a few more *wow*'s and a *huh* before getting back on track. "Well, I guess that makes my ask a bit more real. I was thinking of going to see Mom for Christmas."

What.

The sucker punch hits me square in the jaw and it unhinges. Georgia hasn't talked to Mom in *years*, and randomly in the same year I conveniently don't have plans, they want to drive up to Duluth to see her? The universe hates me.

"Seriously?"

"Well, I was only going to do it if you came with." *Shit.*

"Why now?"

"Why not?"

"George."

They take a deep breath. "Because I've met someone."

"So you're *bringing* them—"

"No! God, no. I've met someone, and for the most part, I think she's it for me. And I don't know, but it just feels like I need to announce it to my parents or something. Even though marriage is a fucked up construct, we're probably going to, like, do the thing, and Dad's not going to be involved, and it just feels important."

They're out of breath and I can tell it's been something they've been holding in for a while. Time to take off my self-loathing sweater and put on my big brother hat. "Hey, that's really exciting."

"Yeah."

"Tell me about her."

They dive in. "Her name's Emma. She's a teacher. A math teacher of all things. Loves calculus and algebra and she treats her students like her own. She came in to buy a pair of clogs one day and then came back the next week, but I wasn't working. A co-worker said she asked when I would be working again and came in specifically to see me. From there everything just kind of made sense." I know how that goes. "We've been pretty inseparable ever since. Her family's in Iowa and I met them over the holiday that shall not be named."

"Thanksgiving?"

"*National Day of Mourning,* Connie." Georgia has taught me more than any school textbook, but I still have to chuckle at their tenacity. Also, they're the only person who can call me Connie. "Anyway. Since you're free, wanna drive up with me? I'm not staying over. It's drive up, dinner, drive back."

I can't let them go alone, and it's not like I'm doing anything anyway. "That sounds awful, George. But I'll muster up the courage somehow."

"Hah! Cool. When's the last time you spoke to her?" Their voice is a bit softer now. Everything about this sucks.

"She texted me over Thanks— *National Day of Mourning* and said some shit about being thankful for God and the orange-haired freak. I ignored it."

They sigh. "This is actually going to be torture."

"Self-inflicted, Georgie."

We hang up soon after and the itch is too painful not to scratch. I can't remember the last time I saw mom and Georgia together in the same room. It's been more than a few years. I can't help spiraling and thinking this is a horrible idea. Why do they want to put themselves through this? Am I being an awful older brother by letting it happen? Would I be an even *worse* older brother if I didn't do it? What's the right call here?

I need to talk to someone about this, and well, self-control isn't something I'm working on these days. I knock three times right under the metal number 311. I hear her footsteps and enough of a pause that I know she's watching me through the peephole.

"Conrad?" she says before opening the door. "Everything okay?"

She's in her pajamas again. This time without the apron. I can see everything and my mind instantly dissolves. I'm trying to look anywhere but her pebbled nipples under her flimsy Rock the Garden t-shirt.

"Uh." I run my nails across my scalp. "Um, yeah I just got off the phone with my sister. Can I run something by you?"

Maeve, of course, lets me in, sits me down, and offers a hot cup of chamomile tea. As I begin, she lights a candle. "Eucalyptus and green tea, it's supposed to be calming."

"Thanks. I know it's weird to just show up."

She shrugs as though it was inevitable. "You're always welcome."

I take a sip of tea to do something else with my mouth besides smile and gaze longingly into her eyes like some idiot. The scalding liquid burning my throat brings me back to reality. "My sister and I are going up to see our mom over Christmas."

Maeve's eyebrows raise just like I want them to. I need someone to react to this the same way I'm reacting to it. "Woaw."

"Yeah. Is it a terrible idea?"

Her eyes travel to her lap, then to a loose thread on her sweatpants that her finger is picking at. "I guess I can't be the one to answer that. What made you want to go?"

"My sister wants to go, so I'm supporting them. They think they're at a point where they're ready to speak with her."

"That's very kind of you," she says.

A tingle runs up my spine. I really like when she tells me I'm kind. I want to believe it when she says it.

"It would be if my mom wasn't going to call them a slur or something. A part of me wants to protect George, but I don't want to get in the way of their... *journey*, or whatever."

Maeve nods slowly. "Well, I think the best thing is to just be there for them, right? If the outcome is great or if the outcome sucks, then just help them through it, you know? But you're not responsible for how your mom reacts. All *you* need to focus on is being there for your sister."

"But what if my mom says something awful? It's not even going to be if, it'll be when."

"Call her out on it."

"But it's my mom."

"What's the worst that can happen? You stop talking to her?" She has a point. "And once again, anything your mom says to Georgia isn't a reflection on you, only the way you react to it is. So, react by being a good brother."

That's all I can do, really. Already my body is relaxing. To be told I'm not responsible for how my mom acts is a wildly new concept for me. One that I've been running away from since 2016. It feels like the key to unlocking my avoidance of her. Where was Maeve then?

"You're right. That's it, you're right. Thanks." She smiles and softens, and if I look at her for another minute I might do something I regret. I've never been able to rely on someone for advice like this. Not only am I enamored by the way she looks,

PIT AND A PEACH

I also want to keep listening to her talk. Because the silence is too tempting. I need the conversation to shift away from me.

"What are your plans for Christmas, then? Any embarrassing family visits, or just me?"

"Actually." Her entire body lifts. "I'm so glad you brought it up, because I have a favor to ask." I respond with a hum. "I'm flying to Seattle on the 22nd. I'll be gone until the 30th, and I have a few finicky plants that will need a watering in between that." *Hah! Take that, Sean.* But also damn, this means she won't be around to debrief on Christmas.

"Okay, sounds easy enough."

"Really?! Perfect, okay. Phew. It gets so dry with the heater on."

My mind goes back into idiot mode. I can't seem to let anything go to chance with her. "How are you getting to the airport?"

"Oh, an Uber or something."

My chin lifts suspiciously. "No."

"I'll be fine."

"When does your flight leave?" She shrugs and bounces her head back and forth, avoiding an answer. "Maeve."

"Like, five...forty...in the morning."

Oh okay, so she'll be completely alone during the worst part of the night when bars close and weirdos are out waiting to steal her suitcases at the bus stop. That's not happening.

"So I'm driving you to the airport, too."

She leans forward, laughing. "You really don't have to."

One.

"Maeve," I repeat, continuing the cherished midwestern tradition.

"No, no. It's too early. Really, I'm serious."

Two.

"I'm happy to."

"Honestly, I'll be fine!"

Three.

Chapter 11

I HAVEN'T SEEN 3 AM SINCE COLLEGE, closing out bars and attending after-parties with Lacie by my side. It was such a different experience than high school, where I was pent up in my room most weekends watching YouTube fail compilations and introductory videos to Photoshop. Now, less than a week before what will probably be the worst Christmas of my life, I'm driving a bundled-up Maeve to the Minneapolis–Saint Paul International Airport at 3:38 am.

It's a bittersweet morning. Her apartment key is secured on my keychain after a walkthrough last night of her houseplants. I'm only needed once during her leave of absence, but she insisted it was a huge help. She even stuck sticky notes on the specific plants that need watering, marked up with amounts like "a little drink" to "count to five when you're pouring," and somehow I'm still nervous I'll get it wrong. On the other hand, I won't see her for more than a week. It's the longest we'll be apart since we've met and that little fact is sitting like a pit in my stomach as I exit to Terminal 1.

"Text me how Christmas goes," she starts, "and remember, it's not about you."

I give her a tired laugh. "Hah. Right, right."

"And call if you have any questions about the plants. Should be pretty straightforward. Can you bring this back to my apartment?" She points at her thermos after taking a sip of coffee. It smells like hedonism. I nod and she pulls her backpack onto her lap, ready to exit my vehicle as soon as I find an opening in the line of cars doing the same.

Even though the sun won't be shining for another four hours, there's a golden glow radiating from the overhead street lamps on the entire scene. It feels so lived in. This is what couples do. They drop each other off at the airport and kiss goodbye and pretend like they're not emotional. They hug for a little too long and get yelled at by airport security. They don't leave until the other is safe inside, waving through a glass automatic door. It's the most romantic place in the city and all I can think about is how none of it is mine with Maeve. I bet when she dropped Sean off at the airport a year and a half ago, they kissed and hugged for fifteen minutes. Fucking Sean.

I sneak into a spot, put the car in park, and begin unbuckling my seatbelt. She gives me a questioning glance. "You don't have to get out."

"Uh, huh. You couldn't get your suitcase *into* my car. You think you'll be able to pull it out?"

A second of stillness later we're both racing to my trunk with puffs of warm laughter floating in the cold air. Everything is more fun with her, even driving to the airport. I pull out her enormous suitcase and gently set it on the ground as she watches with a scrunched-up nose. There's a pause long enough to make my stomach sink again. We both don't know what to do next. Or maybe I'm imagining it.

"Well," Maeve begins. "Thanks for driving me to the airport."

"Anytime." I mean it.

"As annoying as you are, I think I'll miss you a little."

The sinking feeling in my stomach shifts to floating. "Wow, when I die, I want that engraved into my headstone."

Another cloud of laughter rises above her head. She bounces between her left and right foot. "Okay, it's really cold." And like a truck, she rams into me, barely fitting her arms around my parka. I react by engulfing her, breathing her in. As annoying as I am, I'm going to miss her, too.

"Text me when you land, okay?" They're cheap words. She probably has six other people who told her the same thing in the last 24 hours.

"I will!" She grabs her suitcase handle with a mittened hand. "Feel free to make coffee at my place. I'll be bringing back a whole suitcase full of beans." She turns away and I give a small wave, but she walks back a few steps. "Oh! And you can watch my Netflix if you want. I'm already signed in. Oh! And—"

"Maeve, you're going to miss your flight."

"No, I'm not. Happy holidays, Conrad."

"Happy holidays, Maeve."

"Okay, bye. Thank you again!"

And then I get the last second wave through the automatic closing door. Her smile falters for a moment before she turns around for the final time and removes her winter hat revealing a frizzy mess of hair underneath. So here it comes. A week without Maeve. God, how annoying can I possibly get?

My breathing is off as I pull up to my sister's house. Thought that today is actually happening is spiraling me into a minefield of anxious questions. Does Mom even know we're coming? When's the last time she and Georgia have spoken? When's the last time they saw each other? What if the whole day ends in a massive blowout and I'm stuck with a crying sibling in the passenger seat on the way home? All of these are unanswered right now and it's driving my blood pressure up into the stratosphere.

At last, Georgia opens the front door and locks up. "Connie!" they say and approach me with their arms out. Georgia has always followed a path that I don't recognize, but we understand each other all the same. Their hair is bubblegum pink, curly, and short, and their outfit resembles a patch of poppies in shades of yellows, oranges, and blues. While I received mom's thin and frail-ish frame, Georgia is a spitting image of our dad; tall and wide and stable.

"George, how've you been?" I squeeze them a little tighter than normal and it steadies me. It's been way too long.

"So good, so good. Merry fucking Christmas, I guess."

I give them a dry laugh as we settle into the car. "Merry fucking Christmas to you, too."

"Look at this." Before I can start the engine, they lean over the center console with their phone. "Here's Emma." They show me a picture of the two of them in a woods with a black lab I don't recognize. The winter sun is shining on their touching faces, smiling and squinting. This is by far the happiest I've seen Georgia in years. "That's her dog, Shadow. Isn't she gorgeous?"

"Yeah, it's a cute dog."

They smack my bicep. "I meant Emma, you moron. I think when Mom sees her, it'll be impossible for her to call me a demon dyke, right?"

I give them a shrug. "I'll be here if she does." They respond with a noncommittal hum.

In the last couple of years, it's somewhat felt like Georgia has outgrown me, as if I'm the younger sibling now. Little glints of wisdom come out of them when I least expect it. The first time they met Lacie, their immaturity got the better of them. They rolled their eyes whenever Lacie said anything about her Instagram account, kicked me under the table when she mentioned what her dad did, and gave me a look of death when she said her favorite artist was Taylor Swift. However, the most recent time we were all stuck around the same dinner table, their critiques were more nuanced and came once we were alone.

"Does she support you? Like actually care about your well-being?"

"Of course she does, we've been in a relationship for years."

"But how does she show that she loves you?" Georgia's line of questioning short-circuited my brain sometimes.

"Wha— I mean, she invites me as her plus one to events. We spend time together."

"What do you two even talk about, though?" they asked. My response probably foreshadowed our inevitable separation.

"We talk about everything, what do you mean? We talk about the restaurants she wants to go to and I tell her about what's going on at work." That was as deep as I could go with Lacie. Anything with more substance would turn into a coddle session.

When she found out I had only seen my father a handful of times growing up and that I had a queer sibling, she stroked my hair and apologized for my "traumatic childhood." I don't think she even understood what that meant. How could she with a pool in the backyard and lifelong membership to the Edina Country Club? The joke is that we were both living off Daddy's money at the time.

About half an hour into our drive, we're finished with the surface-level updates; work is busy for the both of us, we're in good health, and somehow Dad's Christmas card got lost in the mail for the twentieth year in a row. Normal sibling stuff. But then Georgia asks about Lacie, for real this time.

"How have you actually been? Since the breakup?" This is where that wisdom comes through because when they ask, their eyes drill something into my chest that only a sibling you've been trying to be a father figure for your entire life can accomplish.

"It's been a little bleak, to be honest." They nod their head as it rests on their knuckles. They look more like my therapist than my sister. "I was fine at first, but I think that was just the shock of it all. Now it's a twenty-four-hour pity party. A lot of my life revolved around Lacie."

"It sure did, Connie. It sure did." They shift in the passenger seat. "Have you made any new friends or anything? Do you still keep in touch with her groupies?"

"They weren't groupies," I have to add first because for some reason I'm still defending someone who dumped me in two minutes flat. "But no. None of them talk to me anymore. I don't even think half of them knew my name."

They raise their eyebrows and look out the window. A few minutes pass on I-35 North before they take a deep breath. "You know, the entire time you two were together, I always wondered where you went. Kind of lost you when you started getting serious. And don't get me wrong, your cockiness was at an all-time high during college," — *fair* — "but like two years ago we all went to the State Fair together. Do you remember that?"

"Kind of?"

"It was you, Lacie, me, and my friend, Max, the one who works at First Ave. Every time I asked you about anything, she either dismissed your answers or answered for you." I have absolutely no recollection of this. "You had just gotten the promotion and you were telling us about how you were the youngest department head in the company, and Lacie — I kid you not — said, 'How hard can that be at *North Star Magazine*.'" Their voice is full of uppity mockery.

I, for the life of me, have no memory of this, but I can almost hear Lacie's voice recite those exact words.

"And then Max was asking about what shows you had been to lately, and you couldn't name one outside of Luke Bryan's stadium tour. *Luke Bryan*, Conrad."

"I think his name is Luke Bryant," I say somewhat seriously.

"Oh, shut the fuck up!" Georgia takes another swipe at my bicep and we're laughing again. "You *hate* country music."

"I wanted to be a good boyfriend."

"You don't— That's not— Ugh. Look where it got you." Their voice lowers. "A relationship shouldn't cause your entire personality to revolve around things you don't enjoy."

Maybe Lacie saw through it in the end. She wouldn't even entertain the idea of doing things that interested me. I went along with it for so long that I stopped asking. In our early days, I went to shows alone, saw new exhibits in local galleries alone, browsed the public library...alone. I guess I had hobbies once.

I'm trying to think of what that would look like now. I'm such a homebody that nothing interests me like it used to. The most adventurous things I've done in the past four months are try sweet corn ice cream and go to dinner with the editors. Eating Chinese leftovers for Thanksgiving with Kiara and Zakariya was a first, too. And then there's Maeve. She's definitely an adventure.

"I don't know. I was a dumb twenty-two-year-old when I met Lacie. She was blonde and hot and took an interest in *me* over the wide receiver of the football team—"

"How *dare* you bring sports into this."

"—but all of this is beside the point. It's over. I'm moving on. Can we just drop it?"

Georgia settles back into their seat and crosses their arms. "You deserved better."

I don't really believe it. Why was *Lacie* the one that called it off then? Georgia is becoming a verbal manifestation of everything I've been too scared to confront these past few months. It's true, fine. I didn't have a life outside of Lacie and my sister was fully aware at the onset. Cool. And to make these even cooler, I'm starting to feel the familiar tightness rise in my throat.

Christmas has always held weirdness in the back of my mind. Usually, I could smother it with gravy and cigar smoke and enough whiskey and prosecco to give me heartburn until the morning, but this year it's all coming to the surface. The thought that Georgia has had to deal with these thoughts alone drives me further into my spiral. The silence doesn't make it any better, especially since we're driving seventy-five miles an hour towards a destination that both of us are dreading more than the end of the world. Oh, and I haven't been around Maeve in three days. Things are awesome.

Ten miles pass and it's like she knows I'm thinking of her. A *ding* escapes from my phone and Georgia reaches for it before I do. Privacy has never been their strong suit.

"There's a message from Maeve Thomas."

"Oh, okay," I say, trying to be super nonchalant about it.

Georgia glares at me and doesn't stop until I face them. "What?"

"Who's Maeve Thomas?" they ask on cue.

"A co-worker."

"Bullshit. It's a holiday." See, these sparks of wisdom sting.

"She's a co-worker who I am helping out by watering her houseplants this week. She lives in my apartment complex."

They're not falling for it, I can tell. Growing up as a queer kid in Northern Minnesota has given Georgia superpowers in social skills. They can pick up on the smallest vocal inflection, the most microscopic changes in facial expressions. It was survival for them, and it makes them an excellent manager, I'm sure. And since I'm their brother, there's no hiding. Their grin says so.

"You like her."

"George."

"Ooh, look at you, trying to hold in a smile. Dude!" They hit my bicep for the third time.

"Ouch, stop! I'm going to bruise."

They roll their eyes. "You're way too easy to read. Spill."

"There's nothing to spill. We carpool to work, I'm completely obsessed with her, and she has a long-distance, long-term boyfriend."

Georgia sighs.

"Yeah, so we can drop it. Not totally in the mood to talk about unrequited love while we drive to Mom's."

"Oof."

"I still don't know why we're doing this," I say, taking a deep breath. My stomach is in knots.

"Honestly, the closer we get, the less I know, too."

Things settle again and we approach Moose Lake, a small fishing town over halfway to Duluth from the Twin Cities. We're close. Less than an hour away. The tightness in my throat hasn't loosened, I've just gotten used to it, but now that it's quiet again, it mixes with the acid in my stomach and I'm about ready to pull over to throw up. I don't want to put Georgia through this. Hell, I don't want to put myself through this. They don't deserve this. What they deserve is a brother who doesn't choose his girlfriend over them, who doesn't go for months without buying them dinner, who actually calls once a week rather than texts a meme here and there. If there is one way to treat my sister like they should be treated, it's spending Christmas with them laughing, rather than crying.

I take the Moose Lake exit.

"Everything okay?" they ask before my blinker shuts off.

"Um."

They look out the windows to see what's around. "Do you have to pee or something?"

"No, I don't..." I manage to park us in the parking lot of a tourist trap family restaurant.

"Conrad, come on."

"I don't want to do this." My fucking voice cracks.

"Do what? See Mom?"

"Yes, see Mom. What's the point?"

Georgia takes a deep breath but doesn't look at me. I know they'll be upset at me, but I'm the one driving. "The point is to try and have a conversation. I wasn't at a place before to do that. I think maybe now I am."

It isn't actual vomit coming up, just word vomit.

"But what if she's not? When have we ever known her to be reasonable in the last six years? Even before that. I don't want to put you through this. I don't want today to be another reason why we don't speak to her anymore or why she puts her ideals above loving her own fucking children. We already know what the outcome will be. She's never apologized for anything she's said in the past.

"The real apology you deserve is from me. And if we can promise each other that we'll never spend another meaningless holiday alone from this day on, then isn't that enough? What if we just promise each other that? I love you, George. I'll love you forever, that's the deal. I'll be at every pagan, or heathen, er... I don't know, Norse holiday you can think of if you and Emma will have me, I swear." My dumbass bottom lip won't stop quivering. "I'm so sorry, George. I'm sorry I haven't been around, but can we please just go home?"

Georgia pushes themself back into the headrest, staring up into the sunroof. They blink a few times. I haven't seen them cry since middle school.

"Emma's mom died two years ago. I just wanted to see if there was some way she could borrow ours eventually."

My god.

"But you're right. I don't know what I was thinking. I just want to give her something that no one else has given me."

The dam that's been holding my emotions breaks.

"Then give her a brother instead. Let me do this with you. It sucks being alone on days like this."

"Sure fucking does!" they say sarcastically, but with wet cheeks.

We're usually not the crying type, but everything feels different between us right now. I can't believe I was so caught up in Lacie's life that I forgot about my own. I'm sick with the amount of holidays Georgia spent by themselves, and for what? Six years of this and what do I have to show for it? Nothing.

"Should we get pancakes?" they ask suddenly.

The question throws me off so quickly that my tears practically dry up on command. Before I can let out a mocking response to question them, I follow their sight of vision to a neon-lit OPEN sign in front of us. Coffee lands at the table before either of us has fully taken a seat, and the stale smell of generic brand coffee beans reminds me that I have a text waiting from Maeve. I pull my phone out noting that Georgia is watching my every move.

12:13 PM Maeve Thomas: MERRY CHRISTMAS!!! 🎄 Here's a photo of my parent's cat, Baby Gramps (look him up), with a very stately Santa beard and hat. Hope today goes well and remember: NOT ABOUT YOU!

I open the image and can't help but laugh. The poor cat looks miserable. But what's even better is that Maeve is holding him. She has a toothy smile taking up half of her face and from what I can see, she's wearing a red and white pajama set with snowflakes. Her eyes are looking off-camera at someone she probably loves. I just hope it isn't Sean.

I am now acutely aware that my phone is three inches from my face. Georgia watches me as I come up for air.

The server saves me, but the second we're done ordering the largest breakfast platters on the menu, they lean forward. Their eyes are full of sincerity and I can't sarcasm my way out of this one.

"Okay, cut the bullshit, who's Maeve?"

Chapter 12

WE JAM OUT TO SPICE GIRLS on the way back. It's from a weird era when we both were obsessed with the same thing at the same time growing up. Me with Mel B and Georgia with Mel C.

After letting it all out, Georgia is now the only person on the planet who knows I have feelings for Maeve. Big feelings. Big enough to admit that I miss her even after three days, that I can't wait to see her again. I tell them about the conversation in Maeve's apartment and how she made me feel human again after our phone call. I let it all out. I can't stop thinking about Maeve and once I start, I can't stop talking about her, either.

What the hell am I going to do?

Georgia nodded along at all the right parts, and after I finished splaying my heart out to them, their only remark was, "I think I like her," which was more than they ever said about Lacie. The thought of them meeting was improbable, but still gave my mind's eye fodder for some fantasy where I get to introduce Maeve as someone more than a co-worker.

I invite them to the New Year's Bash, but they already have plans with Emma, and it brings a pang to my stomach.

"Next year," I promise, as I pull back into their driveway, but it's not an obligation this time. I give them a sturdy hug to match the one from this morning, and damn, it feels good to let the guilt turn into determination. We instead make brunch plans for New Year's Day.

Before I know it, I'm back at my empty apartment. It's hollow and barren compared to Maeve's. Colder, too. And I'm not just saying that. Hers is set to a balmy 72°F while mine is at 66°F in the winter because I believe saving twenty bucks a month on my heating bill is the height of financial responsibility.

Technically I don't have to water Maeve's plants until tomorrow. She said they could stretch five days without watering, but I'm feeling a Netflix marathon and I'll be damned if I don't take her up on the offer. The scene when I walk into her apartment, however, tells me I might have saved her entire terrarium by stopping by a day early. Two plants are drooping slightly, but there's one that looks dead. Like, fully dead. The leaves are so sunken that they're resting on the shelf below the ceramic planter they're in. And not only that but all of the sticky notes are scattered across the floor. I have no idea which plants need a teaspoon of water vs. a full coffee mug.

Fuck.

I text her in rapid succession before I start freaking out. Maybe I'm being dramatic, maybe it's a perfect excuse to talk to her on Christmas.

> **6:41 PM Conrad Sutherland:** Uh. I just got home and thought I would check on your plants. Some of them are really wilted
> **6:41 PM Conrad Sutherland:** I'm sorry if I should have come earlier
> **6:41 PM Conrad Sutherland:** Also the sticky notes have failed and I'm not sure which ones need how much water. Sorry again

My hands are already clammy. How did I mess this up already? Can she not trust me with *one* thing? Responsibility has always been my thing. As the oldest child, it had to be. Georgia used to call me Con*dad* whenever I yelled at them to do the dishes or take out the trash. And sure, when college hit and I was dead set on farting around as much as possible. Late nights? Check. Drinking my way through the weekend? Check. Spending my entire allowance on Lacie? Check. But that fell away soon after we graduated. In fact, once I stopped wanting to go to frat parties and football games, Lacie seemed unimpressed. I wanted cozy nights in, she wanted Instagramable nights out. She wanted the appearance of being a perpetual twenty-one-year-old.

This feels like a different kind of responsibility, though. Plant sitting for a co-worker and I killed three of them. That kind of shit ends friendships, right? I'm spiraling into a weird place when my phone rings with Maeve's face. She's video-calling me. I run my hands in my hair to pretend to look more presentable and hit the Call Accept button.

"Conrad!" Maeve says, but an echo of two other voices calls out my name, too. "Stop, Val. Anna! Stop! Oh my *god*." There's a shuffle and the screen darkens on the other end, as if the phone is being pressed up against her chest or stomach. My mind definitely doesn't wander there, too. "One sec," she grunts and moments later there's silence and the faint sound of a door slamming. "My sisters are insane. It's like we're back in high school whenever we get together."

A pinch of sadness reaches my stomach. I wish I had those kinds of memories with Georgia.

"All good. Hey, uh, Merry Christmas, I guess."

I finally see her face as she plops down on her bed. Her bedroom walls are blue and still hold shelves with pictures and trophies of some kind. Everything about her is stable and familiar and yet so far off from my upbringing.

162

"Merry Christmas, Conrad." Her expression softens. "So, you killed my plants, huh?"

"I really hope not," I say and switch the camera to show her the wilted mess on her shelf.

"Oh please, that's just my nerve plant being dramatic. Give it a cup or so." I've never related to a plant more in my life. My own nerves settle slightly as I make her watch me fill up a mug with water and pour it in. We repeat the process for the others that are looking dismal, but she doesn't seem worried in the slightest. This is why I don't have houseplants.

The last one is in her room, a spider plant that she says she's had since college. Glad I didn't kill that one. I switch the camera over to say goodbye, even though I want to ask her the question she always asks me. Little high, little low.

"Thank you, and sorry. I was hoping to avoid bothering you when you're with your family."

Maeve glances back at her door. "Honestly, I needed the break. And I wanted to hear about today. How did it go with your mom?"

I gingerly sit down on her unmade bed. Intimacy, man. She's my *co-worker*.

"Actually, we didn't go."

Her eyebrows raise just like I want them to. "What happened?"

"We got pancakes instead," I say, trying to smile and make a joke out of it, but I can feel the boiling ball of emotion rise in my stomach. Her face is unmoving, she's not having it. "Um, I could say I was trying to protect George, but I don't think that would be the full truth. I chickened out. I didn't want to put them through it and, and I didn't want to have to be faced, yet again," — here it comes — "with the fact that my mom doesn't feel like my mom anymore. And I...I couldn't..."

I face the camera away, but seconds later the call ends. Tears are already rolling off my chin and onto my jeans. I smell like syrup and diner grease, and I probably shouldn't do it, but I fall back onto Maeve's bed so I can smell her. It's both new and recognizable. My phone vibrates in my hand and I answer before I can think.

"Maeve?"

"Tell me everything."

I start with high school and how my sister fought against anything our mom told them, how they snuck out at night to meet up with their secret girlfriend and I covered for them every last time. I tell her about college and how I wanted nothing to do with my family and that meant letting Georgia fend for themself on the frontlines of my mom's changing opinions. Then I explain the fallout after the 2016 election and how my sister didn't feel comfortable being at home without me. Last, I tell Maeve about the day my sister said they'd never speak to Mom again after what she said to them about their "lifestyle choices" being the work of the devil and how she hoped they'd rot in hell. I can still hear Georgia's cries over the phone when I think about it too long and it was years ago.

"The dumb part is that you were right, this isn't even about me. I know that. But I couldn't do it. If one day they regret it and are mad at me, well, at least I didn't drive them to be traumatized by our mom on Christmas."

I inhale a sob and my stomach hurts with how embarrassed I am saying all of this out loud. What am I doing here? Why am I even telling her this? Who gives a shit? I've known Maeve for what...three months?

A sniffle on the other end snaps me out of it. "I'm so sorry."

"No, it's not—"

"I just want to give Georgia a hug." Her pitch raises.

Mine does, too. "Don't cry—"

"I can't help it. The second I hear you get choked up, I'm gone. Conrad, I'm so sorry," she repeats. "I think you did the right thing. Pancakes sound way better than being berated by someone who's supposed to love you." I'm silent for a few moments because if I say anything, I'll break again. "Can I ask why they wanted to see her in the first place?" she asks. "What's changed?"

"They met someone. They're in love. And they just wanted to share it with Mom. How beautifully fucked up is that? It's the proverbial rose-colored glasses. Love makes you do stupid shit, huh?"

"Yeah..." she trails off. And then she's quiet for a minute before she takes a deep inhale and goes, "Hey, I should probably get back to my family."

Shit. I said way too much. I clear my throat. "Mhmm."

"I'm sorry again, Conrad. I'm so glad you told me though. That's a lot for one person."

"Thanks, Maeve," is what I say, but what I mean is thanks for listening, thanks for making me feel like I'm not crazy for caring about my sister's emotional wellbeing, thanks for letting me unload some of this shit that I've been carrying around forever. I've never told Lacie any of this; it was outside the realm of our reality. With Maeve, I can't believe I didn't tell her sooner.

"Oh wait! Before I forget. I don't need a ride from the airport, Kiara is going to pick me up."

A heaviness presses my body into her mattress. "Got it."

"Were you planning on going to the New Year's Bash? Kiara's coming to my place to get ready." Right. This is why we're friends. Back to the business of being her taxi driver. It's partially the reason I RSVP'd at all. That, and I thought Georgia would come with me.

"I am. I can drive you."

"Oh, I didn't— okay." I can hear her smile. "We could all hang out for a bit beforehand? Kiara's bringing her girlfriend. Would you want to stop by before we leave?"

I could easily say no and put some semblance of a wall up between my feelings for Maeve and bowing to her every whim, but the fact that I have to wait almost a full twenty-four hours to see her pushes me to say yes.

Yes, yes, always yes. I'll do anything for you, Maeve.

Chapter 13

AFTER THREE KNOCKS, I HEAR FOOTSTEPS and a muffled, "Conrad!"

I've been counting down the hours, minutes, seconds until I can see her, and here she is, opening the door with a full smile and extended arms. It feels so good to be hugged by her again. She smells sweet and her body is warm under my palms.

I wish we were alone.

She's back. And not only is she back, but she's dressed in a mesh, somewhat see-through black long-sleeve top with only a bralette underneath. Like some sort of shockwave, the excitement electrifies my chest. Ever since I spilled my guts to Georgia, I can't stop thinking about the reality of my feelings for Maeve. Her wide-leg pants whoosh against each other as we walk past the living area. It's the same sound as the blood rushing in my ears.

"We're all in my room." She leads me to her bedroom where three other girls are all sitting cross-legged with curling irons and open make-up bags. It brings me back to the years of watching Lacie prep for dinners with other people trying to make a name for themselves on the internet. They're talking about someone when I walk in.

"No, I think he's going to do it tonight, that's what he told me," Kiara says. She's cross-legged in front of another girl with jet-black hair and smiling eyes, applying eyeshadow to her closed lids. "But not at the event."

"Ew, why would he do it at the event?"

"I know, I know." Kiara spots me, and all three girls on the floor look up. "Ooh, hey Conrad."

I wave meekly.

Maeve points at the girl with one eye covered in dark teal eyeshadow. "So, that's Kiara's girlfriend."

"Hi!" I didn't know Kiara had a girlfriend. "My name's Monica, but I go by Mo Thao."

"Mo Thao, Mo Thao!" Maeve repeats. There's another girl facing the mirrored door to the closet, and Maeve points in her direction. "And that's Claire. She's my soulmate, the love of my life, my everything, and was my roommate at Macalester."

Kiara clears her throat.

"And Kiara was also my roommate for one semester Freshman year before she broke my heart and transferred to the U, but you know her." Everyone laughs as if there was a real joke in there, but I don't get it.

Claire hasn't stopped peering up at me in the reflection of the mirror. She has long curly hair and big eyes that say, *I'm curious about you*, and for a moment I bask in the attention.

Maeve sits next to her and effortlessly slips back into their conversation while I awkwardly sit on the bed. "Wait, so why don't you think he'll do it at the actual event tonight?" she asks.

"Lena wouldn't want that," Mo Thao answers and Kiara nods in agreement.

Maeve takes out a tube of lip gloss and asks, "How long have they been together, anyway?"

"Two years," Kiara says. "Which is kind of a long time in his culture. I mean, Lena doesn't want to get married, like, tomorrow. But I don't know if his family has been on board. I mean his parents are cool with it, but grandparents and stuff."

"Who is this?" I ask at the same time Claire finally speaks and says, "Who are we talking about?" We glance at each other and she flashes me a smile with wide straight teeth.

"Zakariya and Lena, from the office," Maeve says. She smacks her lips together and touches the corner of her mouth.

"Zak said he wanted to propose tonight because they met at the New Year's Bash two years ago." I realize my mouth has been hanging open slightly watching her talk. I'm the most awkward thing in this room. "But Lena isn't Muslim, so he's been spending all this time with her family explaining what will happen if they do get married. It's so sweet. He's so in love with her."

"Even I can tell that," I blurt out and the room looks at me. "What? The dude's always happy. He's like if sunshine was a person."

Maeve smiles at me in the mirror as Kiara says, "That's the nicest thing I've ever heard you say, Conrad." She turns to Maeve. "But Zak isn't expecting her to convert. He's more culturally Muslim. His parents are kind of progressive from what I hear."

"It's like how you're only Buddhist because your mom is," Mo Thao adds, and Kiara nods.

"Yeah, I don't know, it's hard to explain. Being mixed is complicated."

"Maybe it's her, *maybe it's assimilation*," Mo Thao sings, and even though Kiara laughs, she holds Mo Thao's head to still her movements and moves to her other eye.

"What are your religious affiliations, Conrad?" Claire asks innocently, but she might as well have been speaking another language. I'm once again not privy to the joke and am aware of this as all four of them fall into one another spitting, laughing, and slapping each other's arms.

"*Stop!*" yells Maeve. Her smiling eyes land on me.

Each mile on the road brings me closer to understanding the dynamic between the four of them. I've never heard Kiara talk this much in my life, but that's probably because I've never said anything other than, "Where's Kathryn?" or, "Is Kathryn out today?" to her at the office. Mo Thao is like her second brain. They finish each other's sentences and Maeve gets a kick out of it, egging them on from the front seat. *Her* front seat. Claire is quiet for the most part. But when she does speak it's usually something dry and makes the whole car laugh, including me.

Unfortunately, the HOV lane isn't open tonight. Great planning on MnDOT's part, since there's a row of cars half a mile long backed up on 394. As we sit in traffic to take the downtown exit, Maeve shushes the car and we make eye contact briefly. She has something up her sleeve.

"Okay, okay, since it's New Year's Eve, I want to know everyone's pit and peach—"

"Maaae-vuh," Claire groans.

"For the year! For the whole year, come on. It can be something small or big, it doesn't have to be deep."

Claire shoots a glare over to Kiara. "Everyone knows my pit."

I don't.

But that doesn't matter, the car just nods as Mo Thao rests her head on Claire's shoulder. "But my peach was finally getting rid of that self-obsessed, narcissistic ass and being on my own for the first time since I was basically a child." She ends with a soft, dazed smile as Maeve snaps like it's a slam poetry reading.

"Ayyy," Kiara adds before taking her turn. "My pit was probably everything with my dad over the summer. I mean he's fine now, but damn, that was scary."

Maeve's hand lands on my forearm and she whispers, "Kiara's dad had a heart attack this year."

"Oh shit," I say involuntarily and look at Kiara in the rearview mirror. "I'm sorry, I didn't know that."

"Not surprised." Okay, *Maeve.*

"But my peach is that Mo and I moved in together. It's like a sleepover every night."

My mind drifts back to the purple duvet. I missed out on so many of those nights not living with her. The vision of spending a night with Maeve lifts a piece of the heaviness from my chest. Even just staying up late talking to her feels like a childlike dream that will never be fulfilled.

Mo Thao perks up. "My pit is that the Thai place by my work closed."

"Babe, it closed like three years ago."

"Still my pit. They had the best papaya salad," she quips. "And my peach is Kiara. Just Kiara." They share covert smiles and I see the movement of their hands interlinking. They're in love or whatever. Good for them.

We're still twenty yards away from the exit, stopped behind a semi-truck. This is starting to feel a bit like a joke. I'm playing Uber for four girls, about to go to a New Year's Eve party for work, and I'm so painstakingly single it makes my skin itch. I'm already thinking tonight was a mistake. But at least there's Maeve.

"My pit was being mugged," she says with a timid shrug, but the other girls giggle. Claire cackles and I don't get it. I don't know if I ever will with these four. "I guess that kinda sucked."

"Oh, boo-hoo?" Kiara jokes.

Claire leans forward and grabs the back of Maeve's headrest. "Grow up," she says and Maeve laughs along. "It's time to move on." Their form of sarcasm baffles me.

"And my peach is getting this job! Look at where it's gotten me. In a car with the three of you and this weirdo." Just like that, I'm added back into the conversation. "I suppose meeting you was a perk, too. Like a little leaf on the peach."

"There for ornamental value," Kiara says.

"Don't eat them, though." Mo Thao uses her free hand to scratch at Maeve's shoulder. "Cyanide, babe."

Claire's eyes meet mine in the rearview mirror. "Conrad, do you consider yourself a pit, peach, or leaf in Maeve's life?"

"Claire!"

"What?" She winks at me and okay, chalk it up to my singleness, but the vibe Claire is giving me through the rearview mirror shifts. Is she *flirting* with me? The thought vanishes as quickly as it came. Maeve's hands are patting my arm like a drum.

"Your turn!"

"Nah," I answer. We've finally broken through the traffic and we're approaching the entrance to Ramp A.

"Conrad, come on. We all went."

"I don't want to."

"Classic men," Claire says, and I nearly burst out laughing.

"What is that supposed to mean?"

"They're never in touch with their feelings. It's okay, Conrad, you're in a safe space, you can tell us your pit was that your favorite sports team lost the Super World Bowl Series."

"*Claire,*" Maeve scolds.

Kiara gives Claire an elbow to the arm like a set of bickering sisters, but can't resist a chuckle herself.

"Okay, feeling very open to being vulnerable *now.*"

Claire rolls her eyes with a grin and looks out the window. The truth is my pit would make me seem like an idiot. Either I share about my ex-girlfriend dumping me in this very car, or I tell them about the time I chickened out seeing my mom with my sister because I couldn't face the music. I'm a walking coward. Driving, I guess. Driving into Ramp A and spiraling up to Level 7 to park.

And my peach, well...

"Please?" Maeve protests before we get out of the car. The other three girls are already out and shivering. It's like she knows if we're alone I'll break down every barrier I've built during the car ride.

"You know. Pit is Lacie. And I don't know what my peach is." Mo Thao's words come back to me. *It's you, Maeve. Just you.* "I'll tell you when I think of it."

She huffs briefly but is satisfied enough with the answer that she exits the car. It's going to be a long night.

Every year this event is held in the same swanky room in some downtown hotel that's usually booked solid a year in advance. Our first year, Lacie and I tried but ended up stumbling six blocks away to a Best Western that looked very German and was double what I thought it would be. Her dad's credit card was accepted anyway.

The event floor smells of expensive liquor like it always does. Jesse is schmoozing with big advertisers and his husband, *Tom*, is nodding along smiling. There are samples of new dishes from hot restaurants that we've featured over the past year lining the walls. A yuzu-infused cocktail here, a deconstructed tiramisu there. The extravagance, the clientele, the sold-out rooms, it's all still here tonight. Just without Lacie. The best smell in the place is coming from the sambusas directly ahead of me. Zakariya is with Lena, and the whole group gravitates to them. I listen to their conversation, feeling like an outsider. It's my own fault. I'm doing it on purpose.

"Lena! You made it," Kiara greets her first with a hug, then gives Zakariya a wink while she brushes some imaginary dust off the shoulders of his suit jacket. "I guess you can clean up nicely when you want to."

"Hah, hah. Great to see you, too." Zakariya introduces himself to Claire and welcomes Mo Thao and Maeve like a gentleman, but the bro hug he gives me is not something I'm expecting. I guess I'm not yet accustomed to being friends with my co-workers. Unless they're Maeve.

The girls wander off to try sips of newly mixed drinks and there's a stab in my chest that reminds me I have no idea how to handle these events by myself. Lacie and I never got to these things this early. We usually waited until an hour before the ball drop to leave our pre-game at some other bar with her friends.

The New Year's Eve Bash famously transforms into an after-party in the hotel bar. Only the true elite are invited to incestually rub elbows into the New Year. It's a whole thing. Our sales team eats it up and it's been known that at least someone will hook up with a fellow co-worker by the end of the night.

But now that I'm moving from table to table, trying to behave in a way that appears I'm actually interested in what they're trying to sell, all I can focus on is that I'm here alone. I flinch at the sound of a high-pitched sales voice at the table I've been absentmindedly idling by for the last thirty seconds.

"Hi there! Can I interest you in some low-ABV drink options? We have a black tea-infused clarified milk punch that's my favorite and a Negroni Sbagliato that uses a fantastic prosecco over gin." A *clarified milk punch* is probably not going to do great things for my nausea. Every word of that thickens the mucus in my throat. And since I'm having a hard time coming up with anything to say back to him, I nod in the direction of the orangeish fizzy drink in response.

"We'll be serving these at our location in Roseville all through the month of January, because dry January doesn't have to be all that dry," he performs with a wink. Yikes.

I raise my 4oz. disposable plastic cup with a smile and scurry away like the socially awkward rodent I am. Lacie was always the speaker for the two of us at these things. She knew how to handle even the pushiest of salesmen while I watched on with a smirk. I learned early on that I didn't need to insert myself when she was working a bartender or a hostess.

I drag my feet to a high top in a dark corner of the room, allowing me to sulk from the comfort of the outside looking in. It's not about making small talk or the fake smiles. I simply don't want to be here. The only reason why I even entertained the idea was to spend more time with Maeve and she's here with three of her closest friends. None of which are me. Is this who I am? Someone who concedes to every whim of every girl I've ever been attracted to? Lacie had me wrapped around her fucking finger. I attended countless events and appearances that never made me feel anything more than a glorified chauffeur and mobile coat rack. And sure, maybe this time I'm not holding Maeve's purse or folding her peacoat around my forearm, but I wouldn't be here if she didn't need a ride. On top of it, I take a sip of the Negroni Sbagli-blah-blah and immediately my mouth dries with bitterness. What the hell is in this thing? It's somehow watered down and too strong all at once.

"You look like you're having a great time," a small voice says. Claire bellies up to the high-top table I'm leaning my elbows on, and I am suddenly hyper-aware of how hard I had been cringing.

I clear my throat. "Uh, yeah, just waiting until the ball drops."

"You literally looked like you were in pain just now."

"It's this drink," I admit, lifting my bright orange cup. "It's...really bad."

She relaxes slightly and presses her lips together to hide a smile. "What is it?"

"A Negroni Sbagli-thingy?"

"A Negroni *Sbagliato*. With *prosecco*. Stunning." She's talking in a British accent for some reason.

"So you like them?"

"No," she says, falling back into her calm and unfazed demeanor. "But I'll take it." I hand over the drink and she grimaces after her first sip, just like me. Her lip gloss leaves a mark on the plastic rim. "Oh god, that is not a Negroni Sbagliato. That tastes like ass."

"Is that a taste you're familiar with?" The question comes out of me like a reflex. I'm playing defense. "Sorry, I—"

"That was insanely unhinged."

"I know, sorry."

She bursts out laughing, thank god. "Are you always like this? Brooding in the corner and being the weirdest person in the room?"

The flirting feeling is back. I narrow my eyes and hope it looks mysterious and charming rather than pissy and moody. "I wasn't brooding, I was taking a break from the floor because I don't want to be here. And you're the one who brought up ass."

She swipes my arm. "It's just a saying."

"Where are Maeve and Kiara? Why are *you* brooding in the corner?" She followed me here. I was fine sulking alone.

Her thumb wipes off some condensation accumulating on the outside of the drink. "I don't want to be here either. But don't tell them that." Her brows knit together. "I honestly don't even know if Maeve wants to be here, but here we are."

I scan the room to see if I can find where she is, but all I see is a speedwalking Kathryn bopping between booths with a tense smile. Today is her Super Bowl. "Why wouldn't Maeve want to be here?"

"The same reason I don't. Her boyfriend is two million miles away, and I left my ex-boyfriend so he could spend more time with himself. So when the ball drops, we'll be trying not to make eye contact with every couple sucking face. Today is worse than Valentine's Day. You get it. Maeve told me about your whole" — her hand waves erratically towards me — "*situation*."

"Of course she did."

"Sucks."

"Sure does." I can feel our conversation coming to a close, but I want her to linger. A few facts align; she's single, I'm single. She just got out of a relationship, I just got out of a relationship. Her humor is dry enough that I can stomach a conversation. She's cute, shorter than me, and well, did I mention we're both single?

"Have you dated since the breakup?" I'll start off easy. Passive.

She raises an eyebrow. "Nothing serious. A few hookups, but I'm taking a break from the dating apps for now." Her eyes turn up to me with the same curiosity from the mirror in Maeve's room. "You?"

"No. Nothing." That answer seems to satisfy her. Time for another step closer, figuratively and literally. "Also, I'll have you know, my pit this year was not having some football team lose the... what did you call it? Super World Bowl Series?"

Her eyes roll but a hint of a smile appears. "Aren't you special."

"Yes, thank you, I am." One more step and we're home free. If Maeve is out here with her friends, trying to have a good time, why can't we? My answer to Claire was honest. I haven't had any carefree hook-ups. Dating apps sound repulsive to me, and damnit, maybe we both don't have to go home alone tonight.

"Hey." The change in my tone gets her attention. I'm trying to be as sincere as possible now. "What's your number? You're fun."

The blood drains from her face. She doesn't have to say a word. I know I've already been rejected. "Oh, um. I—"

"Got it." I spit out a little too quickly.

"No, I just, I'm not—"

"No need to explain," I say, grabbing the bitter drink between us and wishing it was straight whiskey so I could shoot it back. My eyes trail around the floor and land on Kathryn struggling to carry a folding table with a tablecloth wrapped around her shoulders.

"I'm going to go help with some of the, uh...I have to probably—"

"Yep." She tucks her hair behind her ears. "Sorry."

"Yeah and so..." I lose steam but take my first few steps until I'm speed walking towards Kathryn. My body doesn't feel like my own. Every step fills me with so much anxiety and embarrassment I feel like I'm walking the halls of a high school after wetting my pants. I'm starting to get the feeling that I'll never be as confident as I was with Lacie. She chose me for six years and now no one in the tri-state area is even remotely attracted to me. That's what the heaviness in my chest tells me.

I trash the drink and approach Kathryn with about as much grace as an injured giraffe. "Need help with that?"

Kathryn stops mid-stride and nearly collides into me. For as often as she looks like a deer in the headlights, tonight she's surprisingly focused. "Excuse me?"

"I was wondering if you needed any help?" I don't wait for her to answer and take the table out of her hands. It's heavier than it looks.

She's eyeing me like I'm her next kill. "Did Jesse tell you to do this?"

"No?"

"Then why are you asking?"

I set the table down for a second. It's fucking heavy. "Because I saw you running back and forth and figured there's probably something I could help with."

She checks her watch before eyeing the vendors still sampling out food and beverages. I have no concept of time under the twinkling rope lights, but the ball drop couldn't have happened yet.

She shifts back into focus. "It's a quarter after eleven and we have about forty-five minutes to get every last vendor out of here before the ball drops. Our contracted event workers have no idea how to talk to these clients without pissing them off, and our sales reps are already at the hotel bar. If I can be the bearer of bad news, can you manage the event team and coordinate the breakdown of the vendor booths?"

I nod without thinking about it and she directs me to follow her to a hallway off the back of the showroom leading to the loading dock outside. Six college kids dressed in all black are in various poses leaning against the walls and shelves but perk up when they see Kathryn.

"Team, do what he says." She points up at me like I actually have some authority over these jocks. "If you want to be out of here before midnight, we'll need two guys on tables, one on tablecloths, and three on pipe-and-drape." She whips off the tablecloth, throws it to one of them, and pivots on her heel. I guess that's my cue.

"Hi. I'm Conrad." They stare at me, and for a moment I actually wonder if I'm back in highschool and have in fact wet myself. "Uh, and I have no idea what I'm doing, but let's figure it out. I don't want to be here any longer than I need to be."

A few of them smirk and we're off. Over the next half an hour, it's a barrage of liquor-soaked linens, sticky tables, and physical labor. It resets my nervous system in a way, and by some miracle, I don't see Mo Thao or Claire or Kiara or even Maeve for that matter. My guess is they already joined the afterparty downstairs. The room is empty in no time, only the most extravagant of displays are left as awkward conversations between Kathryn and vendors subside.

Each trip to and from the loading dock back gets me more riled up. Why am I even doing this in the first place? The thought that Maeve is watching me is hovering around me like an annoying fly. I want her to see how helpful I am. I haven't seen her in at least an hour and a half, and on the seventh trip to the loading dock, I'm pissed. I don't want to be here if she's not with me. I don't want to be carrying these tables unless Maeve knows I'm helping out a fellow co-worker.

Okay, that makes me sound like a tool. Isn't that what this is about, though? I'm not actually upset that Claire blew me off, because in reality, I just wanted to date her to spite Maeve. But why the fuck would Maeve care? She has a boyfriend and it's not me.

I'm helping load the last of the tables into the trailer and I'm starting to feel the sinking feeling in my chest, but this tide is bigger than the rest. Something is ebbing so hard, that my entire body is feeling hollow. Did I eat dinner? Did I eat lunch? I was so excited to see Maeve tonight, I think I forgot.

It's the shame that catches up with me. Maeve doesn't want me. My sister's in love. I don't have a dad. I don't have a mom. I don't have a girlfriend. I don't have friends.

I don't want to be here anymore. Nobody wants me here, anyway, why should I insert myself in places where I constantly don't belong? Look what happened with Lacie. It was always too good to be true. God, I wished I never met her.

It's 11:47 pm and we're done. My brain is fried, my arms are sore, and my undershirt is soaked through with sweat. With a fake smile, I thank everyone and am out the doors into the shocking freeze of the night. Guilt dances with spite like the wind picking up the snowfall from the afternoon.

11:52 pm. My car smells like perfume and hairspray and I have to push it all down in order to get through the fifteen-minute drive. No traffic. I'm passing the exit we took to the ice cream place and my temper mingles with the heat of the air blasting out of my air vents.

11:58 pm. There are other cars on the road, and my first thought is, *Isn't that sad?* The year is turning and we're all stuck behind the wheel. Do they have regrets? What was their pit of the year? Their peach? Is everyone else exiting off 394 feeling sorry for themselves as much as I am?

When I stop at the light of the exit, I watch my dashboard clock change from 11:59 pm to 12:00 am and the back of my throat aches. The stupid sting crawls up my nose and my vision goes blurry as I turn into the apartment's underground parking garage at 12:08 am. I already have a plan for shutting out everything I'm feeling right now. And it's an awful one.

I'm three healthy shots of Jameson in as I uncap a beer and take it with me to the shower. That's where I'm at currently. No one's checking up on me. Not a girlfriend. Not my mom. Not my sister. It's just me, my shower beer, and a rising buzz that's lowering my shoulders and IQ by the second.

You know who the culprit of all of this is, right? Lacie. All of this is Lacie's fault. The person who had to break my fucking heart in order to start *living her life*, as if loving me was that much of a prison. That's who I should be taking this up with. That's who I should be calling out. It's not Maeve's fault I'm single and spending New Year's alone. Although, Claire would have alleviated one of those problems. Screw them all. It's my turn to say something.

I don't even bother with a towel as I face plant onto my bed, reaching for my phone. It takes me a few more minutes than normal, but I finally hear the dial tone for one, two, three, four rings. *Damnit*. Again. One, two, thr—

"Hello?"

Holy shit.

"Lacie?"

"Con?" There's music playing in the background and so much noise. "Wha-the hell? Why're you callin' me?" Either her words are slurring, or my brain is, or maybe both. I haven't had this much to drink in a while.

"Whatdyou mean? I can call you if I want to call you. You were my girlfriend for six years. And we need to talk."

"I've said everything I need t-say t-you."

I blow through her. "And that's great and all, but I haven't had a chance to say" — *hiccup* — "what I need to say...to *you*." The pause was for dramatic effect, not because I had to swallow a burp. There's more music and then some sort of loud slam and the line goes quiet.

"Con, don't do this—"

"Why weren't you at North Star's New Year's Bash tonight? You always go. Why are you avoiding having a real conversation with me, face-to-face."

"Because I'm-n LA. I moved two monthssago," she yells even though she's seemingly in a quiet area now.

"What the fuck?" My voice squeaks. This wasn't in any of my preplanned scenarios for how this conversation would eventually go. "You didn't say you were moving."

"I did, too!" she shrieks. "I wrote it in my letter that I was moving out."

"Oh, you wrote it in your letter! The letter!" Now I'm yelling because I can. "You didn't say you were moving to LA. And if you really wanted to be friends, you would've told me. Was that the reason you broke up with me? Why the fuck didn't you tell me?"

"Stop y-yelling." The line goes quiet for a second and then she lets out a high-pitched sob. God, I feel like shit and it's not just because of the alcohol. "I knew you'd try-tah-talk me out of it. I din't wanna fight! This isn't us!"

She's right. We never once got into a screaming match. I'm drunk and angry and this is the only way I can express that without crumbling into a million pieces or doing something stupid. Like knocking on Maeve's door.

"Lacie, we were together for six years. You were a huge part of my life during that time. You didn't think this would affect me?" is what I *wanted* to say.

Here's what I actually say, "I don't give a shit. That's such a bitch move. Just because I'm not some, some" — I'm crying again and I don't know when it happened — "fuckboy who would rather fight than just leave, doesn't mean it didn't fucking hurt when you walked away. Why didn't you let me have any say?" Nice one, Conrad.

She whimpers softly.

"Why didn't I get a fucking say?!" Spit is flying from my mouth and even I hate me.

Her voice is feeble. "I'm s-s-sorry. If I could do it all over again I would." We're a mess. She's crying in some bathroom at a party and I'm feeling sorry for myself naked, alone, and eighteen hundred miles away. We're nothing more than a cliché. But I have what I need. I got to blow off some steam and she got to say the single dumbest thing imaginable.

"You could come to LA? I still love you, Con."

"Fuck off." I hang up immediately and toss my phone on the floor, not caring in the slightest about any repercussions. I crawl under the covers thinking about Maeve and wishing I was with Maeve and wondering where Maeve is right now. Little did I know that three texts are waiting in my unread messages from her.

12:01 AM Maeve Thomas: WHAT THE HE'LL where ate you?

12:21 AM Maeve Thomas: We had to tkake an Uber back thsnks a lot!!!!!!

12:46 AM Maeve Thomas: Don't worry about giving my a ride to workvanymore i'll take the bus

Great job, everyone. Awesome work.

Happy fucking New Year.

Chapter 14

I CAN'T BELIEVE I COMMITTED to a New Year's brunch with my sister and their girlfriend at 10 am. The brunch itself isn't stupid, but every decision I've made in the last 12 hours has been. When I woke up, I saw Maeve's text and instantly felt like an ass. I also saw that I didn't call Lacie just once or twice.

Nope.

I called six times before she picked up, pushing me into absolute idiot territory. I can't deal with it right now. Space is the only thing I have left to give, and it'll benefit both of us.

I shove a beanie over the weird way my damp hair dried overnight. It's doing nothing to make me more presentable, but I'm hoping the extra spritz of cologne and sunglasses will

ANNA POLLOCK

somehow prove that I'm not some delinquent who overserved himself. This will be my first time meeting Emma, and I'm more hungover than I've been in years.

The half-hour drive is a success considering I didn't hurl onto my lap, but the floor-to-ceiling windows at the restaurant urge me to keep my sunglasses on as I try my hardest to smile at the host and tell him I'm meeting someone. I shoot a text to Georgia and fifteen seconds later they're greeting me with a hug I didn't know I needed.

"Hey Connie," they say, sniffing me. "Are you hungover?"

"It's New Year's Day, what did you expect?"

They smack my arm but grab onto me as we walk through the minimalist motif. White walls, light hardwood floors, natural lighting. Everything is too bright.

"I'm so nervous. But I think you'll like her. I just hope she likes you. Don't say anything weird."

"No promises." I don't have time to say anything else, because we stop at a table with who I assume is Emma. She has dark hair and bangs with gold hoop earrings peeking out under wisps of hair let loose from her low bun. She's wearing a muted green turtleneck under a brown overcoat. It's so different from Georgia's technicolor overalls.

"Hi! Are you Conrad?" I nod and quickly learn that Emma is a hugger. "George has told me so much about you. You run *North Star Magazine*, right? I love that magazine."

194

I glance over at George. *My* George. No one else usually calls them that. "Ah, I don't run it. I'm just the production guy."

"You literally put the issues together," they retort.

I shrug. "Sure, I guess." I have no energy to argue with anyone about anything ever again.

The waiter comes around to order, and I stick with coffee and toast while Georgia and Emma order entrees and sides "for the table." Georgia knows what they're doing. Within ten minutes after my first cup of coffee and half a slice of toast, my appetite is back with a vengeance. I'm on my third stolen bite of their eggs benedict when they ask the question I've been dreading.

"So did you end up going to the New Year's Bash then?"

I swipe my napkin over my mouth to give myself a few extra seconds. "Uh, yeah. Hence the hangover."

Georgia exchanges a sly look with Emma. "And how was it? You had fun, it sounds like," they ask.

I wish they were right. "Uh, well."

"Wait, really? Okay, talk," Georgia pokes, but I don't know how much to divulge in front of a new significant other. "Just tell us. Emma knows about Lacie."

So I tell her about Lacie, too. I start with my terrible decision to drink a full glass of whiskey ahead of a shower beer and end on our asinine conversation, very strategically leaving out any other parts of last night that make me nauseous.

"She said, 'I still love you'? And asked you to come to LA?! You have to be joking."

"I'm not," I answer my sister with a full mouth of the French toast in the middle of the table. "I can't believe she moved to LA. I mean I can, but I can't believe she didn't tell me. I would have entertained the idea of long-distance." *No, I wouldn't have.* "But she didn't even give me a choice."

"That's so fucked up!" Emma exclaims. She still sounds innocent and put together, but her tenacity blends in well with our sibling dynamic. "That's not a relationship if you ask me. Relationships are supposed to be a partnership, a choice that you *both* make. I'm sorry that happened, Conrad."

"Thanks." I look at Georgia to signal my unspoken approval. "I think I needed to hear that."

They put an arm around me. "What about Maeve? Any updates?"

Emma's eyes light up. "Yeah! I love Maeve."

"Okay, *George.* Thanks for keeping that close to the chest."

"You never said I had to," they squawk and I feel a genuine laugh bubble up. It feels good to process this with someone other than my inner monologue. Obviously, it hasn't done me any favors.

"Maeve's not the biggest fan of me right now. I might have given her and her friends a ride to the Bash and then left without them."

Emma's eyes narrow while Georgia's widen. "Dick move, did you hook up with someone, Connie?"

"*No*. And that's why I left."

They both give me an unconvinced look. "I'm choosing to believe you," my sister says.

"The event was bringing back all of these memories of Lacie, and Maeve's friend was kind of cute and I swear she was hitting on me, I swear! All night, I'd catch her glancing at me or picking on me. And she approached me when I was alone at a bar table, like, who does that? So I asked for her number and was instantly rejected." I take a breath. "And after everything over Christmas, I was just feeling pathetic, okay? So I left. I went home to drink and call my ex on New Year's. Sue me."

"Sloppy."

"*George.*"

They dismiss me. "So how do you know she's mad? For all you know, they bar crawled the rest of the night. You're not their taxi."

I show them both my phone.

"Ah." Georgia concedes. "Well, at least she was thinking about you at midnight."

Emma's smile shines. "Yeah! That must mean something."

"I appreciate the optimism, but our commute was about the only thing I was looking forward to this year. I'm trying not to think about it."

I cut into a fresh piece of syrup-soaked bread and wash it down with my stale cup of joe. It's nothing like Maeve's coffee. Maybe that was something I was looking forward to, too. Chasing highs I already know is so much easier than fantasizing about new ones.

"Enough about my fuck-ups. What did you two do for New Year's?" They exchange an electric smile and I wish I never asked.

"We stayed in," Emma says, followed by a much more crude Georgia that says, "And got high as a kite."

Going back to the office after the holiday break always sucks, but this year it's ten times worse knowing that I'm avoiding the only person I consider a close friend at work. Even on normal days, our jobs don't interact much. She's out writing about people, places, and things, and I'm stuck in a cubicle begging people to turn in their shit. January is usually an easy month because sales are shit for February's issue, even with the Valentine's Day spike. Our ad volume cuts around this time every year, causing alarm from Jesse that luckily is directed at *not* me, and we hear all about it at our annual all-staff Q1 meeting. *Great job, but everything is on fire*, is the sentiment felt throughout the room.

I speak briefly about Magazine Manager and how easy it is for sales to upload their own ads, but it's overshadowed by Zakariya's engagement. As it should be. There's cake and everything. I try not to be too obvious about glancing at Maeve every five minutes, but she's been sticking to her guns beautifully. It's like she doesn't even know I'm there. Kiara is hellbent on leaning into her Midwestern passive-aggressiveness and puts it on display as she's dishing out pieces of the hastily decorated sheet cake from some grocery store around here.

"Oh, did you want a piece?"

I stumble. "Uh, no, yeah, I'll have— Er, I'll take a piece."

Her expression flatlines. "Okay, just wanted to ask in case you change your mind and bail last second."

I take my one-inch square with nothing more than a nod, and decide to sit at my desk to eat it.

The charade continues as the weeks go by. If there's one thing about January, it's that every day is felt. All thirty-one days drag on. It's a month that demands your attention, but all I can think about is Maeve. I try finding hobbies again. I purchase a few books online, I read the description of some events happening in Minneapolis, I check the Instagram account I made, and then scroll a bit on YouTube. But all of it barely distracts me. She always finds a way back into my mind.

The year's first department head meeting flusters me in an unexpected way. The second Kathryn is asked to share her update for the month, she beams at me.

"Well, I want to give a shout-out. The New Year's Bash went off without a hitch. I think we're on track with the budget to have a live band in the conference hall next year, but the hotel was very pleased with the turnout in the bar, and as always, the rooms were sold out by November. I actually got to enjoy a bit of the afterparty because Conrad stayed and helped tear down in the showroom." Zakariya and Jesse match her enthusiasm. "Honestly, the contractors listened to him so much more than me. Tear down has never gone that smoothly."

"Excellent, Conrad!" Jesse hits his desk with excitement. "Love to hear that. Sounds like the New Year is starting off on the right foot."

If only he knew.

A deadline week comes and goes. The February issue is released, and now it's on to March. Since I'm not getting updates from Maeve anymore, I have no idea what content is coming my way. It isn't until the second week in February that I get an email that sends my pulse into the low hundreds.

From: Maeve Thomas <mthomas@northstarmag.com>
To: Conrad Sutherland <csutherland@northstarmag.com>
Date: Monday, February 21st, 10:03 AM
Subject: March Feature

Good morning,

Attached is the feature for the March issue. Let me know if you have any questions.

M

Maeve Thomas (she/her)
Associate Editor, *North Star Magazine*
mthomas@northstarmag.com
612-555-0281

I swallow hard. A robot could have written that email. It doesn't sound like Maeve. It sounds like two co-workers who work in separate offices on either side of the planet and have never met each other in real life. I must be a masochist; I open up the article and read every word. It's about a family-owned Chinese restaurant off University Avenue in St. Paul.

My mouth is watering. The pictures are vivid and bright. She writes about the food as if it's a romance novel, interwoven with the heart of the people who make it so special. It's a spot that must be well-loved in the Frogtown neighborhood that it resides in. It's a place where families gather after church, on birthdays, anniversaries, and funerals. To celebrate, to mourn, to feel connected. She interviewed the owners and regulars, even stopped by the surrounding locally owned businesses to capture the community. This is on a street that I've driven through maybe five times in my entire life, and yet there's so much I've been missing. I clear my throat before I feel the ache of emotion and plug the feature into Magazine Manager.

For about ten minutes longer than I should, I contemplate replying to play the game with her. It doesn't matter either way, yet here I am.

From: Conrad Sutherland <csutherland@northstarmag.com>

To: Maeve Thomas <mthomas@northstarmag.com>

Date: Monday, February 21st, 10:41 AM

Subject: Re: March Feature

Received.

C

Conrad Sutherland (he/him)
Director of Production, *North Star Magazine*
csutherland@northstarmag.com
612-555-0271

Chapter 15

THE COMMUTES ARE BORING NOW. The weather is dull, even for February. The snow is dirty and the sun never shines. We're lucky if the temperature gets into the twenties, but during an uncharacteristically warm deadline week, it's been approaching the mid-thirties nearly every day, revealing the filth underneath the snow and giving us a glimpse into spring. But it's deadline week. And that means I get to enjoy absolutely none of it.

By Thursday, every client has their ads in except Hank. And because in my mind, that meant my workload was going to be reasonable this time around, I let it go without much fanfare. It's my own fault, but it's a pretty rookie mistake. I've been trying not to focus on Maeve, but it hasn't been working.

I can't count the number of times I've caught myself staring at my computer thinking about what her pits and peaches were for the week or if she misses our commutes. Is she getting home safe every night? And what about me? Does she miss me? I can't stop thinking about how much I miss her. It's a different feeling from missing Lacie. I missed telling people I had a girlfriend, I missed having my weekends planned for me. But this time I just miss Maeve.

Friday morning I hear conversations in cubicles about an ice storm coming to town later that afternoon. No less than six people have knocked on Jesse's door asking if he's closing the office down early. I can only roll my eyes. Everyone else has the luxury of being able to do their work from the comfort of their home, or hell, *doesn't* have a deadline to hit today. So you can imagine my delight (sarcastic) when just after noon, Jesse announces to the entire team that the office is shutting down and we're free to go home.

When I told Jesse about my dilemma on his way out, he huffed in frustration and said Hank had the day off. "Sorry, buddy. I didn't know his were still missing. I swore I saw them come through."

Yeah, well, it's fun to swear but they're not in my inbox. So now I'm the only one stuck here, trying to reach Hank on his cell phone.

I make my way to the kitchen and take a look outside. Oof. It's dismal. Downtown Minneapolis is soaked. Heavy snowflakes are falling to blanket the filth in white. The temperature took a drop about an hour ago and I can only imagine how slippery the roads are getting underneath. Anxiety swarms my nervous system. Sure, it's going to be a bitch driving home in this, but my first thought is reserved for Maeve. The bus stop below on 8th Ave is already packed with people. I'm sure MnDOT hasn't adjusted the bus routes with the higher volume, and damn, that wind looks harsh.

I wish I could text her.

I text my sister instead.

1:19 PM Conrad Sutherland: It's snowing like crazy downtown and I'm stuck at the office. Did the store close early?
1:20 PM George Sutherland: Yes! Go home! It's nasty out there
1:20 PM George Sutherland: If it wasn't so bad I'd tell you to come over. Emma is here and we're making soup

I try to take a deep breath, but I'm having a hard time not feeling sorry for myself again. Maeve and I have to make up someday, right? We were friends, not dating. We didn't break up. She's just mad because I did something stupid and a little selfish. Okay, a lot selfish. I'm confused why it would cause this long of a grudge though. Did I miss some big banner in the sky that leaving four capable women at a party with other co-workers was a crime punishable by ruining a friendship?

And on top of that, it's been weirdly isolating to have no one to talk to. Stopping by Zakariya's cubicle was starting to become a habit after Thanksgiving. Now it would require passing Maeve's desk and having her listen in. What would I even talk about? The only thing on my mind would be to ask why he thought Maeve was so upset. Not really watercooler chit-chat.

It's past 2 pm and I'm on the verge of a meltdown. Fucking Hank. I try his cell phone for the sixth time in an hour. I know it's no use. But just as I'm about to slam the receiver into its dock, by some miracle he picks up.

"Conrad, I have the day off, what is it?" Oh, right, because this is my fault. I'm inconveniencing *him*.

My blood is ice hot. "Hank, I still don't have your ads. The weather's awful, man, I've been calling you for an hour." I try not to be too abrasive with my tone, but one wrong move and I'm going to collapse. It's right at my throat.

"Ah, I'm sorry, I'm up north and service is spotty at best. I don't know…" Static scratches my ear. "…submitted my ads…Magazine Manager like you always tell us to do. I figured I would try to make your life easier…time around."

"Hold on." My mouth is hanging open as I click around to dig into the uploaded internal files. And lo and behold, in Hank's client folder are the ads for some outdoor living design company. "Damn. I see them in here, yeah."

"I probably should have emailed you...my first time submitting them this way, hah!" His boisterous laugh grates against the blood rushing to my ears.

I apologize again and after wasting the last two hours of my life accomplishing nothing, I finally send off the file to the printer. I layer on my scarf, beanie, mittens, and parka for the four-block walk to the skyway. When I get to my car, I'm going to let loose. I'm going to scream into the confines until my voice is sore, get it all out before I have to white-knuckle it back to the Westside.

I don't make mistakes like that. I check those folders almost every day in the optimistic hope that the salespeople will finally wake up one day and be able to listen. I don't know how I missed it. I'm completely off my game and the reason is ten feet in front of me, bouncing up and down on the sidewalk to keep warm while waiting for a bus along with fifty other people. I could make out her navy blue duffle coat and grey backpack from a mile away. The universe is forcing its hand again because at the same moment I'm staring at her, she turns around and catches me. If now isn't the perfect time to apologize and actually do something about it, I don't know what is.

The wind hurts the skin on my face, but I'm determined to shuffle through the snow to reach her. I weave my way through the crowd and she's just as surprised as I am that I'm actually doing this.

"Maeve. What's going on?"

At first, she pretends like she doesn't know me, but she can't hold out for even a second. "Buses are running late."

"Do you want a ride home?"

She looks ahead. "It should be coming any minute."

"You've been waiting for over an hour."

"Like I said, it should be coming any minute."

I blink a few times to get the snow out of my eyelashes and lean in. "Look, I'm sorry. Can we please talk? Let me give you a ride home. It's freezing."

Her hood is up so I can't really tell what face she's making, but after a few seconds, she grunts and slithers through the rest of the bystanders. I don't care if she ignores me the entire car ride home. At least she'll be safe.

And now I have a peach for the day.

We're silent the entire walk to the car. Even in the skyway, away from the snow underfoot and the wind lashing our skin, we don't speak a single word. It's not until we're winding down the parking ramp that she starts in, very obvious about the fact that she's been holding this in for weeks.

"Why did you leave me all alone at the New Year's Bash?"

"Maeve," I scoff. It feels so good to say her name. "I didn't leave you alone at the New Year's Bash. You were with Kiara and Mo Thao and—"

"You were our ride! You drove us there. And I *know* that you hit on Claire. That was weird."

"I didn't *hit* on her. I asked for her number and backed off when she said no." That seems to satisfy her, but her arms cross defiantly. My grip on the steering wheel tightens as we leave the ramp. The snowfall is heavy. I can barely see anything but the car in front of me crawling at 30 mph as we enter the highway. "And I didn't want to be there in the first place. I only went because I knew you needed a ride."

"And you think *I* wanted to go?"

I tense up. "Why wouldn't I?! You literally asked!"

"*No.*" She calms and buries her face in her mittens. "I asked if you were going, and you just responded with, 'I'll drive you.' What was I supposed to say to that?"

"Why *else* would you have asked if I was going?"

"Because I wanted to spend time with you after being gone in Seattle for a week! Kiara slept over after picking me up from the airport, so all I wanted was a night in." She's yelling, but in my gut, I know she's just riled up.

I can't answer her because the car in front of me just fishtailed. The plows haven't been out yet. I get through the patch of ice and we see two cars on the shoulder with their hazards on. I lean forward a bit and feel Maeve soften next to me. I'm trying to get through this commute ten feet at a time.

"But you immediately went off on your own," she continues. "You didn't follow us when we met up with the other editors, and then Claire comes down to the afterparty and she tells me you asked for her number, and that you had to help take down the vendor tables. Like what? Since when are you on the events team?"

"Kathryn needed help," I say, clenching my jaw.

"And all of a sudden it's the countdown, and I couldn't find you anywhere. I felt like an idiot all alone surrounded by strangers making out with each other." Her hands flail around in front of her. Is she insinuating that we would have been making out if I would have stayed?

"What does that even mean? That should be your answer as to why I left. This is my first New Year's without Lacie. You didn't think that maybe I wanted to get out of there as quickly as possible?"

"So you just *left*. Without telling anyone."

I grunt. "I didn't know where you were! And everything you're implying is exactly why I decided to leave. Sometimes I don't trust myself around you, Maeve."

Her eyes narrow and I can only look at her for so long before I'm squinting out the windshield again as I enter the

HOV lane. We're still going around 20 mph, but we're both breathing as if we're sprinting.

"And can you explain what *that* means?"

"That's not fair. I think you know exactly what that means." My stomach is in knots. I'm either about to tell Maeve that I have feelings for her or shut the conversation down.

"I don't. Please. Enlighten me."

"*Maeve.*"

"No, tell me!"

"I don't trust that I'm not going to ruin this, okay? Our friendship means something to me." I glance over to see what her expression is doing. She's listening but her eyes are stormy. "And I left early because if I was with you when that ball dropped, all I would want to do is ki— oh, SHIT!"

The next five seconds happen in slow motion and all at once.

My car hitches to the left on a patch of ice and I immediately veer to the right to course correct, but I've gone too far, and before I can cognitively comprehend it, I'm headed straight into the highway barrier. I blackout for a second, but it could have been five or ten. Time isn't making sense. My mind is trying to take in so much information at once that it decided to register nothing. The only thing I remember of the actual accident is my car spinning out like some sort of carnival ride.

Looking back on it, everything was foggy and had a weird drone underneath like an M83 song.

The next time I open my eyes, we're at a standstill and I feel like I've been punched in the face. My breath is labored as if I've partially had the wind knocked out of me, too.

"Maeve?" Nothing. "Maeve."

Fuck, my face hurts.

"I'm okay. It's okay." Finally, I hear her voice and some of the cortisol in my veins mellows.

For the most part, the car is intact. My front end is smashed in and the windshield is cracked. Both of our airbags deployed and there's powder or dust or...something everywhere. It's covering Maeve's lap. Mine too, now that I'm looking.

"Oh god. Conrad, you're bleeding."

My hands instinctively reach up to my face. That's the only place bleeding would make sense, and I feel it trickle down to my lips. I can already feel the swelling obstruct my nostrils. I bring my shirt up to wipe the metallic taste of blood from my mouth.

"Are you okay?" she asks softly and sincerely.

"FUCK!"

Her question doesn't warrant my outburst and she flinches next to me.

This is the last thing I need right now. My mind races. Do the police need to be involved? Do we need an ambulance? Can we walk? How the fuck are we getting home? Who calls a tow truck? Does insurance pay for that? How am I going to get to work on Monday? How early can my car be fixed? Is it totaled? Where am I gonna—

Maeve reaches out for my arm. "Hey, if you're okay, let's call your insurance. We need to see how soon a tow truck can get us off the highway."

Right. Call my insurance.

The next two hours are a blur. Maeve is fine. The seatbelt got her and she has a tender shoulder, but she can walk just fine and must not have caught the airbag like I did. I'm trying to be as calm and polite as possible over the phone, but the blood on my shirt is starting to escalate my anxiety about the whole situation. It's worse than it looks, but it's still fucking scary.

We get lucky and only have to wait an hour for a tow truck and most of that time I'm trying to stop my nose from bleeding onto every piece of clothing I have on. Maeve is texting Kiara to see if she's able to give us a ride, but she's terrified to get back on the roads, understandably. My sister is probably an hour away in these conditions. I can't bring myself to ask.

Just before the tow truck arrives, we're both starting to feel exhausted and sore. My right shoulder is killing me.

"Should we go to a clinic? Just to see if we broke anything?" I ask, but I know my nose isn't broken.

"No, I'm okay." Maeve sighs. "I just want to go home."

So we settle back into silence and continue that trend as we watch my car get pulled up onto the bed of the tow truck. He's taking it to a shop on the Westside, and our luck continues when he doesn't decline driving us back to our apartment complex. I hand him a twenty because I don't have anything else on me except dried blood and airbag powder. Supposedly insurance will handle the rest.

Maeve hesitates on the elevator, but before she leaves, she gives me a guilty look. "I'm sorry I was so upset about New Year's. Um. Thanks for the ride home."

I involuntarily sigh into a laugh. "Probably would have been better off with the bus." She smiles back at me and it feels like things are normal again.

The pit in my stomach lifts when I walk into my apartment, anticipating getting out of the soiled clothes that I've been trapped in for the last two hours. I run my shower and attempt to wash my face, but as I wait for the sink to heat up I'm met with ice-cold water. My shower's been running for a few minutes now and I stick my hand underneath the spray. Cold. Freezing, even.

It sends me to my phone to email the landlord, and there it is. Sent around the same time my car was being towed down Interstate 394.

Chapter 16

From: Bradshaw & Luther Holdings, LLC
<westwind@blholdings.com>
To: WESTWIDE RESIDENTS
<westwindresidents@blholdings.com>
Date: Friday, February 25th, 3:39 PM
Subject: Water Heater OUT on NORTH UNITS - Fixed Tomorrow

I don't need to read the rest.

All I can do is laugh. Laugh and walk down to the third floor. She opens the door with wet hair and in her pajamas. A small weight is lifted. Even after twenty minutes, it's good to see her again, soft and pliable. "Hey, everything okay?"

"My hot water isn't working." I hoist the ball of clothes I brought with me as a silent suggestion.

"I just saw the email." Her puppy-eyed look of concern melts into squinting eyes and a full smile. "What else can go wrong?"

"Let's not give the universe any more ideas. I take it yours is working?"

She nods and gestures to come inside before grabbing a set of towels from the closet. The air between us is swirling with unspoken words and a type of care that you feel for a wounded animal. I keep wanting to ask if she's okay, but she is. She's right in front of me.

"My shoulder's bruised a bit. Is yours?"

"I haven't even looked," I answer honestly. I'm still in my soiled clothes. "It's sore though. I have a feeling we'll be pretty stiff tomorrow."

We exchange sincere smiles and I head off into the bathroom as she calls from the kitchen. "I'll make us some tea, okay? And sorry about the hair in the drain. Oh! Do you need a washcloth?"

I'm in love with her. That's the word for it, right? When you discover all of the little quirks about the other person and they make you involuntarily smile and your stomach churn in a good way? I'm rethinking it now because when I told Lacie I loved her, it was for a different reason. It felt like something I was selling in order to receive her affection. *If I say I love you, will you keep me around?* This time it's different. It's a feeling, not a transaction. One I'll have to keep to myself indefinitely. I would do anything to keep hearing her go, *Oh!* when she has another thought or before she says goodbye. I want to hear it tomorrow and the next day and the day after that. *Oh!*

I say I'm okay, but she's knocking on the bathroom door, seconds after I pull my shirt off, and holy shit. It's the first time I've gotten a look at myself. The dried blood around my nose is vile. There's a thick pinkish-red line from my left shoulder to my right hip. I open the door and Maeve's eyes go straight to my bare torso.

"Here," she hands me the washcloth and I'm sure I imagine her eyes lingering as I thank her and shut the door.

The warm stream of her shower is exactly what my body needs. I give into the urge to smell every bottle surrounding me on the corners of her tub and on the hanging shelf under the shower head. Vanilla body scrub, lavender body wash, eucalyptus bath soap, two different shampoos and conditioners, one that's citrus and one that smells like expensive mint. I've never understood why girls need more than a 2-in-1 and a loofah, but I'll never complain if it means I get a peek into Maeve's life. The scents are familiar, yet strong and harsh. She usually smells like sweet musk and vetiver.

I close my eyes under the spray and count to thirty so I don't seem like a pervert and gently dry off my aching body. She's in the living area with Netflix on and a steaming cup of tea waiting for me on the coffee table, and I smell like lavender and lemon as I walk out of the bathroom. This whole intimacy thing is starting to become normal for us, but it's like we're playing pretend. This isn't real life. It's just for fun.

"Hey, would you want to stay for a bit?" The question isn't in the words she's saying, it's in her face. I don't have to have Georgia's keen eye for emotion to understand that this request is motivated by a little fear. After all, we were just in an accident together.

"Of course, yeah. I'll stay as long as you want." And then I can't control myself because what the hell is normal these days? "Do you want me to stay the night?"

But her response makes it seem like it wasn't the craziest idea. "Actually, that would be really, really nice. I'm just," she says, trailing off and taking a big, deep breath. She's trying not to cry. "A little shaken."

"Yep, yep. Let me grab my stuff. I'll be right back."

For some reason I'm running, because after what is objectively a fucking terrible day, this turns it all around. We watch old episodes of Futurama and she throws in a frozen pizza for us, and I might as well be eating a 5-star meal at the Taj Mahal with how hungry I am. We talk about everything and nothing. I tell her about the Hank debacle and we laugh, letting the tension from the car live in another timeline. It's in the room, sure, but neither of us will acknowledge it, and that's fine with me. We haven't talked in weeks, and finally, it's all falling back into place. I'll do anything to stay exactly where I am on this couch with her. I guess I don't want to be alone tonight, either.

After a lull in conversation, I look over and she's curled up in a blanket scrolling on her phone with heavy eyelids. I want to ask the question, but I'm afraid of what it will imply. Where am I sleeping? The couch? The floor in her room? Surely not her bed, right? I will be uncomfortable no matter what, the least I could do is work out an expectation of just how uncomfortable.

I glance at her again and she's asleep. *Goddamnit, Maeve.*

"Hey, dude, wake up." I push at her shin and she wakes with a groan. "You're going to be really sore if you sleep out here tonight."

She groans again and gets up from the couch. I watch her waddle halfway to her bedroom with the blanket wrapped around her head before she turns around with a sleepy grimace. "Where are you sleeping?"

"I can stay on the couch."

"But then you'll be sore."

I study her face. I'm trying to read what kind of a request this is.

"The floor's my other option, I suppose."

"Don't be weird. I have a queen. It's fine."

Sean's dumb face comes to mind. He wasn't the one in an accident with Maeve today. I wonder if he even knows it happened. Maeve is a grown adult with free will. Two people can sleep in the same bed without accidentally becoming pregnant. Plus, when I get into her room, she has already put a pillow wall between us and is wrapped in her own blanket. Easy. There's no chance we'll even cross the invisible line splitting the bed in half.

I can keep my hands to myself.

I settle in facing away, gingerly relaxing into the pillow, and just as I'm about to fall into the deepest sleep I've had in weeks, her voice cuts into my consciousness.

"What's your pit and peach for the day?" she asks, then adds a small giggle.

I let out a huff. I was so close to slumber.

"You really have to ask?" I whisper back. More giggles. "Hmm, let me think, ah. My pit was they ran out of soap in the men's bathroom at work. That was the worst thing that happened to me today." The cackle that comes from the other side of the bed fully awakens me. I never had sleepovers growing up, but I bet this is what it feels like. Like Mo Thao said about Kiara. I can't imagine getting this every night.

"And my peach is..." I pause. It could be a few things; making up with Maeve, spending the afternoon with Maeve, spending the evening with Maeve, or being in bed right now.

With Maeve. "My peach is that even though today sucked, I got to hang out with you again." She's silent for a moment and it gives me a window to climb into. "I missed you."

Her voice is small and feels more far away than it is. "I missed you, too."

And that's the last thing I hear her say before we fall asleep. I know what her pit and peach were today, she doesn't need to admit it. They were the same as mine. Even if I had to make a joke out of it.

Chapter 17

TURNS OUT I'M NOT THE ONE who needed to worry about keeping my hands to myself.

Sometime in the middle of the night, I wake up radiating the heat of a thousand suns. The pillow wall has failed and Maeve's blanket is on my side of the bed somehow, causing her to use me as her source of heat. She's nestled into my side, arms folded like a praying mantis and tucked under my armpit. Every inch from her stomach to her toes is flush against my side. I'm on my back with my arm over my head. As slowly as I can, I flick her blanket back over her and roll onto my side.

I try not to think about it too much, but I'm having a hard time falling back asleep. A few minutes later I hear a soft rustle and even though I wake up a few more times, we've learned to keep our distance until the morning.

My brain doesn't let me sleep in past 8 am. It hasn't since I got the promotion to Director of Production. Maeve doesn't seem to be burdened with the same affliction. The other burden Maeve doesn't carry is waking up looking like the horniest person alive. I'm *not*. It just *happens* like everyone else. But when it happens waking up next to a co-worker, it's hard to make a decent case for yourself. On top of that, my entire body is engulfed in a dull ache, including my head. I'm stiff in more ways than one.

I wobble to the bathroom and damn that's a rough bruise on my face. Purples and deep reds drip from my eyes to my nose, and yep, that's where the headache is coming from. Once what's in my pants is halfway presentable, I move to the couch to scroll on my phone and text Georgia.

8:12 AM Conrad Sutherland: Don't freak out but I got into an accident last night. Maeve was in the car but neither of us were hurt. Just some bruising. Car had to be towed but I'll hear back if it's totaled

8:14 AM George Sutherland: MAEVE!! Does this mean you two made up?

8:14 AM Conrad Sutherland: Yes. I also got into an accident

8:14 AM George Sutherland: You said you weren't hurt

I don't know why it makes me so happy to have someone else rooting for me with Maeve. Ever since our New Year's brunch, I've been itching to talk to someone about it again. My initial feeling after telling them was regret. I'm just some guy who has a crush, who cares? But the more I think about it, the more I like that Georgia knows about her. Maeve is the only person who has experienced life with me recently. I actually *like* thinking about these past few months.

That's what Maeve has done to my memories. She's come in and tinted everything golden. Commutes to work were once sterile, now they're my favorite part of the day. I think about breezy fall days with ice cream and crisp cold nights with even crispier sambusas. I taste pumpkin and smell cinnamon. I hear her punchy laughter and see the smile tucked behind her eyes when she rolls them at me, her right dimple visible. Even the memory of Christmas has a stronghold on me now; she's the main event, crying on her bed and hearing her comforting voice. It's what gets me past my shame. Now that we're back to being friends, I can't wait to see what the next six months hold.

A few minutes of daydreaming go by and I hear some...ahem...*noises* come from the bedroom that stop me in my tracks and have me holding my breath. A few more minutes, another one, and I am silently laughing alone in Maeve's living room. So maybe I woke up with a boner, but Maeve woke up with gas. And while it would be so easy for me to say this was the ick I've been looking for, all I can do is smile at my phone and keep this nugget of information deep in my pocket. I want her to wake up already so I can laugh about it with her.

Half an hour later, she stumbles out of her room groggy and adorable. Her hair is a mess, her sweatpants are riding low on her hips, and her shirt is so thin, it's making me blush again. I feel like I'm back in college with how turned on I am by her.

She seems surprised to see me and within seconds I feel like an idiot. Why did I stay here? Why didn't I go back to my apartment? I'm such a weirdo.

"Hey, you're here."

"I'm here." I face her and she gasps.

"Your face!"

"I know. I have a headache." She studies me with upturned eyebrows. "Did you want me to leave?"

Obviously she wants me to leave. It's Saturday. She probably has plans or something.

"No, no. I thought you already did." She carries on with her shuffle to the bathroom but stops and spins around dramatically. "Wait, have you been here this whole time?"

I turn around on the couch and rest my chin on the back.

"Yeah."

Her look of concentration relaxes and she's smiling now. "So you heard all of that." I bury my head into the couch cushion to let out a laugh. Luckily she laughs, too. "Stop. No! I didn't know you were out here!" She buries her face in her hands, and we're both laughing at full strength.

"Are you feeling okay?"

"Shut *up*!" she yells and disappears into the bathroom making a point to lock the door, laughing still. "It was the frozen pizza!"

I'm usually so annoyed with people in the morning, especially if I haven't had coffee yet. But I've listened to Maeve's farts and I still want to be here. Why do I *still* want to be here? I have shit to do today, but it's never enough. I'm never satisfied. Even when we spend an entire evening together, I wake up wanting more.

She joins me on the couch with a rueful smile. "Coffee?"

I want to say yes so bad it hurts. "I wish. I have to somehow find my way to a grocery store today and hopefully get a call back about my car."

"Hmm. Well, I know how to get to the grocery store on the bus. I should probably pick up some actual food, anyway."

I can't help myself and smile while I tell her I need to head to my apartment to change. She jumps up from the couch.

"Coffee will be ready when you get back!" My neck is sore from the whiplash of spending so much time with Maeve after not speaking to her for weeks. And from actual whiplash, I suppose. But damn, everything is fucking rose-colored.

She has coffee and ibuprofen waiting for me when I knock on door 311 once again. We laugh about being in public with my bruising at the bus stop. And because I'm visibly uncomfortable sitting on the stained multi-colored fabric of the seats inside. She makes fun of me because it's my first time, and you know what, I'm able to make fun of me, too. I didn't think doing mundane things with someone would be this fun, but my cheeks are starting to hurt from smiling. Genuine smiling, not obligatory.

The world is bright today. After raging in a wind-struck terror, the snow decided to settle and make everything look beautiful and pristine. It's like yesterday never happened. The snow threw a tantrum and now it's apologizing with sunny skies and a stillness to the air causing it to feel warmer than 15°F. I'm going to remember today fondly, I just know it. It's golden before it even turns into a memory.

There's a dance to weaving in and out of aisles together at Target. Who would have thought Target would be the place where my brain decided to turn on me? We're a couple, we're shopping for our house, our apartment. It's domestic and lived in. It's all I think about in between the aisles of toilet paper and Windex. We're in love. Sean doesn't exist. Why is Target the most romantic place on Earth?

This is what happens to me. I find out about her favorite brand of yogurt and now I want to be a homewrecker. She likes apples, not oranges. She can't say no to a new flavor of sparkling water. She wants to look at the candles, she wants to smell the candles, she wants *me* to smell the candles. She hates scents that smell like baked goods but loves the ones labeled "Fresh Linen."

People are watching us and at first, I blissfully think it's because we're such a cute couple that everyone has to get a glimpse of how it could be, how *love* could be. But then I catch a look at myself in a decorative mirror and holy shit. Those are two nasty black eyes.

We've spent more on snacks than actual groceries. I brought a list, she didn't, but we're both satisfied with our haul as we wait for the bus stop. She remembered tote bags, I didn't. We look like a couple, damnit, and the feeling is just...*there*. It sits in my gut and at the base of my throat. It's the ache behind my eyes coming back to the surface now that the painkillers are wearing off.

Something's gotta give, right? She hasn't brought Sean up for weeks. Granted, most of those weeks we weren't talking, but wouldn't you think if she was in love with someone, she would want to talk about it? Maybe I'm not the person she wants to talk about it with. I'm just the person whose shoulder she rests her head on when she falls asleep on the bus. We're on the ride back to the apartment and I feel a buzz in my pocket, flinching both of us back to life. She gives me an apologetic smirk as I answer the phone. It's my insurance agent. I respond with *mhmm*s and *okay*s and when I hang up, I press my cold fingertips to my eyes.

"They're declaring it totaled. Once the claim is settled they'll send me a check. Could take weeks." The sigh I let out is comical.

There's a weird emotional response that's bubbling up. I've had that car for almost seven years. It was the first car that was completely mine, even if my dad helped pay for it with his absence. The last thing he gave me after the child support checks stopped coming. I fell in love with Lacie in that car. I got my heart broken in that car. I got to know Maeve in that car, and ultimately had the accident with her, too. I saw my future inside those four doors. It was so much more than a twelve-year-old Toyota 4Runner.

Maeve grunts as if this frustration is also something that she carries. "Fuck."

A laugh escapes me. I don't hear her swear often.

"What?" she asks.

"Nothing, sorry. This whole thing is probably my fault, anyway. I needed new tires. I should have been going slower."

"The roads were bad. We weren't the only people in the world who got into an accident yesterday," she says, and it's true. We saw more than one car in the ditch on the way home.

"Hey!" She pops up. "Let's get Chinese takeout tonight. On me."

I don't argue with her because as much as I just spent on some lunch meat and pasta for the week, the last thing I want to do today is cook.

The afternoon marks 24 hours that Maeve and I have spent in the same room, and it's starting to be the only thing I can think about. I'm waiting for the feeling of annoyance — from her *or* me — that signals I should leave, but it never comes. In fact, this is the most calm I've felt since before New Year's. Maybe it's the glass of wine she offers with our dumplings and scallion pancakes. Or maybe the kung pao chicken is so spicy, it's pushing me into delirium. We've been talking all day, but there's more. Always more. The TV is black, there's not even music in the background, yet nothing has ever kept my attention like Maeve. She tells me she was in a minor car accident in high school with her younger sister, Valerie. I tell her I broke my nose when I face-planted off my bike in 8th grade. We're in the middle of her telling the story of how she broke her arm at six while her dad taught her how to ride a bike, and I think of how luminous her childhood must have been. I've heard enough of these stories that the sting of missing out on having a present father is only an itch. I haven't scratched it in years. But Maeve talks about her dad like he's a pillar, sturdy and reliable. Must be nice.

There's only one topic on my mind that we haven't touched on yet. We've spent so much time together. And look, I'm not someone who self-sabotages, okay? At least I don't think I do. But the longer we talk about how Macalester had a Quidditch team, now called *Quadball*, the more my curiosity rises out of me. I can barely contain it. It's the wine, it has to be. Where's Sean in all of this?

I wait for her to finish with, "People from Macalester are dedicated if they're nothing else. Claire almost dated someone who was into LARPing, but she'll never admit it."

I laugh like I'm supposed to. Then take a nosedive.

"So how's Sean? I haven't heard you talk about him lately."

And I think it was the wrong thing to say. Not just for my sake, but for hers, too. This entire time we've been less than a foot from each other on the couch, but she backs away to create space.

"He's fine. Why?"

"Oh, um." *Yeah, Conrad, you fuck. Why?* "I guess, I just was curious if he knows we hang out like this? I mean, we practically just spent twenty-four hours together straight."

"Of course, he knows about you. I mean, we used to see each other every day when we were commuting. It would be kind of weird not to bring that up to my boyfriend. He knows we're friends."

Friends. Mhmm. Friends that spend Thanksgiving together tucked into her apartment. Friends that curl up against each other because they decided to sleep in the same bed after getting into an accident. Friends that order takeout after grocery shopping.

"Does he know about New Year's?"

Someone needs to put a muzzle on me.

"No, why would I tell him about that?"

I don't know, 'cause he's your fucking boyfriend? "I don't know, never mind. Does he at least know about the accident?"

Her eyebrows furrow and she looks around the room as if someone else is going to give her reassurance because it's going to be not me. "No, it just happened yesterday and I won't talk to him until Wednesday." *Hah, so I was right.* She gets up from the couch and busies herself with throwing away the takeout containers that we've finished off.

I feel an intense need to follow her, even though I can't stop picking at this scab that's developed over our friendship. "Don't you think he should—"

"Should what?"

Our eyes meet and she's getting upset not by what I'm saying, but by what I'm *not* saying. What I'm implying. We did Something Wrong™. She's not being honest.

"Know that I slept ov—"

"No! Jeez. What is with these questions?" She lets out a hollow laugh. She's trying to lighten the mood and I get it. I want things to go back to normal, too, back to the way they were before, but I don't have it in me.

This is a dead end.

I'm an idiot.

My feelings for Maeve will only extend to my limbs, achy and tingling with want. Georgia and Emma will be the only ones to know. Then that's it. I'll move on and rearrange my life back into what I want it to be. What it was before Lacie.

So I back off. Literally and figuratively. "Fine, sorry." My hands are up in surrender. "I, uh, think that's my cue to head out."

She rolls her eyes. "Are you taking the bus to work on Monday?" I nod and she softens. I already have my shoes on. "We never got to our pit and peach."

I think for a second and my stomach churns. The highs and lows of the day are intertwined. It all feels stretchy and sticky, like some gum caught on the bottom of my shoe. Spending time with Maeve is my peach, but it's also my pit. I've been delusional. Maeve is with Sean.

I'm a massive fucking idiot.

"I can't tell them apart today," I finally answer.

"Do you want me to stop asking?" she asks and it throws me off. I don't know where this is coming from, but she's still very obviously ticked off.

"I never said that."

"Well, I can stop if you want me to." She's defiant. Like *she* wants to start a fight.

I take a look around knowing that this is probably the last time I'll ever see the inside of her apartment.

Maybe I am a bit of a masochist. "I hope you never do."

Chapter 18

IT'S NOT THE SAME. Nothing's the same after that night. I don't exactly know what's changed, me or Maeve, but we take the bus together for the first few days, and then I have to stay late at the office. Since she doesn't rely on me for transportation anymore, she leaves before I do.

And then it happens again the next day.

And after the first week, we stop catching the same bus in the morning. She likes to sleep in. I like to be at the office before everyone else. It's just the natural progression of things.

We don't talk about that night or that weekend. We don't bring up the accident, even though my bruising is changing colors by the day and our co-workers ask questions about it.

Jesse tells me to take time off. I refuse, even though my gut is in knots most mornings. The ache doesn't go away whenever I bump into her in the fluorescent-lit kitchen, but now it's different. Instead of constantly convincing myself of lingering glances or smiles that mean something, I take it for what it is. Maeve is friendly and is treating me like a colleague, like a co-worker, like a friend. It doesn't matter that I know her favorite Chinese food, or what her hair looks like in the morning, or that she hates the self-checkout lane at Target.

Where does all of this information go? With Lacie, I don't have access to these databases anymore. I know she got her hair done every six weeks. I remember her liking the color pink. Is that it? She had a brother, but fuck. I can't even remember his name now. *Shane?* Is this what will happen with Maeve? For the first time in my life, I want to start journaling. The thought comes as quickly as it goes.

I decide to pursue some old hobbies, so after work, I ask Georgia and Emma to a show at First Ave, secretly hoping that Georgia's friend Max can get us in for free. He can't. But they say yes anyway because I haven't seen the two of them for a few weeks.

"Suki Waterhouse?" Georgia whines as we walk up to the box office on a damp day in March. Their breath is visible as they scoff at Emma. "Isn't she a model?"

Emma tilts her head to read the line-up. "She's opening for Clairo! We have to stay."

I go straight to the bar to grab the three of us drinks, but Georgia gives me a condescending look that predates our teenage years. "I don't drink anymore."

Emma pipes up. "See if they have any THC drinks. I'd take one if it's from Indeed Brewing."

"Oh, actually, same," Georgia adds.

The world is different from when I used to go out. I follow their lead and order my beer and their sparkling THC drinks and awkwardly carry the three beverages back to where they've staked our claim against the side railing. First Avenue's Mainroom is famous for its appearance in Prince's *Purple Rain* movie, but the venue looks just like any other venue. It's dark, standing room only, and the floors are slightly sticky. I love it. Why don't I go to shows anymore? There's so much possibility here. Damn, I could flirt with someone tonight. I could meet someone. I could get a girl's number. Lacie who?

I glance around and there are plenty of girls. Actually, most of the audience is women. Perfect.

I want someone to approach me tonight. I try to open my chest and exude some kind of energy that portrays that. The beer is already doing its job. "We should go to shows more. This is great."

Emma giggles. "Do you like Chappell Roan?"

"Who?" I yell. The live music hasn't quite started yet, but the noise level has peaked.

Georgia nudges Emma's side. "No! Don't ruin it for us."

"She's playing next month and we got tickets. But you'll have to dress up in drag."

"Hah. No." I roll my eyes and Emma laughs. The canned music dies down and the lights lower, causing a stir among the crowd. I haven't been to a show in years, it's true. The last one I went to was a stadium tour of some blonde-haired Country music duo. Lacie got drunk and didn't speak to me on the ride home because I didn't know any of the words to their songs. It's a weird memory to think of at a time like this.

The first few songs keep my attention, and I'm nodding along before I realize it. She looks like Maeve up on stage. Okay, no, but actually. If Maeve had lighter hair and darker eyes and bangs. I look around the crowd and I can't keep running from the thought. What if she's here?

I lean over to where Georgia and Emma are. "Hey, what kind of—" But now they're not here. Three feet away they're talking to a familiar face. Must be Max. They're not even paying attention to the performance.

I'm tall enough that I can look around with somewhat ease to get a view of the room. Poorly lit faces jumble together and I can't make out one person from the next, but suddenly I'm right back into the feeling I had while tearing down for the

New Year's Bash. As if Maeve is watching me, taking note of my mannerisms and the way I sway to the music. I'm turning into a narcissist. The song that's playing adds to it. Come on, Maeve. Put a goddamn move on me.

I'm completely separated from Georgia and Emma, lost in the music while craning my head to see people up on the balcony. Some girl bumps my arm, and I retract my body so violently, I might as well have been electrocuted. I give her a halfway smile and step closer to the railing so I can view the crowd in peace.

"Sorry!" she says. She's short and has dark brown hair. "It's so crowded!" *Yeah, we're at a show, genius.* "What's your name?" she asks. I don't answer her.

This is exhausting. Where are George and Emma?

I escape the conversation and weave my way through the crowd, finally finding Max leaning up against the wall with some guy who's looking at him like the sun shines out of his ass. George and Emma are holding hands and for some reason now I don't want to be here anymore. And yes, I know I'm becoming some sort of flight risk, but I don't want to be anywhere if it's not with Maeve.

Three weeks. That's how long it's been since Maeve and I have had that weird night in her apartment. The way I miss her is how I thought I would feel about Lacie when she first dumped me. I waited for it to come, that ache that consumes your entire body. The white-hot pain that comes with wishing you could change the past and redo everything to change the course of the future. And yet. Only now do I feel it. I wake up thinking about her, I go to bed wishing I was next to her. Because at least I can remember what that feels like with Maeve. I don't with Lacie.

On a Thursday, she doesn't show up to work, and I notice before 9 am. We have an editorial meeting that I get pulled into to brainstorm about our digital content and she's not there. My suspicion is confirmed when Kiara comes by my desk, a little cold but determined all the same.

"Did you ride the bus with Maeve this morning?" I shake my head and she huffs while walking away. "She's not answering my texts."

Cue panic.

It could be a day off. Maybe she is on vacation. Maybe she's sick and sleeping. Maybe she's dead in a ditch somewhere. *No.* Maybe she lost her phone. Because someone mugged her at a bus stop. *Fuck.* She has the flu. Strep throat. Something that would constitute her not replying to Kiara. Maybe they had a fight like we did.

At any rate, I'm not going to think about it, which means I think about it every second of the day. I text George and ask myself over for dinner and of course, they say yes. After six hours of spiraling, I'm finally at the bus stop two blocks from their house.

When George meets me at the front door, they greet me with an eyebrow raised. "You ran off fast at the show. Where did you go?"

I take my shoes off and follow them into the kitchen where Emma is opening a rather large takeout bag. I greet her with a side hug. A sigh escapes me.

"Home. I didn't want to be out anymore."

"You asked *us* to the show," George adds.

"I know, I know. I think part of me was hoping to meet a girl there or something. But the only person I wanted to see was Maeve."

"You were hoping to meet a girl at a Clairo concert? Oh, Connie," George huffs with a chuckle.

We gather around the dining table. Chips and queso are placed at the center and small containers of hot sauce are set aside near George and I. We both like spicy. Emma doesn't. The two of them feel so lived-in. Emma's dog, Shadow, is sleeping on the sofa behind us. An old episode of Survivor is playing on Hulu. The lights are dimmed. I feel so at peace here.

"Why didn't you invite her to the show?" Emma asks, dishing up tacos for the three of us. I am *so* glad I'm here tonight and not alone in my apartment.

I think for a second about how I want to answer, but at this point, I can't keep my mouth shut. "Maeve and I aren't really talking."

"Wait, really?!"

I tell them about the aftermath of the accident, conveniently leaving out the fact that I slept in Maeve's bed, but including all the details about grocery shopping and ordering take out. I don't know how to explain the tension when I left, so I leave pieces out that are still stuck to my throat. It felt final. It felt like a goodbye.

"It's whatever. What am I supposed to do? Profess my love to her over kung pao chicken just because we went on a Target run together? It would ruin our friendship."

"Sounds like it's already ruined," Georgia quips with a full mouth. They're right, but Emma gives them a look. "What?"

I stay quiet, even though it's my turn to say something.

"Hmm. Can I ask you something?" Emma says. Georgia sits up a little straighter. "Do you think Maeve has been leading you on?"

"Hah, no. Whatever the opposite of leading someone on is, that's what she's doing," I respond. "We've hugged, like, twice."

But Emma doesn't let it go. "Maybe not physically, but emotionally. There are lots of different kinds of intimacy, you know."

"She's right, Connie."

"How would someone lead someone on emotionally? Be their friend? Yes. Maeve was — *is* — my friend. How is that bad?"

"Would you have given her rides everywhere if you didn't kinda sorta have a crush on her?" they ask.

Emma nods with enthusiastic curiosity, but I didn't have a crush on her when I found out she had been mugged at a bus stop. I just wanted to make sure she could get home safely.

"I didn't initially have feelings for her."

"But New Year's?"

"New Year's was a joke. I still don't know why she was so upset about that."

Emma leans towards me, placing her elbow on the table. "What about the fact that she didn't tell you she had a boyfriend until *months* after you met? That's kinda weird!"

"That's not even the worst part."

"What's the worst part?" George asks.

I've been biting my tongue for too long. In a sense, I do feel guilty about it. But what good is keeping it harbored away?

"I actually spent the ni—"

My phone buzzes on the dining table, cutting me off. It's a text I've been secretly waiting to get for months, even though I never thought it would actually happen. Just a childlike fantasy wishing for a snow day in June or thinking you'd win the lottery without purchasing a ticket. I never thought it would actually come true. Yet, my stomach drops all the same and I involuntarily let out a laugh. A real laugh. It feels so good to laugh.

8:39 PM Maeve Thomas: Sean and I broke up

8:39 PM Maeve Thomas: Are you home?

Chapter 19

"HOLY SHIT."

I show George and Emma my screen and their eyes widen on cue. All of a sudden they're screaming and standing and jumping around me as I shield myself from their barrage of excitement. And then it stops and George gets serious.

"We have to get you home. Fuck. I'm, like, an hour into an edible."

"You took one without me?" Emma pleads.

George gives her a weak smile. "It was the last one."

"Traitor!" She peeks over the couch at a snoring Shadow. "She hasn't been outside yet tonight. I'll give him a ride if you can take her out and feed her."

George gives a dim-eyed smile and a thumbs-up before Emma and I climb into her Prius. The car ride is somewhat off-topic. She tells me about a trip that she and George are planning for late summer and she's asking me if George is more of an East Coast or West Coast type of person, and while the mental distraction is nice, I have no idea what that means.

When we finally pull up to my apartment building, Emma places a hand on my forearm. Her body shifts.

"Hey, so. Coming from a girl. Can I give you just one piece of advice before you go in there?" I nod and prepare for a very uncomfortable conversation. The mood in the car reminds me of that time I had *the talk* with my mom, aka, don't have sex or else you'll die or end up like your father. I don't know which one was worse in her mind.

"Um, don't make the first move. It's obviously fresh and—"

"I wouldn't do that."

"No, I know. Not tonight or anything, just...in general. I know it seems like she's suddenly available, but like, breakups are confusing."

I try not to let my resentment for that statement show, but I don't think I do too well. "Yeah. Don't worry. I'm aware."

She breaks eye contact and looks down briefly. "Sorry. I didn't mean—"

"It's all good. I'm not going to pounce her or anything."

"No, that's not what I meant—"

"Thanks for the ride," I shout over my shoulder as I shut the passenger door. I wonder if George said something to her. Emma has only known me as someone who's been single and really fucking lonely. My horndog days were in college, and every conversation about my current state should prove that. I'm pathetic, not a predator.

I text Maeve and check my mailbox to stall before I get a response, and the day just keeps getting better. My insurance check of a clean five figures is waiting for me, which means I can finally stop depending on others to give me uncomfortable rides home. My phone buzzes in my pocket.

9:14 PM Conrad Sutherland: Just got back from my sister's. Want me to come over?
9:18 PM Meave Thomas: If you're free, that would be so nice

No Minnesota back and forth, just a sincere response. Three knocks on her door later and I'm on the wrong side of the unknown. Who knows what kind of state she's in? She could be inconsolable, sobbing, a complete mess. She could be angry, vengeful. Hell, she could be looking for something that Emma alluded to, hoping to have someone take her mind off it all. I'm not perfect. I can't sit here and say I would reject it.

When she opens the door, though, it's clear she hasn't been crying. She just looks dead tired. Upon seeing me, she whimpers and immediately is in my arms. I might be the one comforting her, but this is bliss. My hands wind up into her messy hair and I press my cheek to her forehead. God, I missed her. I'm smiling like an idiot before I realize we're standing in the middle of the hallway. She's still squeezing too tight for me to let go.

"Hey, let's head inside."

When she finally releases me, a few wet sniffs escape, but she seems composed for the most part. "Thank you for coming," she whispers on her way to her bedroom. I follow on intuition. "Claire isn't talking to me. I just don't want to be alone."

"Have you texted Kiara back yet?"

She gives me a confused head tilt before crawling into her bed and under the covers. Only the top of her frizzy hair is peeking out. Her voice is muffled when she asks, "How do you know Kiara's texting me?"

"She asked me if I knew where you were today. She may have said you hadn't been responding to your texts and I may have panicked and thought you were dead."

She releases her face from under the covers and smiles. Fully. With her teeth. "You did not."

"The thought occurred." She wiggles back down and internally I say *fuck it*. I crawl under the covers, too. It's not like I haven't been here before. "Do you want to talk about it?"

"Nope."

Fine by me. My eyes travel around the room. Her bookshelves look the same. The plants are alive and well. Her duvet cover is the same beige linen from when I threw myself onto it alone in her room at Christmas. The only thing that's changed is some frames have had the photo removed on her desk. I know exactly which ones.

"Are you mad at me?" Her voice is small but the question is big enough to fill the room and constrict my breathing.

"No." I want to say more. *Why would you ever think that? What have I done in the last six months that would ever make you think I'm mad at you? I've never been mad at you. Not really. Are you mad at me? Please don't be mad at me.*

"I feel like we haven't talked in weeks," she whispers. It wasn't a question so I don't know what to say next. She tucks the covers under her chin and I can't look away. "I'm sorry if I did something. Or said something. I'm just tired and confused and frustrated. My friends are mad at me because they think I'm, like, changing or something. But what does that even mean? Are we always confined to the version of us that our friends meet? How is that fair?"

"Especially because the people we meet change us anyway, you know?" I may not know what she's referring to but I know exactly what she's talking about. Things change. People change. "Some could call it growth."

Her eyes drift off. "Yeah, exactly."

I adjust the pillow under my head and a plume of Maeve makes it to my nostrils. Warm vetiver and her musk. Sweet. Soft. I want to memorize this moment in case I never get another chance. Her sheets are light blue today. She's wearing a Macalester sweatshirt.

"You okay?"

It's the question I've wanted to ask every day since the accident. She rolls onto her back and stares up at the ceiling with heavy eyelids. The only light in the room is the lamp on her nightstand and the yellow glow makes everything feel hazy and soft. It's almost 10 pm, and damn would it feel good to fall asleep here tonight.

"I think I'm more okay now than I've felt in the last month." *Hah, fuck you, Sean!* "Still don't feel good. But I feel okay." Her head lulls to the side to look at me with those curious chestnut eyes that I've been seeing in my dreams. "Are you okay?"

"Why wouldn't I be?"

"You tell me."

Hmm. I wish I could say everything is fine and I've been doing great, but no. This last year has been fucking awful. Between my mom going crazy, Lacie dumping me, and spending every last minute of the past six months in a state of unrequited love, I'd say I'm probably not okay. But with the bad comes the good. I met Maeve, I see my sister more often, and even though being single has been less than ideal, I'm no longer with someone who doesn't see me in their future. I pretend to look like I'm thinking hard about an answer, but my mind is already made up.

"I don't know. Sure, I'm okay."

And then there's silence. At first, it's a bit uncomfortable and I have to get used to it, but then she shuts off the bedside lamp. It's a wordless way of asking me to stay, and of course, I oblige. It feels normal to lay here with Maeve in the dark. There's nowhere I'd rather be, even if I am still in my jeans.

Why do we always pull back to each other? Like two waves that keep crashing into one another. Why did I basically come running to be by her side, yet again, after I told myself I was done? I've tried to drill it into my head enough these past two weeks. We're friends. That's it. But do friends count the minutes until their bodies can be pressed against each other in the middle of the night? Do friends spend thirty-six hours together only to spend twenty-one days apart? Do all friendships feel this fragile? The answer is no. I'm done talking myself out of it. This is something more.

It's evident we both don't know what to say next. Or maybe she's trying to fall asleep and it's all in my head. Either way, I open my big dumb mouth.

"So. What's your pit and peach for today?"

She laughs, full and bright. I was trying to be sincere, but I've never been good at reading the room.

"Oh my god, I needed that. Man, let me think. *What* is my pit? Oh!" — *there it is!* — "You know what, the dryer ate two of my quarters today."

I match her energy. "Unbelievable. Did you call the landlord?"

"Absolutely, filed a complaint with the State of Minnesota."

"Good, good. And your peach?"

She giggles again. "My peach is that I finally did laundry and now have clean underwear." I swallow. Hard. I don't need to be thinking about Maeve's underwear. "Tell me yours, but make it really dramatic. I don't want to live in reality today," she says.

It feels like my whole body smiles. My shoulders release, my stomach lifts. Everything feels better. "My pit was that I thought my co-worker had been kidnapped by the KGB, and that I would have to learn Russian in order to get her back."

"Too much."

"Hah. Okay, fine. Then my peach is that I get to sleep in denim tonight. It's been a dream of mine since I was a kid."

"Conrad."

"Maeve."

"You don't have to stay if you don't want to."

Here we go. "I want to, it's fine."

"I don't think any of my sweatpants would fit you,"

I roll my eyes because she should know I'm not asking to do that. "Would it be weird if I slept in my boxers?"

"You wear *boxers*?" I can hear the judgment in her voice. This is that intimacy thing again. How am I supposed to go back to work with someone who knows I wear boxers? Boxer *briefs,* by the way.

"You know what? This is my new pit."

She laughs again, more of a cackle. "It won't bother me."

I do my business and try not to make it awkward when I climb back into bed a thousand times more comfortable.

"Are you going to work tomorrow?" I ask.

"No. I took today and tomorrow off. I don't want to randomly start crying at my desk or have to explain things to Kiara. Yet. I mean I will in time, it's just fresh and complicated. I feel like I'm still processing it all." Her voice seems far away.

"Yeah, no, I get it."

"What if you took tomorrow off?" she asks.

Deadline week is next week and I need to prepare for how hellish it'll be this time around. But she's asking. The implication is that she wants to spend the day *with me.*

"Maeve, I—"

"Please? I don't want to spend it alone." It should take way more than a crack of her voice to get me to be this irresponsible.

"I haven't taken a day off in over a year," I say as a non-answer.

"Then that means you should, right?"

I should. I could. But taking a day off means so much more to me than it does to most. The last time I took a day off that wasn't an office holiday was almost two years ago. Lacie's childhood dog had died. Growing up without pets, I didn't really get it, and stupidly I told her that. I regret it. The aftershock caused us not to talk for three days.

Another silence falls. I hear a few sniffles before her tired, scratchy voice breaks the stillness in the air.

"It's like my entire future looks different now. I used to have the next five years planned out to the month, and now I have no idea what next week looks like. My friends might change. My living situation. I mean, this apartment was supposed to be temporary. We were going to buy property together! *Fuck!*"

I inhale sharply. Oddly enough, I can imagine what is going on in her head. I had my future planned with Lacie, too. The collapse in her voice brings something out of me that I can't hold back anymore. "Fuck Sean."

"*Fuck* Sean," she echos back, crying. "I will never put my life on hold again. Ever. What a waste of time." More ruffling. Her voice tells me she's facing away from me now. So I follow suit. "He's doing another service term in Albania."

I let the dust settle before turning back around to face her. I'm restless but it's only because I wish I could reach out and hold her. My body is aching for some contact. "I'll take tomorrow off. And seriously, fuck Sean."

She doesn't say it back this time but lets out a small huff and pretty soon she raises the covers to let herself roll to face me, too. Our hands meet and her thumb passes over my pinky, sending a chill up my spine. I catch myself holding my breath as if I can be silent enough to hear her thoughts. There's another stillness coming, and this one lasts until I fall asleep.

I wake up a few times in the night and it's the same charade as before, only there isn't a blanket separating us like last time. It's like her body is magnetized to mine. Her ass is on my back, her cold feet are on my calves. At one point in the night, her head is on *my* pillow. And I would find all of this hilarious, but if I move any closer to the edge of the bed, I'll be on the floor. The next time it happens, I scoot in and wrap my arm around her, pushing us to her side of the bed. She doesn't stir, so as far as I can tell, she hasn't noticed a thing. I rest my head back down and nuzzle myself into her hair, wrapping my senses up in Maeve. It's so familiar. The kiss I plant on her shoulder is out of instinct. It's like muscle memory.

This will all come crashing down, I know it. We'll fly too close to the sun this weekend — maybe we already have — and we'll come out the other end burned and bruised. I'll go back to sulking at home alone and she'll go back to politely ignoring me at work. Up and down, hot and cold, on and off. There's never been a middle with us. Not since New Year's at least. I don't know why.

Once again, I wake up before she does and use the opportunity to get my jeans back on in the comfort of her bathroom. I use that time to text Jesse.

> **6:24 AM Conrad Sutherland:** Thinking of taking the day off today. Got my insurance check and was hoping to look at a car
> **6:26 AM Jesse Schaefer:** Yes! Excellent! Hope it's a successful search! Take the time you need and we'll see you on Monday!

I have a text from George asking how the night went and a secondhand apology from Emma about the unsolicited advice she gave me when she dropped me off. I ignore it for now.

I look up used cars in the area and check my bank account. I'm antsy. Rather than spend the day doing who knows what in the confines of Maeve's apartment, I have an idea that would benefit both of us.

Kind of.

When she finally stirs, she smiles up at me, as if I make her happy or something. "Good morning," she mumbles. God, she's so cute when she mumbles.

"I have a plan for today."

She bunches the covers under her chin. "Can you wait like five minutes before you go all Conrad on me?"

Now it's my turn to smile because Maeve makes me so fucking happy. "I've been up for an hour."

"Doing what?"

"Planning our day off."

She lets out a tired giggle. "Fine, go ahead."

"We're buying me a car. Wanna help pick it out?"

Her eyes pop open, and like the comedian she is, she flips off the covers and springs out of bed. "Only if you promise we can do my taxes later. Oh! And maybe watch some paint dry!"

She doesn't know what's coming.

By the time I'm showered and back in her apartment, she has coffee and a piece of peanut butter toast waiting for me. These small acts mean so little to her and so much to me. It's just peanut butter toast. I don't know why I have butterflies. I'm not used to having someone do these things for me.

We take the bus to the row of dealerships, and I give Maeve the rundown of my budget and process:

1) See what they have for used vehicles, nothing over 75,000 miles, nothing older than seven years;

2) Look up the make, model, and year of the car for reliability and recalls;

3) Don't test drive until we've narrowed it down to three;

4) Make sure to test drive on the highway;

5) Finance through a credit union;

6) Take it to a mechanic.

All things I had been reading on Reddit this morning. I didn't exactly have a dad to tell me how to do this.

"If I ever buy a car, I want you to do it for me," she says once I'm finished with my speech. "Have you even thought about what color you want?"

I shake my head with a patronizing smile. "Maeve, I don't care about the color. I care about the car itself."

She turns up her chin in defiance. "So if there's a car we find that checks all of the boxes and it's hot pink, you'll buy it?"

"I'll buy it for you, how does that sound?"

"Oh please. I would *never* drive a hot pink car."

I love seeing her all bent out of shape about something as frivolous as a hot pink car. Luckily, her silly little outburst didn't matter. About three hours later, we end up finally seated in my brand new (used) 2017 Toyota 4Runner. Same make and model of my last car, only eight years younger. Maeve thinks this is hilarious.

"You hate change, don't you."

"This one is black, the other one was grey."

Her lack of response makes me look over and she's beaming up at me, proud of her work. We're too much alike, getting satisfied from pushing the others' buttons. It's my favorite thing.

"So I'll just drop you off at the apartment, then? Gotta few errands to run."

She pushes my arm. "Hey! I just sat through negotiating APR and...warranty bullshit with you."

"Language, jeez!"

"Hah! You're rubbing off on me." If only that were true. She's laughing in the front seat of my car and everything about this feels right again. Her head is buried in her hands, her phone is in my cup holder. She's with *me*.

"Alright, so first, taxes. Then I have to watch some paint dry," I say as I start the car.

She places a finger on her lips. "On second thought, take me home. I'm breaking my lease."

"It's because of the dryer eating your quarters, isn't it." God, this is easy. It's so good to hear her laugh. "But actually, my plan was to go to Target, then make a stop to get some of that ice cream at Honey & Milk."

Based on the way she lights up, she's game. As the day goes on, I start to find out it's exactly what she needs. She drops little tidbits of information at every stop along the way. At the dealer, she let me know that she finally texted Kiara back but hasn't gotten a response. On the way to Target, she lets out that she and Claire had a fight over a week ago, but she doesn't tell me why. In between the laundry detergent and paper towels, she tells me that her dad was disappointed in the news, and her mom cried with her on the phone. And lastly, on the way home, with sweetened lips from the remnants of vanilla ice cream, she shares with me that she and Sean were on the phone until 4 am the night of their breakup during a scheduled biweekly Wednesday call.

"We were both inconsolable. I barely slept two hours before letting Zak know I wasn't going to make it in. He's the first person I told. I knew he wouldn't tell anyone. Then I called my sisters. Stephanie scolded me, Anna let me talk and told me I did the right thing, and Val basically said I didn't need a man. I just feel so shitty."

"Breakups are shitty," I say as we exit off the highway. "But if there's one thing I've learned, it's that life will move on. For both of you. It'll look different, but isn't that the point?"

She takes a deep breath and looks out the window. I can't tell if she is smiling or not. "I suppose."

As I pull into our parking garage, she's notably quiet and fidgets with the hem of her shirt. I'm sure today was a hard day for her. I have no idea what the right move is to make her feel better. When I put the car in park, we sit in the quiet and she's the one who speaks up first, still focused on her fingers gliding over the fabric of her shirt.

"Thank you for using a vacation day today."

"Yeah. Yeah, of course. It was nice. Plus, the dealership would probably be packed on a weekend. There was barely anyone there," I say back. I'm talking to talk.

"Well, thank you for letting me spend the day with you."

"I...yeah. You don't have to thank me for that." If now isn't the perfect time to confess my feelings, I don't know what is. A voice is screaming in the back of my head. *Tell her, tell her, tell her!* I can't just come out and say it though. "You were my enjoyment insurance," I say instead.

She smiles with her head still lowered and when she peeks up at me, there's something a little smokier in her gaze.

"I have to admit something."

"Okay." *Holy fuck.*

"Last night, I was awake when you kissed my shoulder."

I freeze and play dumb. "Hmm?"

"I was pretending to be asleep." She looks back down to her lap. Maybe if I don't move, she'll lose sight of me and I can somehow escape. "Conrad, I really like spending time with you. That's obvious, right?"

Uh, I have no idea what the right answer is here. "Maybe? I mean, it's been a little hot and cold lately."

She struggles with herself for a split second, and then everything in my memory kind of goes fuzzy because she leans towards me and before I can get a conscious handle on the situation, she's kissing me. Firmly. It's less of a kiss and more just our mouths smooshing against each other. I feel the pressure in my teeth. She pulls away, and the moment I catch the fire in her eyes, I take over, positioning her so that our lips barely touch.

"Maeve?" I sing her name like a question. The only question that I've wanted to ask for months. I'm standing at the edge of a cliff, waiting for permission to jump. The universe is going to let me make the decision this time. The nod she gives me is miniscule. Her eyebrows are upturned, her eyes wild, her breathing heavy. I get that sinking sensation before taking flight. And then I take the leap.

This is the moment I've dreamt of. Wrapping my hand around the back of her neck, tangling my fingers in her soft hair, feeling the tingle of her lips against mine. I want to get closer, I want to envelop my shoulders around hers, get her hips near mine. But the seat belt pulls me back. And when she reaches for me, it stops her, too. Her face falls but bubbles back to the Maeve I'm falling in love with, smiling and laughing. Her hand stays steady on mine where it's gripping her neck.

"What now?"

I plant a heady kiss on her cheek. "We have groceries to put away."

"Oh my god," she huffs with a massive smile, "*after* we put the groceries away."

I don't know how long this step into another reality will last, but I'll do anything to extend my stay. "Ah, well I have to do this…" — I plant a few more kisses on her scrunched face — "and this…and maybe I should start on this. I'm on a tight deadline."

"Wouldn't want you to miss your deadline."

With eager smiles and a few more rogue kisses, we climb the echoey staircase and ride the elevator in a fizzy haze. When it dings on the 3rd floor, it hits me.

WHAT THE FUCK JUST HAPPENED? Holy shit. Maeve just kissed me. She kissed ME. *She* kissed me. And she kissed me before I could do a damn thing about it. I'm not asleep, I'm not caught up in one of my daydreams. She's right here, unlocking the door to her apartment and immediately gravitating back into my space once the bags are on the counter.

She kisses me. *Again!* "Okay, last one until everything is put away."

I race around the kitchen in double time to hear her laugh while I dramatically fling both her and my groceries into the fridge. I'm laughing, too. How could I not be? This is the best day of my life.

The last of the groceries are my tortillas that we stuff into her refrigerator drawer and as promised she grabs my hand and leads me to the couch. She pushes me back, climbs on top of my lap, and kisses me with such vigor the blood drains from my body to my groin. Her hands are lost in my hair, mine are creeping their way up the skin of her belly to reach my final destination. I'm lost in a haze when she comes up for air.

"Hey," she whispers. I can't open my eyes yet, so I nestle my face into the crook of her neck and let out a blissful moan. We're both out of breath. "Do you want to go to my room?"

"*Yes*, yeah. I have condoms, I just have to run and grab them. I'll be two minutes. Less. One minute. Time me."

She flings her head back. I kiss her exposed neck. "Slow down, sweetheart."

Sweetheart. I'm fucking gone. "I'm sorry, I'm sorry."

"Let's just have fun."

That's fine by me.

"I've been waiting for weeks to get my mouth on you," I say and lean back to gauge her reaction. There's fire in her eyes again. I shift her weight so I can carry her to the bed, and gently sit her down before pushing her stomach, signaling her to lay back. I catch her eye and grip the hem of her jeans.

"This okay?"

"Yeah, just come here." She reaches out to my face and guides me down to lie on top of her. I don't know what it means, but we just lie there, my chest pressed against hers. She rubs my back softly and our breathing slows. Sometimes I feel like her body was meant to be next to mine. It's nice when she's in the same room as me. I like knowing she's right here. Safe, warm, mine for the moment.

Eventually, we start kissing again. Our shirts end up on the floor, and pretty soon so do our pants. Her skin is better than any fantasy or dream I've conjured up. It's real, warm, alive under my fingertips. Her breasts are full; even more beautiful than I imagined. I want to lay my head against her soft stomach for years to come, grip her love handles, and tell every peaking goosebump that it's perfect. I haven't been this turned on in years and it shows.

Look, I'm out of practice and she hasn't been intimate with someone physically in over a year, so the way we bump into and explore one another is a bit clumsy. I'm not at my best and even after about five minutes of what I think is excellent head, she nudges me away and simply asks to be held. I don't resist.

Meanwhile, I last sixty seconds with her hands on me.

The difference between any other sexual experience I've had before this is that we're both overwhelmingly excited. Smiling, talking, nodding along, fully aware of what we're doing. I have to remind myself whenever I feel too eager or vulnerable. This is Maeve. The person I've been spending every morning and evening commute with. The one who knows about the best parts of my days and listens to the worst ones. Maeve, the person I love being around more than anyone else I've ever known. I don't know how I got here, but it feels like I stepped into someone else's life.

We end up showering together, giggling under the spray while exploring our bodies in a different way. She points out my moles and I study the soft hills of her belly. We wash each other's hair and I'm in heaven. There is nothing better than a scalp massage by someone who just gave you an orgasm. We dry off with matching smiles.

By the time we're back to wearing clothes and can finally take our mouths off one another long enough to have a conversation, we realize we're extremely hungry. Jokes about our recent activities aside, I've only eaten ice cream since this morning's peanut butter toast. Even with a full fridge, a half an hour later, there's scallion pancakes, kung pao chicken, and lo mein on her coffee table. And of course, xiao long bao.

We can't get close enough on the couch. I'm facing towards her and she's sitting back on my chest, only leaning forward to grab a mouthful of noodles before settling back in. The weight feels nice, but it makes me chuckle against her and she notices right away.

"What?" Her eyes are tired but the corners of her mouth are lifted. I kiss her cheek and she scrunches her nose.

"Nothing, nothing. This is all surreal."

She leans away to grab a piece of chicken between her chopsticks and chews it proudly. "Pit and peach?"

"Oh, like I could find a pit today. Maybe the fact that I drained my savings buying a car, but that was still fun with you."

"Enjoyment insurance."

"Enjoyment insurance." I glance at the plate balanced on my thigh. "I think my peach is the scallion pancake again. Obviously."

She shakes her head and places our plates on the coffee table so she can face me fully. "Be earnest. What was it?"

"Earnest? I'm not a writer," I say, and she playfully paws at my chest. "Okay, okay. My real peach was when you almost let go before. You know, you were quiet for most of it, but there was this moment right before you pushed me away." I can't believe I'm saying this out loud to her. "I could tell you had been resisting something before that, but…"

I lose steam because her breathing quickens.

"I'm sorry."

"You don't have to apologize. I just want you to feel good."

"I do," she says.

"Good."

She takes a deep but tense breath. "I get nervous."

"I'm a little nervous, too," I say because it's true. I grab her hand and stroke over her knuckles. "But I think that's going to be my peach for the next few days if you know what I mean."

With a giggle, she nods and looks around the apartment as if she's debating something. Maybe it's what she says next. "Do you still want to get those condoms?"

"Absolutely. I can run and grab them."

"Yeah," she mumbles, fiddling with the hem of *my* shirt now. She kisses me soft and slow, and when she pulls away, my chest hurts as she says, "I think our peach is yet to come.

It starts off just like before, graceless yet sincere. It's not like the times when Lacie and I did this, even once we were comfortable around our naked bodies and familiar with our pleasures. Maeve and I write our own script, cheek to cheek, chest to chest, hips aligned completely. We can't get close enough. Her legs are wrapped around me, and with each thrust, I'm feeling less and less in control.

She's still quiet. I haven't cracked her walls yet, but the scratch of her nails in my back tells me she doesn't want to let me go. I loosen my grip on her waist and I feel the pressure build in my abdomen.

"I'm about to—"

"Please," she huffs. "Keep going."

I know I have a condom on, but this isn't something I'm used to. "Maeve, are you sure? I can pull out."

Her legs tighten their grip and I can't hold out any longer. God, this is all I want. I just want to make sure it's what *she* wants. It's too late before I can ask her again, though. The bolt of pleasure releases and I jerk my hips into hers. As I catch my breath, I feel her buck against me, and finally, *finally*, her body isn't tense. She ruts her hips into mine, and the sensation is almost too much for how sensitive I'm getting, but when I turn my head, I realize she's still caught up in chasing her own climax. Our hips move in sync and within a few minutes, her breaths are whimpering into my ear, and fuck, I could get hard again just from this.

"Let go, babe, let go. I have you," I say, hoping she feels comfortable enough to allow her gratification to overtake her. A final convulse happens signaling her orgasm and damn, I'm on top of the world. I feel every contraction of her muscles since I'm still...inside. She sharply inhales and presses her face into my neck, and then things go mute. We're on our sides, still tangled up in each other. I'm gently caressing her back. She's catching her breath. And then she says the first words that take me completely out of my body.

"I can't believe that just happened."

I hope it isn't regret I hear in her voice. She's tense again. I try to offer some words of comfort. "Yeah, that was amazing."

"Can you let go of me?"

Oh. "Hey, woaw. Are you okay? Did I hurt you?" She doesn't answer. "Maeve?" Her breathing is choppy for a different reason. "Can you talk to me?"

"I didn't want it to be like this."

"Like what?"

"Like some hook-up. I shouldn't be doing this." She pushes me away and I miss it. My skin misses her skin. Even if my chest is tight with what she just said.

"You think this was a hook-up?" My heart drops. That's what it feels like. It's in my gut.

"What else would it be? This is a classic rebound. I just broke up with someone, like, forty-eight hours ago."

"Wait, you broke up with *him*?"

That wasn't the question to ask, but this is new information to me. So is the fact that she is feeling any regret over what just happened. We were so excited earlier.

"I don't do things like this." She gets up from the bed and grabs the blanket to cover herself and wipe some tears. "I don't think we should do this again."

"Maeve."

"I should be processing and grieving and...I should be sad. I feel like a psychopath. And we work together! Oh my god, I can't believe I let this happen. *Fuck.*" She paces a bit in her room and my brain is catching up on the hard pivot this conversation took.

"Did I pressure you?"

"No! But we should've waited. I've been so confused lately. And this is exactly why Claire is mad at me. I'm not myself! I don't feel like myself."

"Okay, then talk to me. How was I supposed to know?"

Her movement stops and she tries to look at me, but it's obviously too hard. "I think you should go."

"You're kidding—"

"No. Please. Go."

Everything has shifted. The rug's been pulled. The gag is up. I'm due back in the universe where no one wants to be with me. Where Maeve can't see me as anything more than a confidence boost. I've never been on this side of her decisiveness. She knows what ice cream flavor she wants, knows exactly what to buy at Target, never hesitates to tell me her opinion on something. And today is no different. She's as sure as always. She got what she wanted from me and now she wants me to leave. I knew this was too good to be true. My ears start ringing. I'm hot with rage.

"Fucking hell, you couldn't wait until I take the goddamn condom off to kick me out? Feels really great, Maeve."

I get up, still fully naked and in my most vulnerable state. A state that I thought would be protected around her, but now all I'm realizing is that Emma was right. I should have pushed Maeve away when she kissed me. I should have ignored the text about the breakup. I should have left her at the bus stop last fall.

"I just—"

"You know what? I don't want to hear it." I grab my clothes and put them on like some loser who was led to his own humiliation. I'm ready to unload. "Fuck this. Fuck all of this. For the last six months you've done nothing but pull me in and then push me away. All while I've driven you to work and to events, to restaurants, walked through the grocery store with you, broken myself open about my family, sat through conversations about Sean, because I've been in love with you."

She backs up and pulls the blanket tighter.

"But fuck all of it. I'm not going to keep hoping that one day I'll be good enough to keep your attention longer than a weekend." It feels so good to let this out. I fist chunks of my hair in fury, still shirtless. I'm growing reckless.

"God, I've been an IDIOT! I felt like my life ended when Lacie left me, but really it ended when I started believing there was anything more than *this* between us." I point at her and back at me. "I'm just someone to make you feel good about yourself when it's convenient."

"That's not true," she cries. "I care about you."

Tears are streaming down her face and I can't muster up an ounce of compassion to do anything about it. Maybe I'm finally growing a spine.

"Sure fucking feels like it. I don't want anything to do with you." At last, I have my socks on and I say the words that I should have said the first time I felt anything towards her. "Stay the fuck away from me."

Chapter 20

I DIVE BACK INTO WORK ON MONDAY, getting to my desk before 7 am and catching up on emails while the rest of the office rolls in like normal. I wish I could say I got something out of my system, but I didn't. I want more of Maeve and I can't have it. I have to stop myself from gritting my teeth while putting the issue together. Everything pisses me off. I'm annoyed with myself for wasting a vacation day on Friday. I'm angry that we're missing over half the ads for this month. I'm upset that I left my groceries in Maeve's fridge, too, because now I don't have a lunch packed for today on top of everything else.

When Jesse walks in around 9:30 am, his first stop is my desk. "Hey there buddy. Got a minute this morning?"

This isn't a good "got a minute." I'm in trouble. Awesome.

I follow him into his office and he turns around with a chuckle. "The scorn is especially strong today, my friend."

I ease up on my expression. I didn't even realize my brows were furrowed. "Sorry, it was a dumb weekend."

"Yeah, that's what I wanted to talk about." He closes his door and removes his coat while I take a seat and a deep breath. He asks, "How was Friday? Did you end up finding a car?"

If he's concerned I took a day off last minute, at least I can truth my way out of this. My car is sitting in Ramp A. "Yeah, I did. The insurance check came in the mail on Thursday, so I wanted to find one ASAP."

"Well, that's good." He settles into his desk chair and gives me the kind of look that reminds me of my old professors at college. Tired, but curious. "You got anything to tell me?"

Excuse me? How would he know? Did Maeve tell him? Did Maeve tell Zakariya? What is she telling people? I was prepared to keep what happened on Friday between us and the bed. I don't want anyone else to relive that night without being there. I wasn't even going to tell George about it. Am I living in another reality again? My breath quickens. I've never had a good poker face.

"I don't think so?"

Jesse pauses, exhales, and switches topics completely. "You know Hank's been working here for over twenty-five years. Ray Griff was our publisher when he started. Do you remember him?"

I blink a few times. "I know the name, yeah. I never worked with him, though."

"Ah! That's right, that was before your time." He's relaxed and open. Jesse has never been the kind of boss that toys with my emotions, but this is feeling like an ambush. "He was my boss when I started working here." I nod because it feels like I'm supposed to. "Back when I first met my husband. Did you know Tom used to work here?"

"No," I answer truthfully.

"Yep, he was our events director before Kathryn. The job was split in two before her." He leans over his desk and gives me a tight, straight-line smile. The kind you give someone before you give bad news. "Can I put on my friend hat for a bit, Conrad?"

"Am I in trouble?"

"No, no. Sorry, I know I'm doing this wrong. I'll just come out with it. Is there, uh, anything going on between you and Maeve?" *What the hell.* "Again, friend-hat. I'm not about to tell you who you can and can't date."

I get up from my seat, hot and sweaty. "I can honestly say, there is absolutely nothing going on between me and Maeve. Nothing."

"Hey, hey. Listen, I only ask because Hank was at a client meeting at the Toyota dealership on Friday." *Fuck. Shit. Fuck.* "He saw you two together, and he mentioned it to me in confidence. When it comes to inter-office relationships, per our handbook, we allow it as long as both parties consent to sign an agreement, especially if there is a difference in hierarchy, and in this case, there is. It saves us from a lawsuit" — my breath shortens and my chest collapses — "*and* it saves both of you, too. In case anything were to happen."

"Dude."

"Take a seat, Conrad. Like I said, you're not in trouble. I'm trying to be a friend. I'm trying to exercise due diligence."

I fall into the chair again and rub at my face to attempt to gain some semblance of calm. I'm freaking out. I don't want to get Maeve in trouble, but I'm not signing a damn thing saying we're together.

It's not true.

"I know how this goes. I've been in your position before." No, he *hasn't.* He doesn't know anything about the position I'm in. "I was an account manager when I started here. And if you can imagine, back in 2010, it wasn't as cool to have a gay co-worker." I retract my previous statement. "Neither of us were out at the office. I didn't even realize he was gay until we ran into each other at The Saloon. We went on a few dates, and about a month in we understood that if we wanted to continue this any further, we would have to live separate lives at the office. No secret lunches, no after-work happy hours. When we moved in together, we left at different times every morning. We drove separately. Heck, he told people he was still getting over his divorce whenever anyone asked if he was dating. And he did go through a divorce, but I'll tell you right now that man had no trouble dating after her."

I don't know why he's telling me all of this. I get it. Workplace romances are hard. That's why I'm not having one.

He continues, "We were so careful. I was so distanced from everyone at work. Not one person knew except Ray when we had to refile my W-2s after we eloped. And then we went on a trip to Nisswa, thinking we'd be safe two hours away from the Twin Cities. We were at a resort on Gull Lake, and what do you know, Hank's entire family was there on vacation. He saw us holding hands of all things at the resort's bar."

Jesse shakes his head, smiling up at the ceiling. I'm listening now. I can't look away. What are the fucking odds?

"That was our third wedding anniversary. We had almost gotten away with it! But he was nice about the whole thing. He didn't say anything odd, and didn't hesitate to introduce us to his kids. We hugged his wife just like we had at the last New Year's Bash. It all seemed like it was going to be fine.

"But on Monday, when we got back to the office, Tom had his resignation letter written and sent by 9 am. I didn't even have a chance to convince him otherwise. He said he didn't want either of us to be judged or treated differently because we were together, and we're such a small company, we didn't have any policies around workplace relationships back then. It was 'use common sense,' as if people still have that nowadays. The joke was, Hank didn't tell a soul. No one knew. And a year later, when Ray retired, he pulled me into his office and asked me to be publisher."

I have no idea why I'm getting emotional. Jesse swivels around and pulls a box of Kleenex out for me. I refuse even though the tears are pooling. One small movement and they'd be to my chin.

"My first day on the job, I came out to the office, and I wrote this up." He pulls a piece of paper from the binder on his desk. It's a Consensual Relationship Agreement. I wonder what Maeve will think of this. "Now, if it's true that nothing's going on, then we can forget this conversation ever happened. I just need you to know that you're invaluable, Conrad. You could run this magazine with your eyes closed. I half expect you to be publisher in the next ten years once everyone's had enough of me. I can't lose you over this."

There's too much happening in my brain. I'm pissed that I'm being confronted about a relationship I wanted more than anything but will never happen. I'm scared that Hank thinks we're together, even though he technically saw us before anything had actually happened. I somehow feel closer to Jesse than I have in six years. I've never heard the story of how he and Tom met. And he wants to make me publisher one day. I'm an ass.

"It didn't work out." The words escape me just like the tears now running down my cheek. I reluctantly grab a tissue.

Jesse lets the words settle. "Got it."

"Short-lived." I want to tell him more, but the air in my lungs won't move unless I let out a sob, and I'm not doing that.

"Thanks for telling me." Jesse nods. "This looks different from the breakup last fall."

I blow my nose and it's unexpectedly loud, answering his question for him. "Yeah, it feels different."

"Do you want to take today off? You have the vacation time."

"No."

"Heh, alright." He gets up from his chair. "I have to go talk to Zakariya. You can stay in here as long as you need. We'll find an empty conference room."

But Zakariya beats him. He's already outside.

"Jesse?" He's a bit frazzled and I don't think he sees me. "Maeve just gave me her two-week notice."

Jesse deflates. Truly deflates. His shoulders drop. His head lowers. He vocally sighs.

"And history repeats itself." He takes the piece of paper from Zakariya's hands and tries his best to straighten himself up. "Thanks, Zak. Come on in."

"This is completely out of the blue. She loves it here. I don't know what I did—" He stops in his tracks. "Conrad."

"Hey," I say up at him with puffy eyes. The damp used Kleenex is wadded up in my clammy hand. "I guess that's my cue." I get up and give a guilty look at Jesse. "I'm sorry."

"We'll get through it. Take it easy today." He pats my shoulder. Jesse isn't only a good boss, he's a good person. I think they're intertwined.

I speed walk to the men's room to get a few moments by myself to really let it out. This is all so fucked up. Nothing made me happier than being with Maeve. Romantic or not, our relationship was something I looked forward to every day. Our night together was magical. I can't stop thinking about her lips, her hands, her smoldering eyes. The way her body felt against mine, the weight of her pressed against my chest. Her smile. Her happiness when she was with me. Where is she going to find that again? Where am *I* going to find that again?

I gather myself and head back to my cubicle. Zakariya is still in Jesse's office and I think of about a dozen things they're talking about. All of them are embarrassing and humiliating and center around me.

Thirty-one emails are still unread in my inbox, and I can't seem to open a single one. My mind drifts back to Friday night and the emotions that echo in my chest. It was real. That much I'm sure of. There were times when Lacie would want to speed things up, so yes, I know what it's like when someone is faking it, but there was no faking what Maeve and I did on Friday. There was connection, heat, passion. And something more, something that I haven't been able to put my finger on. Something I never experienced with Lacie. Or anyone for that matter. And now I never will again.

I'm checking ads in Magazine Manager and Kiara appears out of thin air above my screen. Her hair is in braids today and her nails are yellow, clicking on my cubicle wall.

"Hey, wanna get lunch? Actually, wait. Let me rephrase that," she says, smiling with an imitation sweetness that can only come from a true Minnesotan. "Hey, let's get lunch. I could go for a chat, how about you?"

We're sitting at a table inside the IDS Center, where the walls and ceiling are glass and make you feel like you're outside at a park, even in the middle of a Minnesota March, surrounded by people wearing business suits and tennis shoes. There's a tree next to us and birds are chirping while some guy is yelling into his phone at who seems to be his accountant.

Kiara baited me with lunch and switched into an interrogation. That's what it feels like at least.

"So first, I'm going to start this by saying Maeve is one of my best friends on this God-forsaken planet, so I will do no smack-talking of her behind her back. So don't go there, okay?" She pauses for my response and I nod on command. Kiara has a very influential presence. "Okay. Second, she knows she screwed up. Big time. And even though I don't speak *for* her, I just want to say sorry. That was a shitty thing for Maeve to do and she knows it. I don't know what I would have done in that situation."

My nostrils flare as I exhale because even if it's exactly what I want to hear, it also means that Kiara knows about my sex life and that's a line I'm not all too pleased that Maeve crossed. "So she told you."

"Honey, Maeve was telling me things long before she met you. Yes, she told me. When our Maeve is being Maeve, she tells me everything! You don't need to worry about what she tells me. You need to worry about what she's *not* telling me. And up until this weekend, she wasn't telling me shit. So be glad that Maeve told me. It means the balance of the universe is finally realigning."

"Well, forgive me if it doesn't make me feel the greatest knowing that a co-worker is getting live updates about my sex life." I scoff. What is the point of this conversation?

"Listen, Conman, I'm the one person between you and any chance of seeing Maeve again. If you didn't have some sort of inkling that this conversation would lead to that, you wouldn't have come."

My armpits are sweaty. This is too much confrontation in one day. "Fine."

She leans back, proud of her work. "Alright. You didn't hear it from me, but Maeve has been losing her mind over you for the last three months. Maybe longer, she won't say. And currently, she's a crying mess at her desk because A, she doesn't have any more vacation time to use, and B, she thinks the best way to win you back is to be as far away from you as possible. Hence the resignation. The long-distance thing really fucked her up, and now she's got this avoidant attachment style that none of us know what to do with."

"Three months? Really?"

"Focus, pretty boy. The other piece of information that I will deny I gave you until my death day is that Maeve is the most stubborn person I have ever met. So stubborn that we didn't talk for six weeks once because of an argument over cookware. That's when I realized I always had to break no-contact first. I mean, she almost ended a friendship recently because she was questioned about some of her life choices. You feel me?"

Things are starting to add up. "Are you talking about Claire?"

"I'm not talking about anyone. I have no idea what you're referring to because I've told you nothing. Either way, I promise you, she will not reach out first. She won't. She's a Taurus through and through. Maeve is a forgiving person, but hell will freeze over before she talks. You can either fight it or live with it."

A part of me already knew this. After New Year's, I was the one begging her to leave the bus stop in a snowstorm.

"Yeah, I'm not doing that."

Kiara's expression sinks into a glare. "Then you're not getting Maeve back."

"I never had her in the first place."

She blinks once and looks around the sunny interior, full of busy people with lives that don't involve childish games that Kiara is suggesting. I'm not playing tag with Maeve. She did something really hurtful, and if she wants to make it right, she can be a big girl and apologize first. I don't know why Kiara is going to bat for her like this, but when she looks back at me, her eyes are welled up slightly.

"This whole thing has affected our friend group. And I don't want her to quit. *She* doesn't even want to quit. You know how fun it is to get paid to work with your best friend?" *Yes, actually, I do.* "Please just talk to her. I know you're the only person who she wants to talk to. She's sorry for what she said."

"Great." I get up a little too aggressively and push the chair behind me over with the back of my knees, causing a few stares from the people eating eighteen-dollar salads on tables around us. "Then she can grow up and tell me that herself."

Chapter 21

PART OF ME THOUGHT SHE WOULD.

I knew that when I left Kiara alone at our table she'd be talking to Maeve immediately, but her little lure didn't work. I'm leaving Maeve at the metaphorical bus stop and this time, not even a snowstorm could knock me off my track. So for the next two weeks, I do what I should've done when Lacie left me.

I hunker down. I become a machine. I get my work done and prove to Jesse that I'm worthy of his praise and trust. I text George and Emma to make weekend plans for the foreseeable future. I take up going to the apartment weight room for one day, then decide it's not for me. Maybe a part of me thought Maeve would be there. She wasn't.

I go to a show by myself. I visit an art museum. I try a new lunch spot instead of eating a dry turkey and Swiss sandwich from home. I wash my bed sheets. I pretend to read in between doom scrolls. I stupidly re-download Instagram and look at what Lacie's up to. Or rather, I look at her follower list to see if I can find Maeve. Still nothing. All within this two-week deadline, I have to show Maeve that I'm fine. I *am* fine. I'm *great*. By Monday she won't be my personal-life problem or my work-life problem. I can forget I ever met her. Well, I can try.

The night before her last day is the worst. I'm too lazy for pick-up. I'm paying for delivery. I order enough Chinese food to drown my sorrows and sit on the couch fantasizing about what tomorrow will hold. I imagine her coming up to my desk carrying a heavy banker's box, tears accumulating in her eyes. "*For what it's worth,*" she'll say, "*I broke up with Sean because I wanted to be with you.*" Or something else that knocks me off my feet like, "*Just so you know, I've always had feelings for you.*" And I'd say something back like, "*Well, isn't that cool. Guess some things are too little, too late.*"

If I had more gull, maybe I'd be the one to do it. After lunch, I'd stop by her desk as she's packing up the contraband wax warmer (it'll smell like lilac for spring), and I'll go, "*Hey, I'm going to miss you,*" or I'll be bold, "*For the record, you were my favorite.*" My favorite crush, my favorite kiss, my favorite hot breath on my neck. My favorite unrequited love. I've had a few, so I have authority on the matter.

A few dozen scrolls later, I hear the soft knock at my door marking the end to my hunger, but when I heave myself off the couch and open the door, I'm met with her brown eyes. *Those* brown eyes. I kid you not, there wasn't a thought in my mind it would be her. I think that's par for the course after you tell someone to *stay the fuck away from you.* I didn't even think she knew my apartment number. My palms weren't sweaty, my stomach didn't drop, I didn't even look at the peephole. That's how confident I was in thinking that beyond my front door would be nothing other than a frantic delivery guy. But in fact, clinging to a notebook is not the delivery guy from King's, but a very frizzy-haired, very tired-looking Maeve. Worse than that one night.

"Oh."

Her glassy eyes stare up at me. "Hi."

"Is everything okay?" I blurt out. *Of course not, you idiot.*

"Yeah, no. Well, um, I just wanted to talk. Can I come in?"

The shock takes over, and for the first time since we met, I let Maeve into my apartment. She pretends not to look around and we land on my couch. Thank god I went into a cleaning frenzy this last week. The carpet's been vacuumed, the blanket on my couch is freshly laundered. I smell like I have my shit together. Because *that's* what matters right now.

I give her a blank stare until she says something. I'm not speaking first; I'm set on it.

"Um," she says, swallowing. "How are you?"

I'm so tired. My body has been in a constant state of flight or fight and all I can do is glare at her. "Maeve."

She takes a breath to prepare. "Okay, look. There's so much I need to say, but before I do, I want to start with I'm sorry." Her mouth is doing that thing where it can't hold its shape because she's about to cry. I can feel it. My throat is starting to close, too. Mine feels more out of anger, though. Yelling would help. She continues, "I'm sorry that I didn't talk to you sooner, I'm sorry that I've been so confused, and I'm so, so incredibly sorry that I told you to leave that night."

My face is neutral because I'm trying to keep the pace of my breathing. It's coming, I know it. I'm not going to cry this time, I'm going to explode. It's going to feel so good.

She continues, "And I don't know if it's fair for me to say this, but it's the truth." Tears are making it to the tops of her cheeks, but she's wiping them away. My cheeks are hot. My temperature's rising. The relief is coming soon. I'm going to tell her to get the fuck out of my apartment. I'm gonna—

"I'm in love with you, Conrad."

Everything slips away. All the anger and resentment. But without those big emotions to feel, I'm frozen. I don't know what to do next. My body is hollow. What am I supposed to do with that?

"Is that okay?" she asks.

I huff out a laugh, but it's the tipping point. I can't hold it together anymore and as my hands reach my eyes to block what's happening, she reaches forward and grabs them.

I barely can form the words when I say, "Only if I can love you back."

She leans forward and wraps me in a hug, kissing my hair. She doesn't smell like vetiver this time. Just musk. Just Maeve. I want to hold her and kiss her for the next twenty-four hours, but she's already out of my reach.

"There's more, there's more. Okay, one second." She smiles through her tears and grabs her notebook. "I am not an indecisive person," — *that much is true* — "but I know I've seemed like one lately. If you'll let me, I want to tell you everything. From my point of view."

I nod and shift to be an inch closer to her. It finally feels like I'm in the right universe. She opens up her notebook and there are pages and pages of words. It looks more like a journal.

"So, you know I'm a writer."

"Yes, I know."

We both let out a wet chuckle and take a deep breath together.

Chapter 22

I DON'T REMEMBER THE DAY I met my family. Duh, right? I was a newborn. My brain was still taking in information like colors and sounds. My senses were forming and getting used to the world. I'm sure it was lovely, but I don't remember it.

I don't remember meeting some of my best friends, either. I know I met Claire during orientation at Macalester. Probably during some icebreaker that we both very vocally despised. Kiara was my roommate and we met online first. There was so much going on around me that I could barely take it all in. Like I said, I don't remember it.

I do remember meeting you, though. I remember you walking towards Zakariya and me, scowling slightly and in a rush. I remember thinking, *that guy has really kind eyes,* and Zakariya telling me that you were *really* good at your job as we walked away. Then we kept running into each other. I'd see you walk by my bus stop after work. You stopped to say hi once, but I don't know if you wanted to. You were always in such a rush. I was so curious about you. When I felt the need to ask Kiara about you, I knew that a spark had ignited somewhere deep in my belly.

If I'm being honest, which is the whole point of this, I felt a little guilty. I knew it was the beginnings of a crush, but it didn't stop me from saying yes to a ride home. It didn't stop me from feeling the flutter of butterflies when I found out you lived at the same apartment complex. And it didn't stop me from asking to carpool to work. Even if it was pretty convenient.

I still think back to our first car ride together. Sometimes I regret how I reacted. My mind often drifts to the pain in your voice as you told me about everything going on in your life. I didn't mean to belittle them, but when you couldn't find anything that could be a peach, I became determined to hear about the good parts of your day. I wanted *you* to hear about the good parts of your day.

Some of my favorite memories are the first few months of getting to know you. Warm days approached fall nights. Rides home with the windows down. Quiet moments with you on

Monday mornings listening to your music. Ice cream after work. Pits, peaches. Pretty soon I found a rhythm through all of it. The worst parts of your days were always something to do with work, but underneath, it was because you cared so deeply about doing a good job. I love that about you.

The best parts of your day usually involve food. I don't know if you realize that. You'd say, "My lunch was good," or "I'm ordering tacos tonight, that's going to be my peach." Some days you'd say it was the sun. Just the sun. How beautiful? I love hearing your peaches. They're my favorite part of the day.

Remember the night after Jaza Allah? Zakariya's Uncle's restaurant? That was two weeks after Sean had first told me he was considering staying another term in Albania. That night we were supposed to talk about it in depth, but he cancelled. Crying in your car and screaming it out the window were the only things that didn't make me lose it that night. Instead of crying as I fell asleep, I smiled and thought of you. That's when I realized I was in an unhappy relationship, and it was the start of my confusion.

The day you told me about your mom will forever be the day I realized how privileged I was to have a family like my own. I've always been surrounded by like-minded people, and in a way, that's made me reject any sort of confrontation. I've never had to come face-to-face with what it would look like to love someone who doesn't believe in my core values. The more I learned, the more I wanted to learn. When you cried over the phone on Christmas, my heart broke for you. And Georgia.

I ended up telling Claire that I had feelings for you after that. Saying it out loud was terrifying, but it made it all the more real. She didn't like that you were coming over on New Year's. It was her job to make sure I was nowhere near you when the clock struck midnight, especially if I had been drinking. She didn't think it was fair to Sean, but she did it anyway. I think that was the night Kiara realized something was up, too. When we had leftovers the day after Thanksgiving, she asked me if something was going on between us. She can see right through me.

The truth is that I rang in the new year crying in the hotel bathroom because Claire told me you asked for her number. A simple and reasonable request. In fact, if I hadn't been going through an existential crisis about my current relationship status and how miserable I was, I think I would have set you two up. Claire is almost as sarcastic as you are. Almost.

But then I messed up. I texted you in a drunken rage. I had a hard time saying I was sorry after New Year's, even though I was, because it would've given too much away. How do I apologize for being angry that I wasn't your midnight kiss? How do I admit that I wished you were near me the entire night? It was easier to be angry about you leaving early. I built it up to be something it wasn't and in turn, almost ruined the very friendship that was holding me together. There were so many days that I typed up emails and texts to apologize. I even wrote journal pages just like this one trying to tell you that I didn't know what to do, but none of them ever made it to you.

Is it awful to say that the day we got into the accident was one of my favorite days? The relief of seeing you at the bus stop, the smiles I kept hidden while walking to your car, the time we got to spend together waiting for the tow truck. It was like my world was back in vivid technicolor after being in grayscale. I knew why you left the New Year's Bash early. I didn't trust myself around you, either. I just wanted you to say it. I figured if you said that you had feelings first, it would spark me to actually *do something*. To take control of my life in a way I was too afraid to do without you.

I flew too close to the sun, though. I woke up intertwined with your limbs and knew immediately I was being unfair to Sean. So when you asked if he knew I had been in an accident and that you had spent the night, it stirred up something that was already sitting at the surface. I hadn't told Sean anything. I hadn't told him about our commutes, our friendship, nothing.

So I lied to you. I lied to Sean. I lied to myself.

Guilt is a funny thing. It can transform us to say things and do things that go against everything we stand for. I think about guilt a lot when I think about Sean. Maybe he was so poor at communicating because of some guilt, too. When I broke up with him, he flung his anger right back at me and said his second service term had already been confirmed six months ago. He never planned on coming back to Minnesota. He had already decided a full month before he mentioned a second term was even a possibility. I like to think that his lack of honesty was because of guilt rather than a core trait of his. I'll never know for sure. And eventually, I hope I'll be able to make peace with that.

Do you want to know where the pit and peach thing came from? I don't know if I've told anyone this, but it came from my younger sister, Valerie. When I first moved to Minnesota, it was really hard on her. Hell, it was hard on me. So she came up with the idea of telling each other the best parts of our day and the worst parts of our day via text.

We called it so many things at first; rose and a thorn, sun and the moon, butterfly and a bumblebee, but we landed on pit and a peach. I started asking it to my friends and pretty soon everyone in my life knew that if I hadn't seen them in a while, I was going to ask what their pit and their peach were for the day. I loved it. It was such an easy way to see over time what people valued in their lives and what caused them pain. In crowded places, I'd imagine what everyone's were. Someone woke up next to the person they love, someone spilled ketchup on their favorite shirt, someone caught all the green lights on the way to work, someone caught every red. The little things that we all take for granted. The good and the bad. I wanted to know it all.

When Sean first moved for his service term, I would ask him every time we spoke on the phone, but after the second month, he started telling me that it was reductive to have a pit and a peach for the day. He said that there are always pits inside of peaches and peaches that bloom from pits and that it was a matter of perspective. To him, it was a question without substance. He asked me to stop, and I did.

But you never asked me to stop. You hoped I never would. That's when I knew I was too far gone to ever come back to a place where I could see my future with Sean. Which is why I all but kicked you out of my apartment that night.

I spiraled after that.

Guilt also has changed me in the last few months. I felt guilty after you spent the night at my place. I immediately called Claire to tell her what happened. She said I needed to tell Sean, but I refused. I was paralyzed by the idea of telling him anything because if I started I wouldn't be able to stop. I knew

I would break up with him if I brought you up. I didn't know how to tell Claire that, and the guilt gnawed at my bones.

I didn't know how to tell Kiara anything either. She likes you, by the way. She thinks you're the perfect mixture of dramatic and sarcastic. And after she spoke with you last week, she said you have integrity. I promise I didn't put her up to it, but you were right. I did need to grow up, and I'm grateful for the hard love that Kiara gave me. It got me here.

Claire started to wonder why I was dragging Sean along if I knew I didn't want to be with him, and in hindsight, it was a fair question. She knew Sean at Macalester. They were both in the gender studies program. I had only met them through a general anthropology course, but the three of us became a trio. The thing with Sean is that he can seem incredibly sincere. He's rarely sarcastic, meanwhile, Claire and I rarely aren't. The three of us clicked, and when we brought Kiara and Mo Thao into the mix, the five of us were unstoppable. It's understandable why Claire fought for our relationship. With the memories of the good old days, there was this unspoken promise that once Sean moved back, everything would just go back to normal, right? But I didn't want the good old days. I wanted you.

So when she pushed me on the subject, I pushed right back. With tears in my eyes, I said that if she was interested in you, she just had to tell me. It was a cheap shot, because when

Sean and I started dating, we didn't tell people at first, and Claire let it slip to me one night that she had feelings for Sean.

Guilt, huh?

She and I didn't talk until after everything fell apart between you and me. I called her crying. I told her that I had finally done it. I finally ended things with Sean so that I could be with someone who makes waking up in the morning feel like a weekend in June, even on the tail end of winter. I told her everything, that I was so nervous to kiss you, but you kissed me back in a way that calmed the stormy sea of my mind and body. I finally felt the exhale, the sit back, the recline. For some reason, she forgave me, but our friendship has survived worse.

Relief. That's what it feels like to be around you. I'm sure that's the reason I let things progress so quickly. I feel safe around you. I'm comforted by you. Enough so that I let my body experience something that up until now, I've never shared with anyone. Alone, sure. With Sean, I tried. But I could never let myself get there. And even though it scared me, it meant something to me. It always will.

I shouldn't have said what I said. I shouldn't have pushed you away. Everything surfaced the moment I came back down, and I took it out on you. For that, I am so deeply sorry.

Conrad. *Conrad.* Conrad!!! I love you. I love every page you're written on in the story of my life. I love your begrudged kindness. I love your sarcasm. I love that you can't outright tell me you loved the sweet corn ice cream, but I know you did. I love that I know you did. I love that you know exactly how to make me laugh and you don't even know it. I love how you listen to me ramble on about everything I'm writing. I love that you care about your job and the work you do. I love the warmth of your chest when I hug you. I love how much you love your sister. I love that when you love something, you love it with everything you have. And that night, I felt loved by you.

I hate that I ran away from it.

I just know you will always be my favorite chapter, and I want to keep reading it over and over again. You were right. This is my life! I've already been living it, but now I want to start living my life...

With you.

Chapter 23

Eight Months Later

I GOT THE DAMN PAGES LAMINATED. I read those words most
mornings when I'm waiting for Maeve to wake up, but
especially on days when I think I don't deserve the kind of love
that she has to give. I think they've rewired how my brain
works, to be honest, and everything in my life feels a bit more
manageable because of it. Because of her.

She ended up retracting her resignation, and because Jesse
is who he is, he accepted it graciously. They hadn't even posted
the job yet. I think he knew all along that it would come to this.

My lease was up at the end of the following month, and
Maeve's was up a month later. We played rock, paper, scissors
for whose apartment we'd move into. I won, but with one look
at Maeve's plants and the amount of artwork on the walls, I
conceded, and six weeks later, I moved into Maeve's space very

willingly. Every night is a sleepover, every dinner is a date, every morning is a sunny day in June.

Maeve had some repair work with Claire and Kiara. They both were pretty upset that she had hidden so much from them, but in time they came around. Now, they're over at the apartment every week in some fashion. Kiara comes after work sometimes, and Claire joins on the weekends. Mo Thao comes when her work schedule allows it. It might not be back to normal, but I think it's better. The laughter never stops with those four. I'm lucky to be a part of it.

Maeve and I had to sign that damn Consensual Relationship Agreement during a closed-door meeting with Jesse in his office, which I hated every second of. Pretty soon I had to tell Georgia and Emma the truth, because the next time I went to dinner at their house, Maeve came along. It's wild how the three of them clicked instantly. I usually can't get a word in edgewise when we're together.

In fact, we just came off the first Christmas our two families intermingled. George and Emma made the trip out to Seattle with Maeve and me to start making their own holiday memories. We were welcomed with hugs and pats on the cheek by Maeve's family at the airport. And I know, it doesn't replace thirty years of dysfunctional parents, but damn, Christmas feels a lot cooler with a family that uses George's correct pronouns and doesn't raise eyebrows at their pink hair. It's also pretty cool that I got to spend the holiday with Maeve's sisters, too, who if I didn't know any better, might all be a little obsessed with me. I think Maeve talks me up too much.

Tonight we're getting ready for our second North Star New Year's Bash together, and my first one as her boyfriend. We're planning on pulling an Irish exit to ring in the new year... alone, but not before meeting up with my sister and their *fiancé*, Emma. Yeah. Crazy, right? It happened in August.

Kiara and Maeve are in our bathroom in various stages of hair and make-up. I'm leaning against the door frame trying to catch Maeve's eye whenever I can.

"Alright, we're meeting Zak and Lena there," Kiara says. Zak and Lena tied the knot two months ago and we still feel like we're recovering. Best wedding I've ever been to. Longest wedding I've ever been to. "Who else is coming?" she asks while carefully laying her edges. Kiara is the mastermind behind tonight. She usually is.

Maeve smacks her lips together. She just applied a lip gloss that I am determined to kiss off before I leave. If I could only get a few minutes alone with her. "Conrad's sister and their fiancé are meeting us later. Both of them are amazing, you're going to love them," she says, smiling at me in the mirror. "Jordan said she was bringing Chris. Oh! I think Sua was coming, too. But I don't know if she's meeting up with us before or during the Bash."

Mo Thao squeezes past me and joins the conversation by plopping on the toilet. Luckily the lid's closed. "Claire can't find anything to wear. She's freaking out because Ryan just texted her that he's meeting us at the bar."

Ryan is the guy Claire has been seeing for the last two weeks. It's new. We're all rooting for it. The main things I know about him are that he's a volunteer firefighter, he works at a college in St. Paul, and Claire is obsessed with him. She's been freaking out for the last few weeks in our apartment before dates but hides it under humor and sarcasm. We're more alike than I tend to admit.

Maeve is just about to leave the bathroom, but Claire intercepts her in one of Maeve's shirts. I recognize it from last year's New Year's Bash. Black, long sleeve, mesh.

"Can I pleasepleaseplease wear this?"

Maeve responds like the good friend she is. "It looks better on you than me. You have to wear it."

So at least that's figured out. I look at my watch. 7:30 pm. I need to be there in thirty minutes. I offered to help Kathryn again this year, which means I'm also now in charge of managing the event labor before the event, so the girls are heading to a bar next door until the thing actually starts. I can't wait to have Maeve to myself this year once it's all over.

"Alright. Time check. It's seven-thirty," I announce. "I have to get going, but you guys are driving separately, right?" They nod, and Maeve sneaks around Kiara to give me a kiss goodbye. Kiara shields her eyes, but she always pulls that shit when Maeve and I do anything outside of a high-five. "Love you."

"Love you."

"Get a room!" Thanks, Kiara.

When the tables are finally torn down, the pipe and drape loaded into the trailer, and Kathryn gives me the okay, I sneak into the bar downstairs and immediately find the group of people who have made me smile more in the last year than in my entire life.

Lena, Kiara, and Mo Thao are dancing in a group near Jordan and Chris. Zakariya and Emma are laughing about something George just said. Claire is dancing with Ryan while Maeve bounces along until she sees me. Her entire face perks up and soon she's breathing in my ear, trying to communicate through the booming bass and rhythmic beat playing on all speakers.

"There you are. How'd it go?"

I nod, waving to George and Emma, pretending to be present. "Good, good." I dance with her because I know she's been waiting for me all night, but after a few rounds of thumping bass and spacey vocals, I'm antsy to get out of here.

It's nice feeling her body on mine in a crowded room, but it's nothing like being alone with her. "You ready to go home?"

"Only if I get to go home with you," she says, driving me wild.

I give her a wink and we announce our departure swiftly and concisely. I hear Kiara yell behind us.

"See you tomorrow, Maeve! We're going to brunch. Bring Conman! Text me for the details!"

"Bye Connie," George screams over the music. "Let me know how you like the shoes, Maeve!" They got her a pair of clogs for Christmas.

Ryan has his arm around Claire as she waves at Maeve. She blows her a kiss and waves back at a few others from the office, but I'm pulling on her hand. I want to get home before midnight.

I've been holding it in all evening, waiting for the perfect time to ask, but it'll have to wait as we navigate the busy skyways of downtown Minneapolis to get to my car. Maeve is in a good mood; I am, too. There's something about the glitz and glam, the finality of the year, and the hope of a new one.

The highway's empty, just a few cars here and there, and just like last year, I can't help but wonder about their lives. This year the sentiment is a bit different. I smile over at her with the question on my tongue that got us into this whole mess in the first place. "Hey, what's your pit and peach for the year?"

Her eyes dart around and she brightens somehow. "You know, I asked everyone this at the bar. I didn't even get a chance to answer. Hmm." She bites her lip. "Pit was not getting to ring in this year with you. And peach is that this time, I do."

"Ah, very full circle. I see." She's got nothing on me, though. I've been preparing. "Do you remember my first pit and peach? The first time I drove you home?"

She points a finger in the air. "Trick question. You didn't have a peach. Only pits." Damn, she's good.

"Right. Okay, ask me what my pit and peach were for the year."

Her eyes narrow, full of skepticism. "What are your pit and peach for the year?"

I stop the car at the stoplight off the exit and rest my hand in her lap. "No pit this year. Everything that happened got me right here, and it's exactly where I want to be. But my peach? Ooh, it's a good one." I look over and she's already smiling at me. "Maeve, it's always been you."

Epilogue

Maeve's Memorable Pits & Peaches

Documented by Conrad Sutherland

(Commentary by Maeve Thomas)

Peach: The hot chocolate I made her was "extra chocolatey" today.

—

Pit: The Chinese place near our hotel in Vancouver wasn't as good as the one by our apartment. Also my pit. (It was Valentine's Day and we took a trip just the two of us.)

Peach: Waking up to mountains, the ocean, ~~and lazy morning sex~~. Also my peach. (Redacted for privacy!)

—

Pit: Zakariya found another job that's way higher paying. It's probably his peach, but all of editorial is in mourning.

Peach: His uncle is hosting a farewell dinner at Jaza Allah. (Zak promised sambusas!)

—

Peach: Kiara and Mo Thao are moving to the Westside. They'll be a ten minute walk from our place.

Peach: Maeve got a promotion! (Say hello to the new Senior Food Editor!)

—

Peach: Forcing me to take a day off so we could spend it together. She can't decide what her favorite thing was; the coffee shop, the walk around Lake Bde Maka Ska, or spending the afternoon at a local bookstore. Mine was holding her hand all day. (Awww!)

—

Peach: Maeve will be an aunt! Her oldest sister Stephanie announced she's pregnant, and Valerie flew in from Colorado to be there.

Pit: Maeve was on deadline and couldn't swing it.

—

Peach: Her pumpkin pie turned out this year. (This was also your peach, too!)

—

Peach: ~~That thing I did with my tongue this morning.~~ (Conrad!)

—

Peach: Our one year anniversary. (Based on our first kiss.)

—

Peach: I peeled her an orange? She doesn't even like oranges. (Orange peel theory, look it up.)

—

Peach: Our one year anniversary...again? (Based on the first time we said I love you.)

—

Pit: ~~She was "really gassy today."~~ (I'm taking this notebook back. It was supposed to be for journaling!)

—

Pit: Our favorite lunch spot in downtown closed. RIP Allie's Deli. I will forever miss the creamy tomato soup.

—

Peach: Our one year anniversary, for the third time. (Based on when we moved in together, you make me sound weird!)

—

Peach: Being George and Emma's witnesses at the courthouse.

—

Peach: New flavor of ice cream at Honey & Milk. Elderberry. (Not as good as the vanilla, but better than the black cap raspberry, IMO.)

—

Pit: Living far away from family is hard.
Peach: It was a girl! (Sophia Rae, 8lbs 3oz.)

—

Pit: She knows I'm hiding something, but can't figure out what.

—

Peach: Getting her nails done with Claire.

—

Peach: A surprise visit from her sisters for the weekend.

—

Pit: She didn't see it coming.

Peach: She said yes! (We're engaged!!!!!!!)

Acknowledgments

Third time's the charm, right?

This book was so fun to write. So many parts of this story feel like a love letter to Minneapolis. It's a city that I have a complicated relationship with, but I'm forever grateful for my time living there in my early twenties.

Additionally, I have some people to thank for getting me here. These books don't become any easier to write, but they continue to bring me so much joy, all because of you.

To Ly. You're my soulmate, the love of my life, my everything, and this book was inspired so heavily by our time working in the magazine industry together. Who would have thought our trauma bonding would have gotten us here? Thank goodness for walks around the block and Skyway sushi bowls. Your fingerprints are on every page.

To Fiza. Thank you for being the first person to read this novel and for your cultural insights. I'm so grateful for the time you spent with this book.

To Jess. Thank you for making the cover of this book beautiful! I think it's stunning, and I'm so glad I stumbled upon your incredible art on TikTok. Your excitement only fueled my motivation, and I'm so grateful that I got to meet you through this process. (Go follow @jesscruzdesign!)

To Jean. I think you would have liked this one. I hope, at least. You're always in the back of my mind, telling me to capitalize things and remove commas. I wish you were still here to be my cheerleader and editor. I miss you every day.

To my family. Thank you for always believing in me. Thank you for getting excited when I tell you about a new plot point or that I finally got the formatting right. It's your love and encouragement that keeps me going on and off the page. I love you, I love you, I love you.

And to you. Thank you for reading this silly story. I hope your pits are small and your peaches are ripe and juicy.

About the Author

Anna Pollock is a community lover and high school theater director when she's not writing heated and wholesome novels about romance. She grew up in rural Minnesota where she currently resides with her orange and white cat, Kinston. Stay tuned for more stories centered around the hope and heartbreak of loving and being loved as a full human.

Connect online at annarbpollock.com.

Printed in the USA
CPSIA information can be obtained
at www.ICGtesting.com
JSHW032230050724
65799JS00004B/20